CW01665639

Nathaniel Sario has always wanted to be a writer. So far, he has made that dream a reality, with several short stories published in Fixi Novo's anthologies (*Chronicles of KK, 2020: An Anthology,* and *The Big Book of Malaysian Horror Stories*). He has worked as a journalist for several newspapers, and is currently doing his best to survive at a local kindergarten franchisor in PJ. *Big Trouble in Little Paradise* is his first novel, but he solemnly swears that there's more coming. Hopefully lah.

FIXI NOVO manifesto

1. We believe that omputih/gwailoh-speak is a Malaysian language.

2. We use American spelling. This is because we are more influenced by Hollywood than the House of Windsor.

3. We publish stories about the urban reality of Malaysia. If you want to share your grandmother's World War 2 stories, send 'em elsewhere and you might even win the Booker Prize.

4. We specialize in pulp fiction, because crime, horror, sci-fi and so on turn us on.

5. We will not use italics for non-American/non-English terms. This is because those words are not foreign to a Malaysian audience. So we will not have "They had *nasi lemak* and went back to *kongkek*" but rather "They had nasi lemak and went back to kongkek". Nasi lemak and kongkek are some of the pleasures of Malaysian life that should be celebrated without apology; italics are a form of apology.

6. We publish novels and short-story anthologies. We don't publish poetry; we like making money.

7. The existing Malaysian books that come closest to what we wanna do: *Devil's Place* by Brian Gomez; and the Inspector Mislan crime novels by Rozlan Mohd Noor. Look for them!

8. We publish books with the same print run and the same price as those of our parent company, Buku Fixi. So a book of about 300 pages will sell at RM20. This is because we wanna reach out to the young, the sengkek and the kiam siap.

CALL FOR ENTRIES.

Interested? For novels, send your synopsis and first 2 chapters. For anthologies, send a short story of between 2,000-5,000 words on the theme "KL Noir." Send to info@fixi.com.my anytime.

Big Trouble in Little Paradise

Winner of the 3rd Fixi Novo Malaysian Novel Contest

Nathaniel Sario

NOVO

Published by
Fixi Novo *which is an imprint of:*
Buku Fixi Sdn Bhd (1174441-X)
B-8-2A Opal Damansara, Jalan PJU 3/27
47810 Petaling Jaya, Malaysia
info@fixi.com.my
http://fixi.com.my

Big Trouble in Little Paradise

First Printing: October 2023

Cover image: @deep.latent.space (Stable Diffusion and Photoshop)
Consultants: Amir Muhammad and Matthew Yap

ISBN 978-967-0042-87-9
Catalogue-in-Publication Data available from the National Library of Malaysia.

Printed by:
Vinlin Press Sdn Bhd
2 Jalan Meranti Permai 1, Meranti Permai Industrial Park
Batu 15, Jalan Puchong, 47100 Puchong, Malaysia

Three 'Thank You's are owed:

The first is for my parents, who put books in my hands and told me they were portals to magical worlds.
To the judges, as well as Amir and the excellent team at Fixi.
And finally to you, Dear Reader, for picking up this book and giving it a chance.

1

About 45 minutes away from the city of Tawau is the small town of Darat Kumut. A tiny splotch on the map, the place had been barely noticed since its incorporation in the late 1970s as a fishing village that somehow, through the miracle that is word of mouth, grew from a few shacks by the sea to an actual, functioning burg run by a group of families.

As the years pressed on, the town grew. Its main contribution to the economy was fishing, supplying fresh catch to other smaller, surrounding hamlets and the larger cities. Then in the late '90s, a very wealthy man from West Malaysia stumbled upon the town and decided that he would build a resort on the deserted island that sat some 45 minutes away by ferry, thus ushering tourism into the town.

From the start, tourists enjoyed Darat Kumut. It came with the trimmings of your average Malaysian small town: peace, quiet, tranquility, serenity and beauty. Its people were friendly. Every person you met on the street had a ready smile. They said *hi*, *hello* and *good morning* to each other because many had grown up knowing one another. Some were even connected by marriage, as was wont in small towns.

At the same time, while the buildings were old (having been erected in the early '80s as prosperity flowed gently but surely in), they were well taken care of and constantly repaired. The streets were kept clean. The roads weren't slathered with potholes.

And barefoot children did not go up to cars and beg for money. The worst you'd see in Darat Kumut were the nighttime drunks. But when in paradise …

Annually, *Sabah* magazine, a little endeavor by the state Tourism Board, awarded Darat Kumut the title of 'Best Small Town in Sabah'. The person who issued the award added in writing that the town had been endowed with the prize as '*Darat Kumut is the place to be any time of the year because you can go from quaint seaside paradise to enjoying a Mojito and wasting away money at the Casino of Pearls on the island. Or laze about on the beach – mainland or the island – away from the stresses of life and the real world.*

Most of that would change after Tommy Asandu's death.

X

The door to the small seaside house banged open.

"Shut up lah!" Tommy Asandu barked as he stepped out of the house.

"For one night, can't you stay at home?" his mother shouted back at him.

"If I did, I probably would OD in my room from listening to you and that bitch!"

There was a pause. Then a third voice – a young girl – began crying.

"You're a horrible, horrible child," said the woman.

"*You* should have aborted me then," Tommy said.

Something was thrown. It whizzed in the air for a moment, then hit the side of the door frame and broke, the pieces raining down on the floor.

"There you go," Tommy said as he lit a cigarette. "Throwing things. Breaking them. It's a wonder Child Protective Services haven't come around to take Tabby from you."

"You animal!" the woman cried. By now, the neighbors were listening in, but these were the keen ones who enjoyed the little drama that once in a while entered their humdrum life. Most were bored. Like a bad *CSI* rerun, after you saw one or five, chances were, you'd seen them all. One would start a fight (it was mostly Tommy), and it would be better entertainment than whatever ASTRO, TV3 or the Android Box had to offer.

Only tonight would be the last time that Tommy and his mother would have this verbal battle.

"I love you too," Tommy said, blowing a kiss at his enraged mother, who stood by the entrance to the house, huffing and puffing, tears streaming down her face. If any of the neighbors noticed, they would have told their significant other that this was one of the bad ones. Normally it would just be barbs in the form of words. But now she was crying, so it had to be bad.

"Don't you dare come home," she said.

The best Tommy could do was offer her the middle finger as he sauntered towards the Beach Path, which extended from the housing area to town. Those who worked in town, or who owned businesses in town or rented here, but worked on the island, walked the path. The wind was strong, and it always smelled of the sea. The lap of waves on the sand had a tendency to ease one's mind.

Even if their minds were drug-fucked like his.

Hands out at his sides like he was a plane (*pilot* had been his profession of choice once upon a long time ago), Tommy shuffled down the path, banking left and then right, the cigarette burning from the corner of his mouth, him making engine noises – *whoosh, whoosh, whoosh* – as he flew.

That came to a pause when his phone buzzed in his pocket.

Tommy lowered his arms and pulled out his phone. He read the message slowly, his heart rate climbing. The supplier wanted to meet up.

Where? he texted back.

The old jetty near the seaside chalets, the supplier replied. Then: *see you there in 10 minutes. Don't be late.*

Tommy pocketed the phone. He didn't want to play airplane just then. No time for it. Adult stuff was going to happen, and the last thing he wanted was the supplier wondering why he was coming down the beach with his arms out, making weird noises and looking like he belonged in the nuthouse. No. There was a problem. The supplier had found out.

"Shit," he mumbled to himself.

The path had cleared out, and now he could see the bright lights of town: the Ferry Terminal to his left, sitting on land and water. The two rows of shop lots that had been constructed in the late 80s to his right. Further on were the newer row of shop-lots. The faint sound of thumping came from near the entrance into town. That would be Palace Neptune, his second-biggest business spot for the goods.

The hairs on the back of his neck prickled. It was instinct, honed from his time in prison.

As he turned, something clattered in the dark. Maybe a bottle. Maybe a can.

Tommy licked his dry lips. He took a long pull from the cigarette, flicked it and said: "Someone there?"

He was met with silence.

"Better come out. Don't want me catching you," he said, though the words came out lacking that steel bite that kept so many others away from him. In fact, he sounded scared, and Tommy didn't like that at all.

He stood there for several seconds, chewing his bottom lip and looking into the dark slices of town that weren't illuminated by the street lamps, which were spaced far and away from each other the further out you went from the town. *Overthinking*, he told himself. *I am overthinking.*

When he was still greeted with no response, he turned and continued down the road. Past the Ferry Terminal was another row of shops. These were the special kind. They had decks that overlooked the Celebes Sea. In front of the first one (which had a sign proclaiming it as the Seaside Bar & Bistro), a bald man with two missing front teeth worked a burger stall.

Tommy locked eyes with the man, then glanced over at his customers. Two of them were dock workers. A quick drink at the bar and then a nice burger right outside that didn't taste like generic, chewed-up cow.

The third member of their little dinner party was dressed in a blue uniform and drinking mineral water. To him, Tommy offered a mock salute.

"Keeping out of trouble, Tommy?" Sergeant Awang Shahmi asked.

Tommy grinned at them, banishing the fearful thoughts that had plagued him earlier. "Unless walking's considered trouble ..."

"Little shit," Sergeant Awang mumbled. The other two dock workers chuckled. When their attention was no longer on him, Tommy offered a middle finger to the whole lot.

Down the road he went. On this end of town were the evenly spaced seaside chalets. There were four of these beautiful wooden monoliths along the south side of the beach. They were outfitted with rustic wooden paneling and artistic-bordering-on-obscene furniture. The chalets cost up to RM2,000 a night and could fit up to 20 people. The last unit was currently being rented by a group of young adults. College students, said his source in the management office of the Darat Kumut Seaside Chalets.

He slowed a little as he passed and listened to the sounds coming from the place. There was music. There was laughter. Several playful shouts. A lot of cursing. He'd offered to sell them drugs, but they'd asked for the T20 shit. High-end party pills. Acid. Premo weed. He had a supply of Ketamine, weed (no special names like Purple Palm Tree Delight), and syabu, almost all of it fresh from the proverbial oven. Would that float their boat?

The dude had asked for the weed. He'd smoked an *entire* joint and then, with his broad chest, friendly grin and an aww-shucks attitude, had told Tommy that his weed tasted like shit and no thanks, they'd probably just stick to the booze. Cheap fucks.

The last thing to see Tommy Asandu alive was a cat that he would aim a failed kick at. The cat had been minding its own business, but had the unfortunate luck of being in his way. The next time anyone saw Tommy Asandu, it would be a couple from the party chalet.

The duo, in search of some nice, passionate sunrise sex, were making love on the pier for about 10 minutes before discovering Tommy's body floating there, face down, hands spread out, like an airplane almost, just without the engine sounds.

2

Wesley Lawrence Moysin woke up just before the alarm rang.

He was getting used to it: waking up at 7 am or just before. He had a routine now. Well, *before*, there was a routine, only it wasn't like this. The routine before this, before Kumut, was unhealthy. After two months in town, that was slowly changing. The gloom had begun fading away at the edges.

His eyes focused on the ceiling fan that spun lazily. *This is good. This is what I need.*

Wesley swung his legs over the bed and faced the bamboo blinds that let in sunlight. The windows were open and he could smell the salty sea air and hear the waves lapping up on the sand. It was the start of another good day.

With a stretch, he got up, grabbed his phone and towel and made for the bathroom. Showered. Back to his room to put on some clothes, then to the kitchen, which faced the living room. It was 7:25 am.

Aunt Zara and Margie were already at the table.

"Morning," he said.

"Morning," Margie said, waving her Nestum-covered plastic spoon at him. Next to her chair, Lucky woofed at him.

"Sleep okay?" Aunt Zara asked.

"Slept great," he said, rubbing the space behind the dog's ears with both hands, making his tail wag.

"Breakfast?" his aunt asked.

"Gonna have it at the shop."

"Who's holding the keys?"

"Delilah."

"Great. I'll see you in the afternoon."

"Roger that," he said.

"Wes?"

"Mm?" he said, as he took Margie's spoon, scooped out some Nestum from her bowl and fed her with it. His cousin clapped her hands in delight as she chewed.

"Ever think about getting a haircut? It's a little shaggy here," she touched the top of her head, "here," the right side, "and here," the left side.

"Nah, I'm thinking of keeping it long." He passed Margie back her plastic spoon.

"Okay."

Out the door he went, backpack strap around one arm. The neighborhood – if that's what you could call the messily organized clutter of houses here, there and everywhere by the beach – was just waking up. He could hear breakfast being made, people telling other people to hurry up. Others were already on the way out for work. A few of those who knew him waved. He waved back.

He walked down the beach path and glanced down at his right hand. Zara had been looking closely at it earlier with concern. It wasn't a pretty sight. The skin over his knuckles was still recovering. The scabs had yet to heal. It had been over a week, and he cleaned the wound regularly, but still … he touched the red and purple mark on the middle-finger knuckle and winced. It was the worst one.

Life was supposed to be good …

He smiled and nodded at a couple of joggers. Some still running. Some on the way back. Some walking. He replied to the cyclists who called out to him. Fist-bumped a dude who worked as a bouncer at Palace Neptune who did power-walking until dawn when his shift was over. A group of workers from the resort on the island waved. He waved back.

The beach path opened up to town. Mrs Fazila, who made fresh kuih cucur, pisang goreng and nasi lemak, called and asked in Dusun if he was in the mood for breakfast. He replied to her in his broken Dusun, saying he was not hungry. She laughed heartily at his attempt. Maybe he said he was not angry. Who knew?

He crossed the road.

"Good morning, Wesley," Aunt Joanna said. She stood outside her café Aunt Jo's and was enjoying her first cigarillo of the day. The hand that usually held a cane was now free and came up to fan the air around her. Even from six paces away, he could smell the floral perfume that she doused all over her massive dress.

"Readying the kitchen?"

She bobbed her head several times, causing her two chins to jiggle. "Apple and Oliver are inside. The other two should be on their way. You want something?"

"Hinde, tiya," he said.

Aunt Jo chuckled and blew smoke rings at him. "Your Tagalog is still terrible, bata. Stop relying on Google translate."

He laughed. "See you, tiya."

Aunt Jo continued smoking and smiling.

The All-Convenience Store was the first building that you'd see if you were walking down Darat Kumut's Main Street. There was no 7-Eleven, CKS, Bataras, Giant, Lotus's. If you wanted something, you came to the All-Convenience Store.

Leaning against a street lamp was a bicycle. The owner of that bicycle was on her knees, working the bottom lock of the shutter.

"Morning," Wesley said in a sing-song voice.

Delilah Loh looked up and gave a quick wave. "Morning, champ."

Wesley looked into the basket attached to the bicycle's handlebars and picked out a book jutting from her tote bag.

"Oooh, someone's feeling classy," he said, waving the copy of Virginia Woolf's *To the Lighthouse*. "How was that book I lent you?" he asked, noticing that the Stuart MacBride paperback in her tote bag as well.

"Do you ever feel bored when you're just reading the same commercial stuff day in day out?"

"Nope," he said, placing his backpack by her bike to help her lift the shutters. "It's like eating fast food every day. You can never go wrong."

Delilah made a gagging noise. "You're weird."

"This coming from the person who believes in UFOs?"

The store was unlocked, the shutters rolled up. Delilah got up and threw a playful kick at him. He dodged it, laughing. "How was it, though?"

"Good. I actually get the dark humor."

"The Scottish stuff wasn't too hard?"

She shook her head. "Easy-peasy. Can you park my bike at the back? I'll go in and get the coffee ready."

"Got it."

3

Inspector Rabbil Harris rubbed sleep from his eyes before pawing at his breast pocket for cigarettes. He'd promised Syafiqah – his wife – that 2022 was it. That this year would be the last year he'd ever light up a cigarette. Well … half the year was over, and here he was, peeling the cellophane tape off a fresh pack. He did say he wouldn't be quitting cold turkey anyway. One every two or three hours … and that had worked while he was with her. But his wife wasn't here at the moment, was she, so that meant he was free to do whatever he wanted.

He rolled down the window of the rented Hilux, tossed the piece of plastic out and fired up the cigarette.

"How much longer?" he asked after that first, glorious puff of nicotine and about a thousand other chemicals.

In the front seat, driving, was Constable Rudolph Lim, the tour guide, and sitting in the passenger seat was Sergeant Atiqah Lajis.

"Ten minutes, boss," Atiqah said.

Rabbil produced a jaw-cracking yawn and leaned closer to the window, allowing the cool wind to blow at his face. He saw nothing but green on both sides of the two-lane black top. But here, the air was cleaner. It didn't smell like the city where there was this awful layer of something that didn't sit right in the nose.

"Ticks," he said, "why is CID sending us over to investigate a drowning?"

"It's not much of an investigation," Atiqah said. "From what I understand, this small town-"

"Darat Kumut," said Rudolph helpfully.

"This town," said Atiqah, sounding mildly annoyed at being interrupted, "does not have the proper personnel or experience to handle any kind of police investigation. We're being sent to cross the t's and dot the i's. If there's no foul play, we go back to Sandakan and continue with the seminar. If there is foul play … well, we'll have to stay and look into it."

Rabbil grunted and smoked.

They passed the Klink Desa Darat Kumut, and then an ancient-looking Petronas with three pumps, two of them exclusively for diesel. Once they were away from this, Rudolph, excited that he was working with actual CID officers who specialized in murder cases, announced that they were nearing the town proper.

"What can you tell me about this place?" Rabbil asked Rudolph.

Rudolph said, "Darat Kumut started off as a fishing village, but somehow it grew. Before Arthur Krishnan came and built the casino-resort, no one really bothered, and the place was just another dot on the map. After the casino and the resort though, everyone wanted to come. Forget Sipadan, that's just Instagram fodder. You wanna have a good time and blow up your 'gram likes, you come to Darat Kumut."

And suddenly, as Rabbil was in the process of lighting up his second cigarette of the morning (Syafiqah would blow her top if she knew), he hoped they *were* going to see a murder scene. Murder meant that they would be here for a few extra days. The killer would be caught by day three or four, and he only needed the one day to go off to the casino. You were allowed to have fun while working, right?

Just a couple of days ago, he had been two numbers away from winning RM160,000 from Sports Toto's Jackpot 2. Syafiqah wasn't keen on gambling either, but if he came back with another closed case and … RM50,000 (even half of that wouldn't be that bad) for the kid's Pampers and college fund, would she really be mad? Nope.

"As you can see," Rudolph said, his words cutting through Rabbil's 50,000 ringgit fantasies, "we're already here."

The first thing Rabbil saw was a massive patch of asphalt surrounded by a wire fence. This, according to a sign, was the bus terminal. It didn't look like much. Just the patch of asphalt half the size of a football field, a small office, and an open-air waiting area that looked like it could double as an oven during the hot season.

They drove past the bus terminal and saw the first row of shops. These were the more modern set pieces of the town. One was a bakery. Then a nightclub, and lastly, a Chinese restaurant/kopitiam. Down the single strip of road (another sign on the side read 'Main Street/Jalan Utama) was the town. Two rows of older shophouses on either side. Old bones, his father, a retired architect, would've said if he saw these buildings.

The first was a single-story, cream-white corner piece which was the town's convenience store. Next to it was a coffee shop, a store selling hand-crafted items from across Borneo, a café called Aunt Jo's and, at the end, a barbershop. Across the road were more stores. All family-owned. The signs looked old and withered, but they fit. Take a picture and you could put it on a postcard and sell it to tourists. A slice of the Land Below the Wind.

Main Street ended at the Ferry Terminal but branched off in two directions. There were signs here as well. The one on the left said 'Kawasan Kampung' and the one on the right said 'Pantai Pasir Balung'. Rudolph went right. Rabbil took note of the police outpost, and then blinked at the seaside chalets.

"Here we are," said Rudolph, gliding the Hilux to park in front of two other vehicles. One was an old Ford Ranger that had seen better days, and the other was a beat-up Saga from the '90s sporting a fading police logo. One tire was sagging.

Rabbil checked his pockets, lit another cigarette, and climbed out of the car.

4

Wesley liked it when the customers came into the store to do more than just buy things. A small town in Sabah isn't like a small town in another country. The people were neighborly. They liked talking to one another. Gossiping. Their center would be the one convenience store in town. *Did you know so and so are sleeping with one another? Is it true that he or she ran away to KK to make their fortune? Think the weather will be shit tomorrow?*

Aunt Zara said that when her father realized this, he made a small adjustment to the store. The front area was converted into a bar of sorts that could sit seven or eight, if they didn't mind squeezing in.

The rack on the right side, which contained the newspapers, magazines and secondhand books, was moved to the empty spot by the front doors, and this allowed for several mismatched tables and chairs to be placed there. Behind the coffee bar was a dual hot plate coffee warmer with two pots constantly cooking. There was also a little sign above that said *Coffee Never Rests Here*.

Lolo Zebedee didn't expect it to take off. He thought one or two people would mengopi while they talked, and at first, that did happen.

And then fishermen, who wanted something strong and sometimes sweet, had decided this was the place to go to after returning from their morning excursions in the Celebes Sea. By 8:15, they came in droves. And soon, they brought with them the night-shift workers at the terminal, who in turn, brought the morning-shift crew. Word spread that if you just wanted a place to sit down and drink black coffee, the All-Convenience Store was the place.

Soon, he added pastries made by Mrs Rozita, whose daughter would fly through culinary school and open a bakery next to the town's one nightclub. He split the profits with her 60-40.

"Coffee's just about ready," Delilah said. "Everything okay in there, Wes?"

Wesley was sorting through the written orders from yesterday. So and so wanted a couple jars of this, an extra rasher of that and a few packets of those. He had a dozen orders to pack before the first drop of what would be a torrent of customers came in.

"How's your aunt?" Wesley asked as he filled up the seventh paper bag with goods.

"Stuck. She's having one of those weeks," said Delilah as she loaded the ancient oven by the coffee machine with pastries. "Nothing's coming into her mind. She sent Lester to KK to find her more material."

"Publisher gnawing at her?"

"Like the customers when they see that we're open."

He chuckled. "What's this one about?"

"She doesn't know if it's a murder, a robbery then murder, or a kidnapping with murder as the red herring."

"Exciting."

"If you like mysteries like her, then yeah. The best I can do is offer ideas about what the kids are up to these days."

"And what are kids up to these days?"

"TikTok and selfies?"

Wesley snorted. The bell above the front door jingled.

"Eh, first customer is here. Drop your cock and grab some socks."

Wesley sealed up the paper bag with a short strip of tape and got up. "That's what the kids are up to as well?"

"Ha-ha."

X

The person who broke the news was Kak Tonna, who did the cleaning for the managing officers of the Seaside Chalets. Around 11:30am, she walked into the store with her pink Thermos that was stained because of the amount of coffee she liked. This was her first round. Before the end of the day, she would come in for two more refills of coffee.

"Tommy Asandu is dead," she said by way of greeting.

At the bar counter was Muzir, a fishing boat captain who, on that day, wasn't feeling well, but at the same time, wanted to be miles away from his wife's nagging at home. "I go to work, I kena. I'm sick also I kena," he'd told them this morning, shaking his head mournfully. He'd been there for some time now, sipping his fourth coffee and reading *Utusan Borneo*.

Along with him were several other customers. Two were tourists from Korea. One was a local, but rarely spoke, and the last was Mrs. Rozita, waiting patiently with her first coffee and waiting for Zara to come around for their daily dose of gossiping.

The atmosphere chilled right then. Delilah had been counting coins and Wesley had been leaning against the back shelf, nose buried in a Tana French paperback. Everyone stopped what they were doing and just stared at Kak Tonna as she ambled towards the counter.

"Did I hear you right?" Muzir asked, lowering his paper. He was just about done with the news from the world and was ready to enter the more thrilling sports section. Apparently MU had screwed the pooch at home again, according to the big story with massive headlines and long quotes that had been blown up for dramatic effect.

Kak Tonna placed her scarred Thermos on the counter and slapped a five-ringgit note next to it. "Found him by the old jetty. You know, the one everyone thinks is haunted. Happened this morning. Two teens staying at the last chalet went there for a 'walk'," Kak Tonna made air quotes.

Muzir looked at her, confused. "What do you mean?"

"Diorang tengah amput bah," Mrs. Rozita said.

Kak Tonna nodded. "The boy was almost at the station—"

"What station?" said Muzir.

"Pancut," Mrs. Rozita translated.

"When the girl, who was riding the boy, saw Tommy floating by the side of the jetty."

The old woman shuddered and then shook her head for good measure.

Mrs Rozita had managed to silently slither her way towards the seat adjacent to Kak Tonna. This was material for her. She was the town courier. Telephone, telefax, tele-Rozita, as the town joke in the coffeeshops and the bar went. Tell her something, and by tomorrow, half the town would know. Why bother with *Utusan* when you had Rozita, with added dramatic effects that would put Kak Tonna's to shame, of course.

"The police came this morning. Big Hilux truck. Three of them. Looked very interesting."

Muzir whistled. "Well, it's sad. But the boy's mother, she must be relieved."

Kak Tonna said, "He just died lah, Muzir."

"I know. But do you think she'd be sad? Ten ringgit says that when the cops go and talk to her, she'll be glad. Tommy Asandu was nothing but trouble."

5

“In my experience,” Sergeant Atiqah Lajis said as she sat down in the swivel chair directly under the air-conditioner, “death notifications are the worst. Like, they’ll break down, cry, scream. Break things. Hit something. Or just crumple. With Mrs Asandu…” Atiqah shook her head.

Rabbil had one buttock on the table in front of her, his arms crossed and there she was, just leaning back against the chair, her heels airborne, the tips of her toes touching pointed up, not saying anything.

“Cepat lah, Ticks,” he said.

“Mrs. Asandu was relieved.”

Standing behind her, Rudolph nodded. “It was weird.”

“Didn’t even seem mad. Just said that she was expecting this to happen for many, many years.”

Rabbil touched the stubble that was already growing on the bottom of his chin. He turned towards his notebook. No need to pick it up. No need to open it. The details were very, very sparse.

Back at the beach, the attending medical examiner, a pretty and petite woman named Dr Nitta Siddhu, had told him that they were looking at drowning as the cause of death.

“So close to the shore?” he asked, biting down on the cap of his ballpoint. It was the only substitute for a cigarette when he was at a crime scene. Seeing bodies gave him a sudden longing for nicotine.

"Stranger things have happened," the doctor said. She had an assistant who was holding an umbrella open for her as she took down notes about the body, which in turn, was lying in a black, yet to be zipped up, body bag. The victim had long, stringy hair. A couple of lip studs, earrings in the right ear, a thin, bony frame and needle tracks on his arms.

"My guess," said Dr Siddhu, as she continued scrawling over the papers attached to a Hello Kitty-themed clipboard, "is that he came here to shoot up, maybe the stuff was tainted, you know, cut bad, mixed bad." She shrugged. "Or he got the dose wrong because he did it at night, lost his footing, fell into the water and drowned. Wouldn't be the first one."

"Really?" Atiqah asked.

Dr Siddhu nodded. "Had a sailor in Sandakan do the same thing. November last year ka, or around there lah. He worked on a luxury yacht. Offered oral for extra tips, apparently. One night, during a party involving some politicians," she offered the cops a wink, "he ends up overshooting the ketamine, falls into the sea and drowns less than five feet away from the yacht. There was a big hoo-ha because a body was involved. Cooled down faster than this guy," she pointed at the dead body with the butt of her pen, "when they realized it was no one important."

"Time of death?" asked Rabbil, wanting to change the subject.

"We did a rectal check and I'm putting TOD between eleven and one in the morning."

Then there was the forensics. The officers had been a pair of idiots who were caught smoking under the shade of the beach trees. Thinking that Rabbil, Atiqah and Rudolph were tourists too curious for their own good, they began barking, only to stop and instantly turn amiable at the sight of Rabbil's blue kad kuasa. You could actually see their balls float up to their throats.

They had given their reports in what could best be described as babbled sputtering punctuated with the occasional long pause or the much-reached-for 'umms' and 'ahhs'.

But brief it was. A wallet had been found. Some change. A pack of soggy Marlboros smuggled from Indonesia, and that was it.

"No phone?" Rabbil asked.

Idiot 1 (this was the one with the mustache) had said no. When Rabbil asked if they'd checked, Idiot 2 (this one with the bigger belly) had sputtered out an answer about how they didn't have the right equipment.

"Then call someone who does," Rabbil snapped.

A quick conversation with Sergeant Awang, who was in charge of the outpost, had been somewhat fruitful.

"Tommy Asandu," Awang said with a sad shake of the head. "I never expected much from the boy. Used to be of the mischievous ilk, you know?" Rabbil shrugged. A short, quick one which said he didn't really care, and nodded so that Awang could continue: "Skipping school, stealing candy from the All-Convenience store. Vandalizing property. Minor stuff till he ended up doing drugs and killing that poor girl."

That accident happened eight years ago. A massive tragedy for a town like Darat Kumut. The girl had been a local taking the last ferry back from the island. She'd been working there, saving some money for vet school. Everything had been fine on the ride back, but while she was on the road and making her way back home, Tommy Asandu, brain cooked from booze, came barging down the very same blacktop that Rabbil had been on, car swerving from left to right.

According to the police report, Tommy only realized when his fender sent her and her bike into the air. Gravity took hold of her, and cruelly brought her down. The impact cracked her head open. Tommy, on the other hand, managed to crash his car into a tree and knock himself out.

Tommy got sent to jail. Came back last year. Got hired to work at the very place he'd been stealing from, but that didn't last long either.

"And now," said Awang, a short and stocky man in his early 40s with a receding head of curls, "this happens. I'm not going to lie, Inspector, but I can tell you, confidently, that there are a number of people in town who are sad, but glad this happened. Kid was a bad egg. It's a miracle he didn't take anyone else with him."

"Boss," Atiqah said, "what's the plan?"

"We'll wait for the medical examiner to get back with a detailed report. In the meantime, I want you to put pressure on Tawau Forensics. I want to make sure that the kid's phone is found. Those two idiots still around, kan?"

"They're having breakfast and trying to get someone down here to help them find the phone."

"Right. Work on that." He stood up and shoved his notebook into his back pocket, then touched his other pockets to make sure that his wallet, phone, cigarettes and lighter were all on his person. "I'm going to do a door-to-door."

"Need help, boss?" Rudolph asked.

"Help Sergeant Atiqah."

He nodded at them and made his way out of the tiny and cramped police outpost.

6

"That's not gonna change anything, you know," Delilah said. She sat to his left, away from the billowing cigarette smoke.

Wesley had been at the back of the store, by the dumpster, sitting on the steps, cigarette in left hand. His right hand was clenched into a fist, and his eyes were on it, the marks on the knuckles. The broken skin. The bruising. The scabs that had yet to heal.

"The cops are gonna think I did something," he said.

"Did you do something?" Delilah asked.

"Of course not," he said. "But you know how it looks ..."

"He tried to assault me, Wes. Imagine what would happen if you weren't there? If the cops call you in, I'll go in and talk to them as well." She extended a hand, her index finger tracing the injuries on his knuckles. "You used the ointment I bought you?"

"Yeah. Hurts like a bitch, though."

"You sound like one right about now."

He found himself smiling. Delilah was smiling as well. "It's painful–"

"A couple months before you came, I took a nasty fall. Scraped my knee. Skin turned into this mess of red. I used the ointment every day, without fail, and whenever Aunt Mabel or Lester came to ask if everything was okay, the one word I would refrain from using was–"

"Let me guess, *painful*?"

"Finish your smoke and get back in there."

"Yes, ma'am."

She gave him a playful punch on the arm and walked back into the store. He watched her go. Then leaned against the rusty stair railing. There was one good puff left, so he took it. As the smoke slowly trailed out in twin plumes from his nose, he heard someone clearing her throat. It sounded so familiar that …

The cigarette fell from his hands. Standing by the dumpster, hands across her chest, was Ashini.

Wesley felt the gentle ache in his chest. Then came the tingling in his fingers. He couldn't breathe and his heart was trying to set a new record for how many heartbeats it could pump without actually killing him.

"Ah …" he said, choking on his own voice. "Ah …" His left hand, now free of the cigarette, went scrambling for something to latch on to. Because if there was nothing, he would've definitely fallen.

Lucky poked his head out from the store, stared, transfixed at Wesley and then angled his head towards the dumpster. He let out a low whine, ears pressed flat against his skull before running back into the store.

"Wes," Ashini said. She had a smile on her face. Not the kind of smile that the demons, monsters and ghosts with bad intentions had, but one of genuine happiness. A smile that looked odd on the face of someone who had been dead for over nine months.

"You …" he sputtered. "You …"

"This could be stress, you know," she said. "It could be your imagination."

"I …"

"You need to let go, Wes."

"I …"

"Shit happens, remember?"

"Wes?"

He gasped and looked at the door, where Delilah stood, concerned. He turned back to the dumpster. Ashini – if that was her – was gone. What in the blue hell had happened?

"Wes?"

"Yeah, just … just had a little panic attack," he said, trying for a smile and coming up short with a grimace. Before entering the store room, he turned one more time and looked at the dumpster. No one there. Just a rubbish bin. Nothing special.

7

When he walked back into the store, he saw a man speaking with Zara and sipping coffee. He wasn't one of the locals. But he wasn't a tourist either. Tourists didn't come to the beach in a long-sleeved shirt, slacks and tie. And most importantly, tourists didn't come to the beach on holiday with a gun.

"Hi," the man said, turning to notice Wesley. He reached for something on the table and lifted it up. Wesley took a few more steps and saw that it was a police authority card. This one was blue. On the left was a picture of the man, younger, hair shorter. On the right were three lines of information. The first was the man's number. The second was his rank (Inspector), and below that, the guy's date of birth and IC number.

"Inspector Rabbil Harris, CID KK," the man said, offering a friendly smile. "I'm looking into Tommy Asandu's death."

"I'm Wesley Moysin."

"You look familiar, by the way," said the inspector. "Have we met before? Or are you one of those people? You know, the ones with faces that everyone thinks they've seen before?"

Wesley shook his head. His heart, which had calmed down from whatever it was that happened earlier, was picking up a new beat. "Probably that second one."

The inspector was silent, eyeing Wesley closely. When the quiet got a little too quiet, he said, "Probably. Look, I'd like to talk to you about Tommy Asandu."

The only sound that remained came from the store room, where Margie was in a chair watching *Barney & Friends* on Aunt Zara's tablet. Delilah stood by the door to the back, arms crossed. Aunt Zara, who'd been watching their exchange, locked her eyes on the inspector. Her posture went rigid.

"Inspector," Aunt Zara said, "need I remind you that I'm a lawyer?"

"Yes, but in conveyancing, not criminal law," he said calmly, digging through his back pocket and pulling out a notebook. From his shirt pocket came a ballpoint with a scarred cap. "And, this isn't an interrogation, Ms. Mudis. It's simply me asking some questions. Looking for pointers. No one is talking about murder. And no one is pointing the finger at your nephew." His eyes were on Wesley as he said this. "I'm sure you're good at Q and A, right, Wesley?"

Wesley nodded once.

"Okay then. Oh, I'll need another cup of coffee as well, Ms. Mudis, if that's not a problem?"

X

"So you came here a month ago? Just packed your bags and moved here?"

"Two months," Wesley corrected.

The inspector nodded, cut out something, scribbled another thing. "And before this, you were working in KL?"

Wesley nodded. "PJ, actually."

"As?"

Wesley felt the tremors in his hands and shoved them into his pockets. A bead of sweat slowly slid down the back of his head.

He was very sure that soon, the inspector would see how bad he was doing because of guilt. He mumbled an answer. In his mind, it came out clear. But Inspector Rabbil cocked his head to one side, leaned closer and asked him to repeat himself.

"As a news reporter."

"I'm very sure that's what I heard," he wrote down something. *Scritch, scritch, scritch* went the pen. "And you left that job?"

Deep breaths, he told himself, deep *fucking* breaths. "Yeah."

"Why ah?"

"I ..." Deep. Breaths. "I just couldn't cut it, you know," he said, "working in KL wasn't like anything I could do. It was just full of politics, and you know the editors always had their own little pets, and if you were one of the new guys, you needed to pay your dues and ..." Realizing that he was on the verge of babbling, Wesley paused, took a short drag of air, and said, "One day I just crumbled. Had a panic attack. Handed in my resignation. Came home."

"And then moved here?"

Wesley nodded.

"Why here?"

"I wanted to get away from the big city. I felt stifled. Crowded in."

"I thought that him moving here would give him a new start," said Aunt Zara.

Inspector Rabbil turned to her. "You invited him here?"

Aunt Zara nodded.

"Now" – his gaze shifted back to Wesley – "when you arrived, Tommy Asandu was still working here, right?"

Wesley nodded.

"And you met him when you arrived?"

Wesley nodded again.

"Was he the first person you met?"

"No. The second."

"I see. What did you think of him?"

"Well ..." *Uncomfortable* was the first word to come into his mind. When Tommy Asandu had swaggered into the shop from his 45 minute-long smoke break, he smiled at Wesley, and 15 minutes later, when Delilah went into the bathroom, tried to sell him meth. Or, Tommy had said, if ice's too strong for you, maybe we can settle on some weed?

Wesley had politely declined, and Tommy, still with that wolfish smile, called him a pussy. Things got worse when Tommy found out that A) Wesley was Zara's nephew and B) Wesley would be working at the store. From then on, Tommy was actively hostile to Wesley. Shooting him dirty looks. 'Accidentally' bumping into him. Stealing his lighter. Making lewd jokes because he and Delilah were growing close as friends. Once he'd even sung: *Wesley and Delilah sitting on a tree, F-U-C-K-I-N-G,* which had caused Delilah (by then, the verbal pokes and prods had been going on for two weeks) to pull off her shoe and throw it at him.

That had led to a big fight, which in turn, led to Tommy storming out of the store and disappearing for an entire week.

Scritch, scratch, scritch, scratch went Inspector Rabbil' pen as he wrote Wesley's filtered version of events. He kept things pretty diplomatic. The sudden drug sale wasn't in there. But he did add in the part about how Tommy had been a pain in the ass from the moment he started working there.

"Did it get to you?" Inspector Rabbil asked.

"It got to *us*," said Delilah.

"And you are?"

"Delilah Loh. I work here. Have for some time now."

"Mmhm" – then back to Wesley again – "anything else happen between you and him?"

Wesley wanted to answer, but the sight of Ashini standing right behind the inspector, checking out a box of Koko Krunch, knocked the wind out of him. He just stood there, staring at a point beyond Inspector Rabbil's shoulder.

"Wes?"

"Uh, sorry?"

"Did anything else happen between you and Tommy? He was ribbing you, right? You must've been unhappy with him."

"I ..." He had been looking at the inspector, but he was momentarily caught off guard by movement behind the inspector. Ashini had placed the box of cereal back on the shelf. She looked at him, her cheerful smile up and ready.

"*Wes*," she said in a clear voice, "*if you don't speak, he'll have more questions. Journalism one-oh-one remember? Oh, and you not saying anything* says *something. Remember that too.*"

"Right," he said.

Deep. Fucking. Breaths.

"Sorry?" said Inspector Rabbil.

"I ... well, I got into a fight with Tommy about ... well, he was being a terrible customer."

The Inspector nodded and scribbled some more. "Was that here?"

"No," said Delilah. "At the Seaside Bar. Wes and I went there for a drink one night. About a week ago. And when I went in to order a round, Tommy approached me and ... he uhh ... he tried – no – attempted to assault me."

The scritch and scratch of the pen stopped. Rabbil looked at Delilah. His lips were now pursed. He took a few moments to process this bit of information and then said, "And then what happened?"

"I fought him off. Slapped him. Wesley saw this and–"

"I, no, we – me and Delilah – were sitting on the deck. I saw what happened, and just rushed in there."

"And then?"

Wesley wasn't sure at all. Delilah had told him later that she had never seen him so angry. Neither had Tommy. Which had probably been the reason he kicked Tommy's ass so hard that the guy just ran away. He'd blanked out.

"We fought."

"Outside the bar?"

Wesley nodded.

Scritch and *scratch* went the pen.

"And you beat him?"

"I think so."

"You think so?" Inspector Rabbil said. "Why do you say that?"

"I don't remember much of the fight. I just blanked out."

"Blanked out, no memory?"

"Yeah."

"Is that normal?"

"I've never been in a fight."

"But you kicked the shit out of him."

"I think so."

"Mhmm. Can I see your hand? The right one. It is the right hand?"

Hesitantly, Wesley pulled his right hand out of his pocket. Ashini (if that had been her and not his brain slowly fragmenting into madness) was no longer there.

Inspector Rabbil looked at the scabs. "Damn." Looking down at his notebook, he flipped a couple of pages and checked out some earlier notes and said, "According to witnesses who were present at the fight, you *mauled* Tommy Asandu."

"Okay," Aunt Zara said, "I'm putting a stop to this. You're trying to implicate my nephew in some way in Tommy Asandu's death, and I am having none of it. Charge him or stop your little fishing trip, inspector."

Inspector Rabbil turned to her. "Just poking my nose around. If he was *killed*, and even though he sounds like the resident scum, Tommy Asandu deserves some kind of justice." He reached for his wallet, paid for the coffee and then placed his card above the 1 ringgit note. "If you remember anything, please call. I'm not on a witch hunt here. Just curious. Cheers."

8

With a strangled yelp, Wesley jumped up from bed, gasping. A cool wind blew into his room from the window, but he was sweating. His breathing was going places, and his heart was beating with a mad frenzy. He reached for his phone and saw that it was 3:53 am. He'd had about two hours of sleep.

It had been a nightmare. After months of peaceful sleep where all he experienced was darkness, his mind had formed a new nightmare to scare the living shit out of him.

Deep breaths, he told himself. Deep, fucking breaths. Maybe count back from 10 as well? Anything, really, to calm him down.

He swung his legs from the bed, wrapped himself with the blanket, grabbed his cigarettes and stepped out into the hallway. Aunt Zara's door was closed. As was Margie's. Lucky slept on the front porch and offered a soft whine when he stepped out. Wesley sat on the porch, bare feet on the sandy grass. Lucky moved positions and sat next to him. Wesley ran a hand over the dog's head and back as he smoked.

He reached back for the nightmare that shocked him awake. It had played out in first person. It's nighttime. He's walking along the beach path. Only there's someone in front of him. He recognizes the clothes. Start with the jeans: a dark shade of blue once upon a time, but now washed to a pale color. He has long, oily hair that looks like it could use a good wash. A black T-shirt. Beat-up sneakers. The guy is smoking a cigarette. But he pauses in the midst of a puff to spread his arms out, and now he's banking up and down and side to side, making weird noises. Like a jet engine, almost. *Whoosh, whoosh, whoosh.*

But Wesley knows that it's not just any guy. Wesley knows that the person in front of him is Tommy Asandu, the biggest asshole a nice little town like Darat Kumut could produce. Sure, he'd kicked his ass a few days ago, but Tommy's a piece of shit, and he could be plotting all sorts of ways to harm Aunt Zara. Margie. Shit, even Lucky. But most importantly, he could be thinking of hurting Delilah, and no way is that ever going to happen.

So do something about it, he told himself. Remember what happened the last time bad people were allowed to hurt, no *take away*, someone you cared about?

There's a short blackout, and then he's there, at the rotting, old jetty by Pantai Pasir Balung. Tommy stands by the edge, zipping up. He'd just peed, and is rummaging through his pockets, searching for his cigarettes, because he flicked the last one away before he released a golden stream into the clear blue sea.

Wesley takes several steps forward. The wood under him creaks. Loudly. Tommy turns, hands still in his pockets. His fly half up, a shocked look on his face.

Which is when Wesley woke up with a gasp.

"I didn't kill him, Luckster," he said to the dog.

The dog whined softly.

"Really," he said, bending down and shoving the burning end of the cigarette into the sand. "I couldn't have. Right?"

And that was what worried him, because truth be told, Wesley couldn't exactly remember where he was the night Tommy died.

Just like how he couldn't remember *mauling* Tommy outside the bar.

Wesley reached for his cigarettes. Sleep wouldn't be coming for him tonight. That's a fact he was very, very sure of.

9

But somehow, sleep did come.

Because the next morning, Delilah was there.

His eyes were closed, but he smelled her. It was a smell that was so familiar. Lily of the valley. Light enough that it wasn't pervasive. He smiled because it reminded him of the first time he saw her, standing behind the counter. Book open in front of her. Her short, shoulder-length hair, dark brown with blonde tips from an old dye job. And when she'd noticed him standing there, she hadn't been rude. She'd smiled at him.

He opened his eyes, and the first thing he saw was her. She sat on the floor, legs tucked up to her chest, back against the couch, reading her battered Virginia Woolf paperback, humming a tune quietly.

Wait a minute. This is happening right now?

"Delilah?" he croaked.

She turned and smiled. "Finally. Zara said you might be out till noon, but I knew she was wrong about you."

"Noon …" he muttered.

"Yeah. She's given us the day off."

"What about …"

"The store? She's there right now running things. Told us we could use the break."

"Huh. What about Margie?"

"In her room. Watching *Sesame Street* with Lucky."

"You've been here long?"

"Got here at seven. Zara was already up. You were dead to the world on the couch, and based on the number of cigarette butts out there by the porch, we figured out that you ended up not sleeping."

"Had a nightmare."

"Well, it's morning. No more nightmares. Hopefully."

Wesley then realized that other than his boxers and the blanket, there was nothing else covering him. "Uhh," he said, sitting up and wrapping the blanket around him as fast as he could, "what's the plan?"

"Breakfast, for you, shower and chill at my place? Mabel was very excited last night when I told her about what happened. She says that she wants to talk to you about your experience. Hopes that it'll help get her out of her slump. We can bring Zara and Lucky with us."

"Sure," he said. "Uh … I'm gonna go shower, okay?"

"Don't let me stop you. Love that your boxers are so colorful, by the way."

"Oh fuck off," he said, loving the tinkling of Delilah's laughter, which followed him to his room.

×

"It wasn't exciting, I can tell you that much," he said.

"Oh hosh-posh," said Mabel Mah with a wave of her massive fingers.

"Sugar?" Lester Rungam, Mabel's personal assistant asked, taking a step back from the table, both hands still on the pot.

"In green tea?" Wesley asked back. "You can hear the entire nation of Japan weep."

Mabel chuckled. "Smart boy," she said as Lester slowly filled her cup.

"Cool T-shirt, bro," Wesley said as Lester filled their teacups.

Mabel raised her lips in something that might've been mild disgust. "I'm a big believer in the freedom to express yourself, but really, Lester …"

Lester grinned. He placed the pot back down and got to work slicing the cheesecake that Mabel had baked this morning. The T-shirt in question was black, covered on the back with a massive white skull, with a mop of hair over its head and a lopsided, forked tongue hanging out of its grinning mouth. At the front, over the chest, were the letters *BSF* in bloody red print.

"Secret society?" Wesley asked, nodding at the letters.

"Band," Lester replied. "Borneo Skull Fuckers. Best hair metal band in all of East Malaysia. Saw them at the Rainforest Rock Festival before the pandemic hit, and," he whistled, "they were fire."

"I'm sure they were," Mabel said. "That'll be all, Lester."

There was a sound of screaming. All three of them glanced down to see Margie, pigtails flopping, running from Delilah. They were playing tag downstairs because Mabel wanted a private word with Wesley. Delilah looked up at them and smiled at Wesley. He smiled back and waved. And then she was gone, chasing his little cousin around the massive lawn and garden.

"If you want to," said Wesley, "you can call the inspector and tell him you're a viable suspect."

Mabel snorted as she blew on the surface of her teacup. "What's my motive then?"

"Book research?"

This time she laughed, a deep boom that transitioned into a loud cackle. The sound did not match the woman in front of him who was dressed today in a fuchsia dress and bunny slippers. Bracelets of gold, silver and pearl lined her wrist. Rings covered eight of her fingers. There was a cross around her neck. Her nails were painted a shade of light blue. And though she wasn't going out, Mabel Mah had her long hair coiffured and ready as if in a few hours she'd be at a ball or hosting it.

He didn't tell her that yesterday wasn't the first time that he'd been interviewed by the cops. Nor was it the second.

"All life is sacred," Mabel said. Done with the little sips of tea, she reached for the massive pipe sitting by the pot. The bowl was carved from meerschaum into the shape of a lion's head, the top now open and stuffed with tobacco. In turn, Wesley pulled out his cigarettes and lit one. "All life is sacred," she said once more, after a puff of her pipe. "I believe that. Even the life of Tommy Asandu, who tried to assault my niece. Though I believe karma would have finally gotten her nails into him. But to end up drowned in less than five feet of water…" Mabel shook her head. "How are you, by the way? Have you managed to put words on paper?"

He shook his head. When he'd first met Mabel, she was delighted to know that he was an artist of the alphabet. Her excitement had doubled when he told her that he was a big reader as well, and she clapped when he mentioned some of his favorite writers. At that moment, she introduced herself as a Lady of the Letters as well, a mystery writer who went under the pseudonym Martha Lee.

Wesley had heard of Martha Lee, celebrated author of the Diyana and Dante Chen mystery novels which chronicled two amateur teen sleuths who started solving crimes in a fictionalized version of Sandakan, but now, according to the series, were young adults working in KK and doing the whole detective gig part-time.

Authors like Rozlan Mohd Noor, Chua Kok Yee, Heidi Shamsuddin, Maizura Abas, and Hanna Alkaf had written blurbs comparing her work to that of Enid Blyton by way of Roald Dahl, with a little seasoning of Sue Grafton and Val McDermid for that noir flavor. There had even been talk that local film production company Kuman Pictures was thinking of adapting one of her books for the big screen, with big honcho Amir Muhammad all but confirming it on his Twitter account.

That had made Mabel Mah a very wealthy woman. Her house wasn't a cottage, but a bungalow further down the road from the other houses. It was massive, with a lawn, a small swimming pool and a conservatory that overlooked the sea.

"No," Wesley said. "I haven't been able to."

"Have you tried notebooks? Stephen King writes long-hand, you know. I used to have a typewriter, but I realized that nothing beats pen and paper. Well, except Lester, who does the typing, of course," she added with a chuckle.

"I just can't," he said. "It's like what happened just knocked the wind out of my sails, you know?"

Mabel nodded gravely, though it was a known fact that every year (for the last 20 years), without fail Apex Publishing, a semi-independent company now with ties to Penguin Random House in Singapore, would receive a typed manuscript from Martha Lee just after Halloween. This year would be no different, of course. "I've only had ..." – she suckled on her pipe for several seconds – "three writing blocks. Including this one, of course. The first two were solved with a little marijuana over the course of … an entire week, was it? But since my sometime dealer is now gone, well …"

"Tommy Asandu sold you drugs?"

She nodded. "Where else are you going to find a supplier in this place? I always knew that boy was trouble. Even before he killed that poor girl years ago. He was already selling by then, you know. Only 23 and involved in drugs. Didn't start taking it until about a month from that stupid accident."

"Is that why you summoned me?" Wesley asked. "You wanna see if I know something about his death? If I was … *involved* in it somehow?"

She raised a finely threaded eyebrow at him. Her eyes, already magnified and massive behind the thick lenses of her glasses, widened even more. And she laughed again. "Wesley. I applaud you for standing up to that little shit, God rest his soul, and giving him a good beating for trying to defile my niece. But anyone can see that you'd never have been capable of killing Tommy Asandu."

"People are capable of anything."

"Maybe. But did he threaten to hurt you? Your family?" She paused when they heard Margie's laugh and Delilah saying, "I've got you!" Mabel glanced in the direction of their voices, very close to the little gate leading to the beach, and nodded. "Maybe he threatened Delilah. What would you have done then?"

Wesley didn't answer because he didn't know the right answer. He was not a fan of violence and had never resorted to it. But what happened the other day at the fight … what might have happened two days ago the night Tommy Asandu died, the dreams …

"I … don't know," he said.

"And that's why you couldn't have done it. You're a good person, Wesley. I knew it the moment we first met. So no, I didn't invite you here to see if you might've done something to Tommy Asandu. I invited you here because I wanted to see if you wanted to do something about it. Say … look into Tommy's death, maybe?"

10

X

"Why would I want to do that?" he asked. "Isn't that why the police are here?"

"Oh, would you humor an old woman? I'm not saying that the police wouldn't do their job. They'll do it, or else why pay taxes, yes? I'm saying that it's likely that the cops wouldn't want to take an interest in the death of the town pariah. I mean … let's review the facts as Lester here has managed to collect them."

Lester stood by the double glass doors, vaping. He winked at them when Mabel said his name and continued scrolling through something on his phone, occasionally swiping left or right with a nod or a shake of the head.

"The known gossip is that Tommy Asandu was found dead without any wounds or signs of a struggle," she began.

"How do you know this?"

"Officer Radus, one of the new guys under Awang," said Lester without looking up from his phone, "the kid talks too much. Especially after a few drinks. All I did was buy him a bucket of Tiger last night, and he got it in his mind that I need to be plied with information."

"Uh-huh."

"I shall continue," said Mabel. "While we wait for the impressionable Officer Radus to get us more information, specifically on the autopsy, which I suppose will confirm whether or not Tommy Asandu was *murdered*, we have to take into account the manner of his death."

"This is normally how she starts a book," Lester whispered loudly to Wesley. "I'm the sounding board."

"Most of the time. Now shoo away you," said Mabel with a smile. "Anywho, as I was saying, Tommy Asandu's death is very odd. Have you heard?"

Wesley shook his head.

"He drowned. In five feet of seawater. Or that's what they're saying for now. The theory, according to our lovely leak at the station–"

"AKA *Deepthroat*," said Lester.

"Shush, you. The source at the station said that his foot was caught in one of the jetty's pylons. But it's still a weird way to drown."

"Unless he was under the influence of drugs," added Lester.

"Yes, precisely. But we wouldn't know any of that until our source gets back to us. In the meantime, we're going to put some question marks on COD. That's Cause of Death, if you're wondering."

Wesley just nodded.

"So, the theory I developed," said Mabel, taking another puff from her pipe, "is that Tommy went to the old jetty to get high, got high, and while in the midst of such an exceptional high, was tossed into the sea where the killer or killer*s* forced his head into the water until he stopped breathing."

"Wouldn't he have heard them?" Wesley asked. "The old jetty is creaky, isn't it?"

"Well, I was thinking about that as well, but over some nice and fluffy scrambled eggs, I noted that two things must have happened. And mind you, these are just *theories*, so bring some salt to sprinkle."

"Got a whole bag in the kitchen," said Lester.

Ignoring him, Mabel said, "Theory one is that Tommy, a known and frequent addict, would've shot himself up with a lot of drugs to … I don't know, numb the senses, send him up into euphoric bliss, and he was so high, he didn't hear the perpetrator or perpetrator*s* until the last minute and then they pushed him over the jetty, into the sea and," she paused to wet her lips with some warm green tea, "force him under, I suppose, would be the gentlest of terms.

"The second theory, and this is me delving into some Tom Clancy, so it's a little … dramatic and far-fetched, is that the killer or killers was already waiting for Tommy and was hiding *under* the jetty. I could be wrong, but there is some space under the jetty, right, Lester?"

"Might be. I could take a look if you wanted me to. But yeah. The jetty sits a few feet above the sea, right, so there's a little breathing space under there."

Mabel nodded. "And then, as Tommy is slowly succumbing to the sweet poison that's doing a number on his senses and his mind, the villain slowly climbs up onto the jetty – if there were two of them I'd imagine them coming from both sides – subdues Tommy, gets him into the water and drowns him. If there were two, I suppose the attack would have been easier. Faster."

"Or," Wesley said as he crushed his cigarette into a chipped plate, "what if he just slipped while he was high, tumbled into the sea and drowned there?"

"Unlikely," Mabel replied. "Remember, even though he's high, there's something in him telling him to keep some of his wits about him. Not all, or else he'd still be among the living today, but enough that if something were to happen, say falling into an ocean, he would have enough brainpower to find a way to get back to land. So no, I don't believe that he just fell into the sea and died. What'd be the fun in that?"

"Too soon, boss," Lester said, with a shake of his head and a dramatic whistle.

"Hush you" – and turning back to him – "Wesley, from what I understand, the cops are looking at you for this because of that little spat you had with Tommy. Everyone in this town has a story or is related to someone who has a story about how Tommy Asandu made their life miserable. Some worse than others. But you were his latest piss bucket. From the start, he did nothing but push you. You pushed back because you were just fed up, which is a normal thing, and now here we are. With a dead body and a lot of curiosity. If you don't want to treat this like you are clearing your name, why don't you treat it as an article? A special feature. And I'm not talking about a one-thousand-word piece, but a long-form thing. A cozy mystery made real. The most hated person in a sleepy little seaside village is suddenly killed. The village has questions. Of course, no is asking loudly because why rock the boat, but you get it, right?"

"I think so. But if I research it, speak to people, write it, what then?"

She shrugged. "Show me. If it's a good story, I'll find someone to sell it to. My friends in Apex know someone. People will want to read this. Especially with your skills."

"I haven't written in a long time."

"I've always looked at writing as a sort of muscle memory. Just like riding a bike or playing an instrument. Constant practice eases things. With writing, it's all about forming the words in your mind and then arranging them on paper. Or you can go the path of Neil Gaiman, just put the words down and then edit later. You can do it, Wesley. Don't tell me you're retired at 24, and now you just want to pour coffee and hit the keys of a cash register?"

"No … It's a calming job …"

"Calming and *boring*. You were put on this earth to write, boy. It's your vocation, and I only say that because of how flawlessly you write." All this talking made her thirsty. She took another sip of tea, several long pulls from the pipe and then: "I called Edna, you know."

Wesley, who was in the midst of lighting up another cigarette (*last one*, he promised himself), paused. *Now there's a name I haven't heard in some time.* His former editor. Tough old bird. Had seen a lot of shit in her almost 40-year career as a news reporter. The Abu Sayyaf kidnappings in Sipadan in 2000, Lahad Datu in 2013, as well as a series of other news reports of great fame and history-making that earned her the sobriquet 'The Queen of the Front Page'.

Most had thought she would walk the beat until death came for her, but one fine day, while covering for a colleague in court, Edna suffered a vicious heart attack that opened up two new paths for her: assistant news editor, followed by the big chair as news editor, or a career in teaching. She had been new to the role of editor when he walked into the famed hallways of *Daily Malaysia*, a fresh-faced cub reporter, so green he was practically pissing kale.

"How did that conversation go?" he asked.

"She was a bit sad that you never called to tell her that you're still alive. But other than that, she's content. Said a lot of good things about you before … well, before *that* incident. And wishes that you'd consider coming back. 'One of the best' was the term she used to describe you."

He just nodded. Thinking of Edna brought him back to a scene that felt like it belonged to someone else's life. He saw the desks in the newsroom. The massive clock above the doors to the conference room telling everyone that it was 10:30 pm. Most of the day-shift crew were out.

The night-shift people were in, but so were Wesley, Edna, Shaerine and Tara. They had been working on a big story then, a group effort being led by Shaerine, who was a new writer, assisted by Tara, with Wesley playing the role of the sub-editor. The story was simple, but still shattering in the right spheres: pangolins being smuggled and sold in the heart of the capital. The dalang of the matter being a respected businessman (Datukship included, par for the course) with ties to several prominent politicians, who had, three weeks before Shaerine stumbled on this story, launched a massive partnership with WWF Malaysia under the banner of going green and keeping the earth clean.

At 10:30 pm, they were waiting for one final detail from their source in this whole mess (the businessman's PA, who happened to be the older sister of Shaerine's boyfriend) to furnish them with some pictures of the man in question visiting the site where pangolins would be auctioned off. Wesley wanted out of that scene. It was too strong, too vibrant, too many memories he couldn't bear thinking about. Mabel brought him back to reality by speaking. He was thankful to her for that.

"This might be a redundant question, Wesley," said Mabel, "but do you miss it? The hunt for the story, speaking to people, watching as they shower you with information? Stumbling onto documents, adding more questions to your questions? Watching as the pieces slowly fit? The whole Woodward and Bernstein thing?"

"Believe it or not, I've never seen *All the President's Men*."

She chuckled. "You didn't answer my question."

"I … I do," he said. As he said the words, a breath of clean air, with gentle hints of salt and sea, brushed against his cheek and ruffled his hair. The wind seeped away, and its absence felt like some kind of finality. *No*, Wesley thought, *not a finality but a sign*. Something had shifted, and he was going along for the ride.

11

"She talked you into it?" Delilah asked.

"Not exactly. I..." he paused and considered his words, then let them out slowly, "miss doing it. Being a journalist. Finding things out. The whole Woodward and Bernstein thing."

"Who?"

"A couple of reporters. They brought down a president. A nice read on Wikipedia if you need to sleep."

"Right, so anyway, Mabel wants you to solve a death."

"I think it's 'solve a murder', you know, 'cause a death sounds definite, no questions at the end, just something set in stone. But if you're feeling technical, then yes, she wants me to probe Tommy's death. She's convinced that it's murder."

They paused when Margie squealed. She was on the beach, running with Lucky, holding the string of a kite in both hands. The kite was about 30 feet up and climbing. The wind from the sea blew and blew and blew, making it flap and shudder in the air. The sun had decided that it had basked the earth with too much heat and was now taking a little break behind the clouds. The effect was a windy day that was bright, not hot and cloudy. The perfect time to go out and just enjoy God's earth.

Wesley and Delilah sat on the concrete side of the beach path. They'd taken off their slippers. Warm sand floated and slithered between their toes. They were sitting close, but not too close, because he needed another cigarette to tell Delilah about everything that Mabel had just told him. She listened with barely a reaction. Her question came after a short break to stare at the sea, the island in the distance and the horizon further on.

"Would it bother you that Mabel might be using you?" she asked.

"Is she?" Wesley asked back.

"She's having a writing slump at the moment, and sending you out to gather clues might just help her with her next bestseller."

"The thought did cross my mind for a moment there. But like I told you …"

"She wants you to write it? A story that parallels hers? She would have detested it."

"Mine's about the facts, you know. Hers … well, she could always write 'based on a true story' in the preface."

Delilah laughed. Then brushed a rogue lock of hair that had fallen over her eyes. As she tucked it behind her ear, she said, "You said you wanted to do it. Do you, like, really want to do it?"

"I don't see why not," he said. "The cop yesterday rattled me, Lilah. I mean … he was being coy and shit, but he really was looking to see if I was involved in Tommy's death. And the truth is I don't even have an answer for that."

"What do you mean?"

"I never told you this, but the fight at Seaside, I don't remember it."

"What? But you were lucid. You … even after they pulled you off Tommy, you looked … well *fine* isn't the right word for it, but you looked like you were there, like you were aware of what you just did."

"Lilah," he said slowly, "I remember you screaming at Tommy. I remember that I was leaning against the railing at the deck. I remember moving and then this brief nothingness. Next thing I know, we're outside Zara's place, you're washing my hands and asking me if my ribs hurt. And they did. I lost about thirty minutes of my life there, and I was scared shitless."

"Is that why you asked if he was okay?"

Wesley nodded.

"Was it the first time?"

He shook his head. "No. But it was the first time in a while. The last time was … before I got on a bus and came here. Back in KL. Back in KK … I'd wake up in another place. I'd be doing something and then blackout. And when the lights came back on, I'd be somewhere else."

"Does it have to do with …"

He nodded. "My therapist told me that there's a small population of people who, after experiencing trauma, have these memory blanks. Back then … before I came here, they were bad. I was in a bad place and …" He shook his head.

Delilah placed a comforting hand on his shoulder and squeezed. "You didn't kill him."

"You don't know that."

"I do," she said firmly this time, "you could have done that in front of the bar when you were beating him. You could have just knocked him into a coma, broke his neck. Not stop when they were pulling at you. You had the chance to do that, but you didn't. That's how I know you didn't kill Tommy."

"Thanks," he said.

Delilah removed her hand from his shoulder, found his left hand, which was free and resting on his knee, and entwined her fingers between his. His grip was limp, so she gave him a squeeze. "If you want to do this, then I'd like to do it with you."

"You sure?" he asked, mildly shocked to see their hands together, and a little happy as well, the beat of his heart picking up rapidly, but in a good way, a way that he hadn't felt in a very long time.

Wesley squeezed back. Suddenly he felt reenergized. What had happened nine months ago was still there, still haunted him, but he knew right then that although he had to live it with, he could not allow it to define him. Just like a tattoo you got during a long night of drinking and making bad decisions.

Ashini's voice was suddenly by his right ear. "Heal up, Wes. I'm right here with you."

And for that, he was thankful.

12

Wesley stared at the items on his desk. The pens sat on one side. Next to them was the notebook, a gift from Mabel just before he left her house earlier.

The front was leather-bound. Embossed on it was the logo of the Mystery Writers of Malaysia Association – a bloody keris buried into a skull – at the center. The notebook was chunky, the paper thick, premium stuff you might find used by lawyers when drafting an agreement.

"They give these things out to me every six months to check up on me and see if I'm still alive and kicking," said Mabel as she cleaned out her pipe. "Honestly, I don't really bother, and I think the damn things are a bit too tacky for my tastes." With a very thick forefinger she'd tapped a legal pad on the side of the table, which was filled with her tiny, cramped handwriting. "Wrote my first book with three of these. Been using them ever since."

The first page was a blank sheet of paper. On the center, at the top of the first page, Wesley wrote Tommy's name. Then a short arrow. First, *location*. Then *cause of death*, and finally *theories*, which were the ones he and Mabel talked about. Then, using a Watson's gift card, he created a line at the center of the page.

In that blank spot, he adds another title: *Suspects*. Then the number *1* below that on the left side of the page.

He flipped the page. And at the top, he added *witness/sources/statements*. This would be a summary of his findings when he started asking questions, poking his nose in the bushes and shaking the trees to see what fell out. The adjacent page was for his ramblings and doodles that might make sense. He began with *family members* – Tommy's sister and mother – and then the first of the many unknowns: *friends*. Friends would mean … customers? Fellow junkies? Other suppliers? A girlfriend? These possibilities were listed without any order. And they were categories, not actual people.

"Maybe all of them did it," he mumbled. In the living room, Margie and Delilah were watching an episode of *Sesame Street*, Delilah constantly prodding Margie with questions about the characters. This time she was asking about Big Bird's feathers for some reason. Margie, on the other hand, was explaining everything patiently. Lucky was outside by the washing machine, eating.

Wesley stepped outside. Dusk was slowly spreading into town. The sun was dipping behind the horizon. The wind from the sea continued blowing.

Delilah got up from the sofa and left Margie in peace to enjoy the antics of the Muppets. She joined him on the deck, which faced the little stone path leading to the front gate. It was the same spot he'd sat on this morning after waking up from his nightmare.

"You and Tommy," he said as she sat down next to him, "did you guys talk much?"

"Not really. After he realized that I wasn't interested in sleeping with him or buying his drugs, he just stayed well away from me. Didn't dare do anything stupid. Especially since Zara and Margie were constantly in the store."

"Did you guys ever talk? You know, not the important stuff, just talking for the sake of talking?"

She nodded. "A few times. But I don't remember most of it. Why?"

"I'm trying to find people," he said, "people who might've been friends with Tommy. Someone who could point us in the right direction."

"Well, there's Syakir. He's the only person I ever heard Tommy talk about."

"Another junkie?"

"A functional one, apparently. He works on the island as an IT guy for the resort. Lives on the mainland, though. Tommy told me that this Syakir is a friend he lepaks with sometimes. Said they spent time together at the Pearl-0."

"What's that?"

"The club on the island. Extremely expensive, but I heard it's fun."

"*Heard?*"

She smiled at him mischievously. "Okay, so I went there once because a customer *asked* me."

Wesley wanted to ask if the club was just the limit, or if she and this mysterious person took things to another level. Those rooms at the resort were pretty nice. The brochure (both physical and e-version) emphasized the stunning views of the ocean, the comfortable beds, the floor-to-ceiling glass panes that surround the expansive bathroom, as well as the morning view when you step out onto the balcony. Only, he decided that maybe there are questions that you shouldn't ask. Ignorance can be bliss. After all, she'd never pushed him about KL.

"That's the only person, Syakir?" Wesley asked instead.

"That's the only person I heard of."

"Next, there's the family."

"His mom rarely leaves the house. Can't stand the way people in town look at her. Associating her with him. His sister, Tabitha, is someone you can consider getting answers from."

"Does she normally come to town?"

"She does. Normally it's to tapau food or buy groceries. She'll only come into the store if it's empty. Like her mom, doesn't like the way people look at her. Guilty by association."

Wesley rubbed the back of his head and sighed. "Anything else I'm missing?"

"The accident. The one with the Everett girl?"

"Ah."

"If you're lucky you might bump into Julian Everett at the ferry terminal. You can ask, but I doubt he wants to talk about Tommy Asandu. Did I tell you about the one time he bumped into Tommy in the middle of town? Tommy was coming back from lunch, and Julian had to pick up some batteries from the store. It didn't end well. Took three men to hold Julian back. I think it was the first time he saw Tommy since the sentencing. He was livid that Tommy had come back to town and was working in a store."

"When was this?"

"Uhh … about two weeks before you got here? They fought right outside the store. Margie was taking a nap in the back, so it was just me and Zara."

"Any recordings?"

She shook her head. "The town doesn't air its dirty laundry, remember? A couple of tourists saw, the older guys fed them a cock and bull story, and that was that. They talked, warned Julian about shitting on the town in front of outsiders. Didn't bother with Tommy because he knew the rules and he didn't swing first."

Wesley absorbed all of this. He was staring at an ant between his feet, running back and forth in a kelam-kabut way.

"You know what I don't understand," he finally said, leaning back, hands spread out on the wooden porch, "the town cares so much about having a shitty image, right?" His eyes were on the darkening sky. "Do you think they know about Tommy selling drugs?"

Delilah was quiet for a moment, then said, "I don't know. Maybe he was smart enough to be quiet about this. Maybe he was actually good at something, you know, like reading people?"

"If that's so, why did he try and sell us drugs?"

Delilah shrugged. "We're young, so naturally, he thought we would be interested? I'm not really good at this detective thing."

"Ditto," Wesley replied.

However, when he looked down at his notebook, he saw a list of questions, and that was a signal telling him that something was afoot. This wasn't just the story of a junkie who'd ended up dead at sea. There were layers he would have to peel.

Wesley felt his heart rate speed up as his eyes looked at each question. The one at the bottom read:

If Tommy was murdered, who did it?

13

Two days after the body of Tommy Asandu was discovered, Dr Nitta Siddhu called.

Inspector Rabbil Harris answered at the first ring when the opening jingle of Boney M's 'Rasputin' began ringing away.

"Rabbil here."

"Inspector, good morning. Dr Siddhu here from the Tawau Hospital Morgue. Did I catch you at a good time?"

"Yes you did, Doc," said Rabbil.

Knowing they would staying in town for a few days, he got them a booking at the town's only hotel: an elderly shop-lot across from the Ferry Terminal. The rooms were small and simple. The price was cheap, and that first night, before he collapsed into a dream that involved him as a father, he wondered if youths used this place as a love shack. He was not with the religious squad (nor was he religious), so the thought escaped his mind as exhaustion took over.

"At first, we wanted to rule it as an overdose. In Tommy Asandu's system, we found more than 200 milligrams of heroin. Now there isn't exactly a definite amount as to how much of the stuff is needed to kill you, but I'd say 200 is lethal enough. And way beyond the amount needed for a quick high."

Murder, Rabbil thought to himself. *Alrighty then*. "Okay. Go on, doc."

"I was about to call you yesterday evening with my findings, but I decided to check the body once more. Just to be certain.

And I found what could be a needle mark on the victim's neck. Right on the jugular vein, which isn't normal at all. Addicts would prefer something more accessible. A spot they can hide. Say between the toes, or along the wrist, or even in the fleshy area between the wrist and bicep. Tommy Asandu was a drug addict, right?"

"He was, but nothing too heavy. Dope and syabu, mostly."

"My exact thoughts. He's never done heroin, yes?"

The pieces fit and clicked into place. *Well, well, well,* Rabbil thought as he used his free hand to uncage another cigarette from his pack. "Seems that way, doc."

"Bah, that's good. I'll need your email to send my findings over."

"Sure. I'll WhatsApp it to you after this."

"Thank you, inspector."

"Much obliged, doc."

X

The mood in the little space the local cops call an office went deathly silent when he broke the news.

"Murder?" Atiqah said.

Rabbil nodded. "Murder."

"Tuan," said Sergeant Awang, "are we sure about this?"

"Tommy Asandu was a drug addict. His crime sheet indicates that he's big on syabu, ganja, party pills, acid and the occasional snort of ketamine. He's never had heroin before. Or 200 milligrams of the stuff."

"Maybe he's open to trying new things?" said one of the officers.

"When you *try* new things," Rabbil said in a patient tone, "you *try* a little, and when you get the hang of it, you continue to add a little more every single time. Does it apply to drugs? You bet it does. You try a little, you get a little high, and once it wears off, you want a bigger hit. You'll continue upping the dose. You don't just take the whole thing." He realized that his voice was getting a tad louder, and that patient tone from earlier had started to fray at the edges.

"So," he said, after a deep breath and thoughts of zen – which to him were artfully designed koi ponds with limestone edging, green shrubbery here and there, an artificial waterfall because those are very nice, and most importantly, those gold and red fish floating happily about – he continued with, "This death has been labelled suspicious by the medical examiner and as the senior investigating officer at hand, I am declaring the death of Tommy Asandu as a bona fide whodunit."

14

Slowly but surely, the town began to unravel as news of Tommy's death – now a murder – floated into the ears of the townspeople. It began, as it always does, in the social spots: Aunt Jo's Cafe, the eating joints, and even (silently, though) at the All-Convenience Store.

The point of origin was the Seaside Bar.

That very night, over several pints and bottles and even a few shots of bahar from Kota Belud, Officer Jackson Radus – free of responsibility (which in this case meant leaving his uniform in the backseat of his ancient Kancil) and away from his colleagues – announced to whoever was listening that Tommy Asandu was murdered.

Everyone in the bar had been murmuring because of Tommy's death. But the moment the word *murder* was thrown into the mix, the silence in the bar was deafening. Sure, people didn't like him – and many believed he would have died with a needle proudly sticking out his arm – but they hadn't expected murder.

See, murder meant messy, and no one in town liked a messy affair because the end of it meant that one of them, one person in this little paradise so far away and undisturbed by the outside world and its complexities, was responsible for taking the life of another, even though the person in question wasn't well-liked.

And when the silence became a little too uncomfortable, the patrons began talking, while also shaking their heads at the new turn of events.

"Maybe that detective guy is wrong?" said one of the regulars, a boatswain for one of the two ferries to the island. "He's a West Malaysian, after all. When have those guys ever gotten anything right?"

"What about you?" someone called out to the boatswain. "You never *get it right* when you play cards. Even a halfwit like Tommy Asandu managed to cheat you."

"Yeah, yeah, yeah, and I threw him out for that," said one of the boatswain's drinking buddies. "You, on the other hand … didn't he throw up on your shoes once? New, weren't they?"

"Gave him a mighty shove out the door as well," said another voice.

"You're one to talk," someone else said, "you got sold bad weed. Gave you a headache for a whole week."

"More like a whole month," chimed another patron.

"Ah, there we go. Didn't he get your son into trouble at that fancy club on the island? Heard he went full Sabahan and climbed one of the fixtures like a monkey."

"A monkey looking for the Wi-Fi," said the boatswain, which got him some laughs.

"Okay," Owen Gunsillan, the owner and bartender of the Seaside Bar said, "enough." He could see that the room was uneasy. The combination of murder and booze had gotten most of tonight's patrons (the Seaside Bar was at about 99 per cent capacity by then, locals all) in a frenzy. They'd start with the finger-pointing. The good-natured tone was slowly turning sour. Give them 15 – no, make that 10 – more minutes of this, and the shoving would start. Then would came the fists. Maybe a couple of barstools. One or all of the cues, and lastly, the mugs. Nope. This shit wouldn't happen if this were a juice bar or a cafe, but the power of alcohol is such that it gives normal men this odd notion that they could say and/or do anything they want, consequences be damned.

Well, forget 15 minutes. The action had just started.

Someone pushed someone. The two combatants now began shouting at each other. Owen sighed. Imagine if the tourists could see this. Or that poof of a writer from *Sabah* magazine. Or even the old man on the island who technically owned *both* the island and town?

With a sigh, he reached under the bar counter and found the cricket bat from his high school days, and shouted very loudly for everyone in *his* bar to "SHUT THE FUCK UP FOR JUST A MINUTE," before slamming the bat down.

The impact was hard enough to make a couple of guys jump, sending a few glasses shuddering. He slammed the bat down once more, and a tumbler, empty, thank God, leapt up, landed on its side, rolled, and hit the wood-paneled floor where it broke.

That got everyone's attention. When the only sound was Waylon Jennings on the speakers, Owen pointed at a sign above the glass and mirrored shelves behind him. ALL BUT STUPID TALK ACCEPTED HERE had been carved on a piece of wood that had been bleached by the sea. "More of that stupid shit and Mike there will drag you out of here. Paid drink or not. Fight and I'll ban you forever. Feel free to play young and wild at Palace Neptune."

Mike was the sometimes bouncer who spent his mornings helping out at the Terminal if there was work to be done there. A former army man, Mike was big, muscular – most of that had gone to fat by now, though he still sported the severe crew cut, which he kept in shape twice a week – and when he glowered, people stayed away. He was at the end of the bar, nursing a mug of Tiger and finishing up the last of a thick burger from Abu Bakar's Burger Bakar. He'd been quiet during the whole ruckus. But now, he aimed his flat gaze at the crowd who, seconds ago, had been on the brink of raising hell in the always peaceful Seaside Bar.

The men, knowing they were seconds away from being tossed into the doghouse, shrugged and stared sheepishly at the floor. A few mumbled apologies. Some to Owen, others to their neighbor. For a moment there, they'd forgotten that most of them knew each other. Most had shared drinks. Attended birthdays. Laughed. Agreed and disagreed on politics. Bitched about their wives, in-laws, kids, work – and not always in that order.

"Radus," Owen said when the threat of violence had ebbed. "You were telling a story earlier?"

The officer nodded. Took a sip of beer (he was a little scared that he'd be handling a riot armed with nothing but a blue pen) and said, "The medical examiner spent two days checking the body" – with a pull from his bottle of Tiger. "That's how she found the mark."

The music was lowered so that everyone could hear Radus. A waitress was cleaning up the broken glass on the floor, but she, like the patrons, was listening raptly. The prospect of a very interesting story had knocked the idea of beating each other to a pulp out of their heads. Here was a *story*. Here was something to keep them entertained and maybe keep their own evil intentions at bay. Where minutes ago, they might had been on the verge of violence, now they huddled closer to Officer Radus, waiting for the good parts that they could later share with friends and family or in WhatsApp groups. Even Mike, who kept a poker face, was looking up from his tattered copy of Stephen King's *Needless Things*.

"What mark?" said Owen, reaching for a cigarillo. "Don't end the story there. Tell the whole thing, bah."

"Well, this was what I heard," Officer Radus said. "The medical examiner checked him one more time. Head to toe, and she found this puncture mark on his neck. Above his … his … apa tu … the…" – he tapped a spot on his neck as he fought through the fog of booze to find the right word – "… juggler vein, yes that's it."

"*Jugular*," Mike corrected.

"Whatever lah," said Officer Radus. "She told the inspector–"

"You mean *detective*," said the boatswain.

"Or de*fective*," said someone, which earned him a ripple of laughter.

"It's inspector lah," said Owen. "Jack, continue your story."

"That's why they've re-classified his death as murder. Or at the very least, death by mysterious circumstances. But I doubt this inspector is gunning for anything short of foul play."

"What about suspects?" Mike asked.

"No one yet," said Officer Radus, "we've just started, so what they're doing now is trying to build a profile of Tommy Asandu."

"A what?" someone asked.

"Profile," said the off-the-clock police officer. "It's like they get to know everything about a person and build their case around that. Like who he was friends with, who was the last to see him alive, who had a problem with him, like that lah."

"What about Zara's boy?" said Yee Liang, who owned the Chinese seafood restaurant next to Palace Neptune. "I heard Tommy got his ass kicked by him."

"Yeah," said someone else, "gave him a good ass-kicking. From a skinny kid with massive glasses, that must have been pretty humiliating."

The majority of the patrons, most of whom had been at the fight and had relished the image of Tommy Asandu getting ass-kicked, nodded.

"If someone insults the woman you're in love with," said Owen, cleaning a glass with a cloth, "do you think you'd just stand there and say 'thank you, carry on'? And Tommy did not insult Delilah. He was going to do something" – using the cloth this time, he pointed at the sign, focusing on the word STUPID. "I don't blame the boy one bit. Tommy was lucky Wesley only gave him a shiner. If it was me" – instead of completing the sentence, he placed the towel down and took a long pull from his cigarillo – "well, let's just say that inspector would be visiting me first."

More nods.

Among them was Tommy Asandu's actual killer.

15

"Murder," said Delilah, "damn."

Wesley was silent. He wanted a cigarette, but he'd already had one after the morning rush when the news was delivered by one of the men who'd been at the Seaside Bar last night. A few of them glanced at him in that knowing way, as if they'd already passed judgement on the case. You could actually see the thought in their eyes: he'd beat up the asshole, why not kill him as well? He'd kept his eyes on them as well. He had the temptation to look away, but screw it, do that, and they'd have a stronger case in their minds.

"We should start immediately," he said.

"We've got work, dude," Delilah said. "We can't just–"

The door opened, and Tabitha Asandu walked into the store.

Tabitha looked nothing like her brother.

For starters, there was the hair. Tommy's had been long, stringy and oily, left to hang around his shoulders when a haircut would have made him look much better. The widow's peak didn't help either. Tabitha's hair was pitch black, long and thick, styled into a braided ponytail that hung low, touching the small of her back. Her face was smooth where Tommy's had been oily and pimply, with craters around both cheeks. Her nose was longer, with a gentle downward curl. Tommy's had looked like a squashed tomato. And unlike her brother, Tabitha was short, compact and a little fuller at the waist. Her clothes looked a little better than Tommy's choice of whatever T-shirt had been lying around in his room and his naturally distressed denim. And unlike Tommy, Tabitha wore glasses.

Delilah had met her a few times when the girl (she was sure Tabitha was 15 or 16) had come into the store to buy groceries. When this had happened, Tommy pretended as if she were a stranger, barely saying a word, or disappearing into the back, like it was wrong for him, the town druggie, to be seen with his sister. Tabitha, on the other hand, had always said hi to her brother, even when he couldn't be bothered to say a single thing back to her. She didn't seem to take it personally.

Now, though …

"Hi, Tabby, good morning," Delilah said.

Tabitha, still standing by the entrance to the store, hands clasped in front of her like she was in mass, looked around for a bit. When she was happy with whatever she was looking for, she made her way forward towards the counter-cum-bar.

There, she passed a list to Delilah. "Some things mama needs," she said. Her eyes were on Delilah the whole time. She didn't look at Wesley.

"Tabitha," Wesley began. What was he going to say? *Sorry for your loss? My condolences? I hope God – if He's a real thing – doesn't decide that your brother deserves to roast down there in hell?*

She didn't look at him just yet.

Delilah, who was just standing there, twirling the little scrap of paper that Tabitha had given her, decided it was best to intervene and said, "Tabby, this is Wesley. You can call him Wes. He–"

Tabitha turned to Wesley, cutting Delilah off by saying: "Did you kill Tommy?"

Beyond the lenses of her glasses, Wesley could see that her eyes were red, the skin around her eyes puffy. She'd been crying. He suddenly felt bad for her. Yesterday when he'd spoken with Mabel and played with this idea that here was a story that could help him deal with his own problems, he never took into consideration how Tabby or her mother must be feeling.

When he'd been dealing with that horrible accident back in the Klang Valley, everyone had been there for him. Colleagues, friends from college, family members. His parents had called every night. His friends had faked MCs and taken ELs just to make sure he didn't go off the deep end and do something stupid while in the throes of survivor's guilt.

He'd had support. Did Tabitha and her mother, perhaps unloved by the town as they were related to its pariah, have support? Was anyone coming around and checking up on them, making sure that they were fine, that they had someone to listen to them, someone to hug them, someone to just be there?

Wesley wanted to go around the counter and hug Tabitha because right then, he felt bad. But maybe that wouldn't be the best way to show he cared.

"No, Tabitha," he said. "I didn't kill him."

"But you beat him up pretty good."

"He gave me a few reminders as well." Wesley pulled his T-shirt up, revealing the slowly fading bruises that covered the left side of his torso. "I just got lucky, is all."

"My mama hasn't cried once," Tabitha said. "When Officer Radus came over with the announcement this morning, do you know what she said?"

Wesley and Delilah don't say a thing. They waited for her to speak.

"She said, 'We need more milk. Tabby, can you run over to the store to get some milk? And a new broom, some cleaning wipes and garbage bags. We'll need to clean your brother's room'. She wrote a list, gave me some money and asked me to leave. She didn't cry, didn't ask about his … about his … his…" Tabitha paused, took a deep breath and shook her head a little as if shaking away cobwebs from her mind. She composed herself and said, "His remains. She decided that a room needed cleaning and now was the best time to do it."

"Tabby," Delilah said, "do you wanna maybe sit down?"

Tabitha didn't respond but chose one of the stools. Delilah then asked if she wanted coffee, to which Tabitha said yes, coffee would be great. "Might not fall asleep till about 3 in the morning," she added as Delilah fetched a clean mug (yellow with a waddle of penguins waving happily at the drinker) and poured some coffee for her.

Tabitha didn't immediately drink it. She made the cup go around in circles, staring down at the black liquid, which was steaming up to her face. "I love – no, *loved* Tommy," she said slowly. "He deserved a lot of things. Dying isn't one of them. Murder either."

Delilah glanced at Wesley. Wesley glanced at Delilah. The look they exchanged said: *What do we say to her?*

And maybe Delilah's next look (to Wesley, she was attempting to convey a message of some sort with her eyes) confused him, so he decided that since Tabitha was here, they might as well try and get some answers out of her. He filled his own mug, pulled out his phone and switched on the phone recorder and set that on the counter. Close enough that it wasn't intruding, but near enough to Tabitha that it would come out clear.

Back when he was still a hot-shit news reporter, he had done his fair share of bugging-the-victim's-family for-a-good-quote. The trick was timing. Right after the accident or outside the morgue would get you a good beating, some spittle and maybe a flying selipar. After they realized that this was it and that the spilt milk couldn't be shoved back into the bottle, they'd open up. Nice and easy. That was lesson two.

"Tabby," Wesley said, "Can I call you that? You can call me Wes if you want to."

She just nodded.

"Can I maybe ask you a few questions about Tommy?"

With her head still down and her hair covering the rest of her face, Tabitha asked in a small voice: "Why?"

"I'm curious about what happened to him."

"Why?"

"Because ..." *I want to revitalize my career. Because no matter how much I tell myself that* this *is what I want – a peaceful life in a small town with little to no distractions – I still want to be back doing what I do best, and that is to tell real stories about real people. I got into a bit of a slump for a few months because just the thought of living when someone who was better than me should have survived,* deserved *to survive, makes me embarrassed. Makes me feel ashamed to live. Because I know that there are people who wonder, 'Why did he survive?' Something along the lines of: 'Does he even deserve it? Ashini was a better person. He ...'*

"Because I want to care," he said.

And this got a reaction from Tabitha. Her head went up, a blank look on her face. "You care? About a guy like Tommy? He didn't like you. He said a lot of mean things about you. Wanted to make your life here miserable."

He took a second to process this. But he knew the answer. It was something he discovered when he tried to give himself therapy via Google.

"Hurt people hurt people," he said slowly. "People behave in the way that they know. Tommy spent a lot of time being hated. The whole town didn't like him. They knew he was no good, was up to no good, but they never tried being nicer because … well, because being nicer meant enabling him, giving him a free pass. Imagine if people actually tried showing that they care. I knew I didn't. I could have asked him for a smoke and tried my best to get to know him. But from the moment I met him, all I saw was another …" he hesitated, but the way Tabitha was looking at him, in a way that implied that he had all the answers, made the decision for him, "All I saw was another piece of trash in human form. I judged him when I should've been trying to understand."

He took a sip of his coffee. Placed the cup down and continued, "I was part of the problem when I should have tried being the solution. It's too late for that now. But I guess it's not too late to try and make amends."

16

At 8 am, the sky had been blue. Fluffy white clouds hung about like good decorations and prevented most of the sunlight from giving anyone at the beaches on Darat Kumut and Pulau Kumut sunburn. But by 10:45 am, when Tabitha Asandu walked into the All-Convenience Store, the bright and cheery day had turned a shade darker, and the rain, which had been threatening to fall over the last few days, finally made good on its promise.

It fell slowly at first. Little drops that slowly grew and grew and grew until they became a steady downpour. Then came the crackle and snarl of thunder and the darkened sky was lit occasionally by a flash of lightning.

Inside the All-Convenience Store, all was silent. Tabitha seemed to be contemplating Wesley's words. Delilah stood by the door to the back (she'd moved there to make sure the backdoor was closed). Wesley had both hands around his now-cooling cup of coffee, waiting for Tabitha to say something. Anything.

"I don't want you to feel sorry for me. For us," Tabitha said. "I … we don't want that." A quick sip of coffee, a grimace on her face, a clearing of the throat, then: "I know that the people in town who don't hate us, or don't look down on us, pity us. 'Look at them', they'll say whenever they see me and mama going to church, 'the wife with no husband and the child with no father. And what's worse, the brother is no good trash'. I know they say this because I've heard the other kids at Sunday class and the adults say that."

She said all this slowly. She had thought a lot about this and to say it would require clear delivery so her audience would understand her.

"Mama and I, we try our best to make do with what we have. It's not easy when you're related to a killer, but ..."

Wesley didn't interrupt. She was on a roll; she was readying herself to say something, something that might help.

With her finger drawing random patterns on the surface of the coffee bar, Tabitha said, "Tommy didn't deserve to be killed. Prison maybe, but not ... that."

"Do you know who did it?" Wesley asked after giving her several seconds of silence.

"If I knew that, I would've gone to the police," she said. Not angrily, but calmly, like she was talking to an idiot child.

"Who do you think could have done it?" said Delilah.

Tabitha's shoulders went up and then down in a half-hearted shrug. "I don't know. Tommy was into a lot of bad things. Once when I was cleaning his room, I saw that he had some ... things in his guitar case. Little bags of green-like stuff. Some powder. Something that looked like sugar, but wasn't. I wasn't snooping," she added. "Mama asked me to clean his room because when he caught her doing it, they got into a big fight and he disappeared for a whole week."

He had drugs in his room, Wesley thought. He wanted to pull out his notebook from the center pocket of his apron and write all this down, but it wouldn't look good to Tabitha, plus he had the recorder going.

"What about friends?" Wesley asked. "Did he have friends over?"

She nodded. "There was a group of them."

"Did you know his friends?" asked Delilah.

Tabitha shook her head. "I saw them once or twice. They usually came at night. Or midnight. There were three of them."

"Can you describe them?"

"One's a guy. Always in T-shirt and jeans and selipar. He's bald. I think. And then there are two women."

"What do you remember about them?" Wesley asked.

"Um … they're women."

"No. I mean, was there anything about them that made them stand out? Like their clothes, their behavior. Was one of them nervous, angry? Unhappy? Anything like that?"

"Uh …" Tabitha lowered her head and pondered. "I remember that one of them was short and the other was tall."

God in heaven, Wesley thought. *Off to a great start, aren't we?* "Anything more specific?"

"One of them …" her left index finger, which was slowly drawing Rorschach patterns on the surface of the coffee bar, picked up the pace. "One of them was wearing a uniform."

"Can you remember it?" Delilah asked. She had crossed over from her side and was now standing by Tabitha, leaning against the bar, waiting for Tabitha to say something.

"She had a shirt on … no, a blouse. White. With the frills over her chest, I think? And a red vest. Like the old-timey ones."

"With a pocket watch?" Wesley asked.

"No. But it didn't look like she enjoyed wearing it, because she kept on talking about how they should've gone back and let her change first."

Delilah snapped her fingers. "The casino. On the island. What Tabby's describing sounds like the uniform for the casino workers … what're they called again …" she rapped the side of her head with a knuckle.

"Croupiers?" Wesley asked.

"Right. Those."

"And what about the other woman?"

"She was dressed in normal clothes."

"Did she look familiar to you?"

Tabitha nodded. "I've seen her before."

"Where?"

"The Chinese kopitiam. She owns a stall there. I think." She paused. "Do you think that they could be the ones?"

"I don't know," he said. But he did know a way: Tommy's phone. But if Tommy was the kind of dealer you saw in *The Wire,* he would've had a second phone. One for personal use, one for business.

"Tabby," Wesley said, "will you be helping your mom to clean Tommy's room?"

She shrugged. "Maybe."

"Could you do me a favor? Might help us get more answers."

"What do you want?"

"A phone. Not anything expensive. Think of an old, cheap phone. Something that's good enough for calls and texts. No need for social media."

"A second phone? I think Tommy had one. Because there were sounds from his pocket that didn't come from his usual phone."

"What was his usual phone?"

"One of the old iPhones, I think? But that one's normally on silent mode. The phone I heard sounded like the old ones. Like beeps and tinkles."

"Did you see him with it?"

"That second phone? I don't think so. But I can try and find it."

She took another sip from her coffee and then asked for the things that her mom ordered. Delilah went off into the backroom. It was now Wesley and Tabitha.

"Who do you think could have done it?" Wesley asked.

"I don't know. A lot of people didn't like him."

"Anyone specific?"

"You know he killed a young woman a few years ago? Maybe her father? That man lost his daughter and then his wife in less than a year."

Wesley was aware of the story. But the problem was the timeline: Those two deaths happened six years ago. Why wait six years to kill the person who killed your daughter? Edna would have labelled 'Weak Sauce' to that theory.

"Anyone else?"

"I don't know. A lot of people seemed content to just ignore him. Not … kill him," Tabitha sighed, and Wesley watched as her shoulders slumped in defeat.

"You cared for him."

"I thought that if I loved him, or you know, showed him enough love, maybe he'd love me back."

Thunder roared in the dark gloom. Rain fell harder and drenched the town from the Ferry Terminal, along Main Street and everywhere in between. Tourists and locals scrambled to find shelter. Some ran for cars. Others raced for home. A few made for Aunt Jo's, or the kopitiam. A few even found their way into the All-Convenience Store. Out there, the sky rumbled and rocked and rolled.

Delilah returned with Tabitha's goods packed in two paper bags. Wesley had pocketed his phone and was serving coffee to three tourists: a trio from Japan and a single man from Sri Lanka, here, he claimed, for the sights and the casino.

"Don't go just yet," Delilah said to Tabitha. She placed the paper bags on the counter, went back into the storeroom and came out a few seconds later with a large umbrella. "Come on. I'll walk with you."

"I …" Tabitha made a warding-off gesture.

"I insist," Delilah said, adding the spice of finality to her tone. "Now come on. I'll carry one bag, you get the other, and I'll walk you home."

"But …"

"No buts," said Delilah, already holding one of the packages. To Wesley, she said, "Wes, you can hold down the fort bah kan?"

He nodded.

And with that, they were out the door and into the pouring rain.

17

"Chua? Busy ke?" Rabbil asked.

"Uhh, no, boss."

Chua was the senior digital forensics officer at KK HQ. Once, during an informal speech, the head of KK CID stated that no one could lube a firewall down like Chua. The investigating officers, many of whom turned to Chua when a digital trail ran cold, cheered at this. Right now, the man sounded a little out of breath. Odd at – Rabbil glanced at his wristwatch: 12:09 pm – such an hour. Outside, rain poured like there was no tomorrow. Thunder and lightning added their own magic, screwing up the phone lines a little. On the louder side of the tiny police outpost, Atiqah was performing her duties in the search for a suspect in the murder of Tommy Asandu. Tawau HQ had called, and they'd promised to lend whatever support they could, though Rabbil preferred the help of his own people.

Chua, one of the best computer geeks in KK HQ, was one of his own people. Like Atiqah, he was a little strange, but Rabbil didn't care. The man excelled at getting answers from the digital world. He was also fast. And Rabbil was constantly his priority.

"Writing those weird hentai crossovers?" Rabbil asked. "What is it this time? Annie from *Attack on Titan* and her need to transform into a giant to bang Goku?"

Chua chuckled. The raspy chuckle told Rabbil that he sort of hit gold.

"Don't give me ideas, boss," the strange little man said.

"Right. Look, I need you to track a phone."

"Um. Okay. I need–"

"I know what you need," said Rabbil. "I've got a warrant underway, and we're getting info on the victim's telco. I'll get you all that and then you track his phone for me."

"You do know that tracking only applies if the phone is switched on or if the SIM card is still in the phone."

"I may not know about anime, bro, but I can tell you a few things about catching bad guys. I'll get Ticks to send you the info. How fast can you get it to me?"

"Uhh ..."

"*Uhh* is not an answer. I need a timeline."

"Tell Sergeant Atiqah to get it to me quickly so that I can get you some answers."

"Okay. Good luck on the erotica." He hung up before Chua could say anything, got up and made his way to the bullpen, where Atiqah was in the midst of a briefing with Sergeant Awang, the officer in charge in these parts. Awang was a short and portly man. Once upon a time, he might've been muscular, but those days have long gone. Today, he was the kind of cop that Rabbil envied. The man was stationed in the country, where the worst crime you could be accused of was being a silly drunk twat. And that meant that other than patrolling the streets (or just the one, really) Sergeant Awang had very little to do in a town like Darat Kumut.

Now, the man looked like he was far and away from the element he had become comfortable with. Sergeant Awang was sitting on a swivel chair, arms across his chest, a concentrated look on his face as he tried his best to make sense of what Atiqah was talking about. On the whiteboard that they managed to scrounge from the tiny storeroom at the back, several names had been written. Tommy Asandu's known associates. Assisted by Atiqah, the small group of officers were doing their best to track these people down. Of the eight, two were in jail, one died in a car accident (while under the influence of substances) and the other five were undetectable. The officers stationed in town had looked at these five and declared that these men were not townies.

Atiqah was in the process of finding known associates and narrowing them down to the Tawau area. Rabbil was going through their backgrounds. All eight names were involved in drugs. Two of them were suspected of murder, three were most probably rapists, and one was a bona fide pimp who had an entire sheet of crimes involving illegal gambling. The final two looked clean, though he was waiting for more results from the Eastern Sabah Security Command and Immigration to see if any of those lovely faces were involved in people smuggling.

And then there was the missing evidence. The preliminary report from Tawau HQ's Forensic Unit stated that the only thing unaccounted for was Tommy Asandu's phone. The on-going theory was that Tommy's phone fell into the water. But if that was the case and the body was found in such shallow water, where did the phone go?

The killer took it. Simple as that. No need for a hundred pages of theories on what might have happened. A phone could have sunk. Forensics could've found it. They didn't. Which meant that the killer took it. Why? Because the phone could link Tommy Asandu to the killer. And that meant two things. First, that the killer was chummy enough with Tommy Asandu to worry about their safety. Second, the killer intended for this to happen. Which meant premeditation. Killing Tommy Asandu was an extreme decision. What led to that decision ... well, the answer to that question lay in Tommy Asandu himself.

Questions, questions, questions and more questions. Rabbil ran a hand through his hair and took a sip of his coffee. It had been lukewarm before the call to Chuah. He gulped down half the mug with a grimace and moved over to where Atiqah was standing. She had her arms crossed and was staring at the board, specifically at the names of men still alive and breathing.

"Rudolph and the others are chasing up on them, boss," she said.

"Mm. What about the other list? Where are we on that?"

Atiqah made for the door leading to the outpost's tiny kitchenette. Once the door closed behind her, she said, "A lot of people in town hated this guy. You've got a long list."

"*We*'ve got a long list. Any standouts?"

"Julian Everett. Remember the story Awang told you about the young girl Tommy killed a few years back? He's the father."

"Anyone else?"

"A few serious ones. That young guy you spoke to the other day is in there as well. Wesley Lawrence?"

Rabbil nodded. "Make a top ten list, then start calling them in for interviews."

"Okay."

After she left, he walked out the backdoor and fired up a cigarette. Most murder cases he had cleared since rising up to the rank of inspector had been straightforward. Jealous spouse. A business partner who was skimming a little too much. A fight gone too far. But this case: an overdose that was actually murder. It didn't feel like a run-of-the-mill case. It felt complex. More than one-dimensional.

To Rabbil, it felt like an actual challenge.

18

"The good news," said Delilah before blowing on her tea, "is that she doesn't blame you for Tommy's death."

"What's the bad news?" Wesley asked.

"She won't say more about her son. Well, outside of the stuff that she told me lah."

"Was she sad?"

"She was knitting and watching TV. Didn't seem too sad. Told me the cops came over this morning to tell her that her son was actually murdered."

"How did she take it?"

"Just shrugged and said she hoped the cops catch whoever did it."

"Damn, she's cold."

"Is she?" Delilah asked. She looked around the store, saw that it was empty and walked around the counter to perch on one of the stools facing the coffee bar.

"You think she isn't?"

"I think that she's relieved."

Wesley whistled.

"Not when you understand what her life is like."

Delilah had given him the low-down on the Asandu family after Tommy threw a hissy fit over 'not being respected in the store's hierarchy' and chose to just walk out the door, tossing his apron behind him as he left. The family was one of the founding pillars of Darat Kumut. They had been one of the richest, starting their short-lived business empire with a fishing company that grew from just one boat to a fleet of 12, the biggest in town. Then it branched out to logistics and then construction. However, a bad investment and an economic crisis bankrupted the family. By 2000, their shipping company had shrunk down to two boats, with the business as a whole nearing the point of no return.

Tommy's father then sold the last piece of his business and used the proceeds to start a fish farm. This worked out well. Money started pouring in. One celebration later, Tommy's father found new love with a woman who was barely legal and had an over-reliance on the drink. Just a year shy of operating the fish farm, Tommy's father secretly sold it off and used the money to run away with his new mistress, leaving his original family in the proverbial financial shithouse.

Outside of his father, there were no other Asandus left in the vicinity. There was an older sister, but she had married into some blueblood family in KK and had no reason to connect with a woman whose greatest achievement was giving birth to two more children bearing the Asandu name.

But somehow, Eloise Asandu nee Rubyson managed just fine with her two kids. Well, until puberty hit and transformed Tommy into a hellraiser.

"Do you think she'll cooperate if we ask nicely?" Wesley asked.

"I was asking nicely, and she barely gave me enough. I think she just wants to bury her son and put this whole thing to rest."

Delilah continued sipping her tea. Wesley had his eyes on the window that overlooked Main Street. Rain fell hard and strong. There seemed to be no end to the volume of water that was falling on the town.

"Oh," Delilah said. "I've got one more surprise for you."

"Am I gonna like this surprise?"

Delilah reached into her pocket and pulled out an ancient cell phone. The type that still had buttons and a tiny screen.

"Tommy's second phone," Delilah said. "Tabby found in there, and here it is."

Wesley wanted to lean over and kiss her. Decided that that wasn't too professional and just smiled. "Is it …"

"On? Yep. No saved contacts, but there's one recent phone number in the call logs."

Wesley offered his phone. He was pretty new in town, and no one would've saved his number just yet. He punched it in and then hit 'speaker phone'.

"Hello?"

Delilah looked at Wesley. Wesley looked at Delilah.

"Someone there? Hello? Hello?"

Click.

Slowly, Wesley and Delilah turned their heads towards the kopitiam across the road.

"Was that Su Yen?" Wesley asked.

Delilah nodded.

X

"What's next?" Delilah asked.

Wesley stared at his notebook. There were now two new names to check out. He decided on the IT guy.

"We'll start with this Syakir and get some answers. Tommy might've told him something."

"Not Su Yen?"

"Not just yet. Why don't we go for the one person who was good friends with Tommy? With Su Yen, there might be a group dynamic seeing as Tommy met her and two other people. She might tell the others, whoever they are."

"But Syakir seems isolated?"

Wesley nodded, though he didn't feel very comfortable with that assessment. Oh well, part of the fun of detective work, right?

"Isolated means that there could be things Tommy told him." Another maybe. Nothing solid, but they'd find a way to work on that. "We just need to know when Syakir comes back from work."

"I think I know someone who can help us with that," Delilah said.

X

"Is it normally this boring?" Delilah asked. It was 5:15 pm. The rain had calmed to a drizzle and looked like it would stop any second. The sky, already gloomy with rain, had turned a shade darker at the approach of dusk.

Delilah had spoken to her 'source'. The call lasted less than five minutes. After, she told him that Syakir would be on the 5 pm ferry from the island. That meant he would arrive at approximately 5:45 pm. The call was made at 1 pm. Which gave them four hours to plan the right way to corner Syakir and get some answers. Then came the bad news: Syakir wasn't working today. Maybe he'd come tomorrow.

Wesley groaned. Delilah slapped her forehead.

They decided the best thing to do was wait for tomorrow. In the meantime, they'd kill time.

"What do you mean?"

"This investigating thing we're doing," she said.

Wesley, who was sitting by the cash register and nearing the end of the Tana French paperback he'd spent the last week reading, nodded. "Imagine if you were dealing with the government. It's even longer. This is normal."

"It's boring."

"Kan. But back then, while waiting for another source to get back to me, I'd probably be trying to contact another source. And even if you don't, you get used to it. Waiting hours for someone is not too bad. Try waiting for an entire week. Patience not your style?"

"It should be. I wanna be a lecturer. An academic. I think patience is a job requirement. Unfortunately, I don't have any of it."

"A lecturer?"

She nodded. "I ever tell you what my degree was?"

"Nope."

"English Lit. Before that, I was studying Pharmacy. My parents wanted me to be a doctor, but my SPM grades didn't cut it. Pharmacy was the closest thing. Then I went off and changed my degree to English Lit, and my parents lost their minds."

"Really?"

"Argued with them for a whole month. It was messy. I thought that being the baby of the family, they would allow me to do whatever I want since I already did two years of something I don't care about, but ..." she shrugged.

"So they shipped you here?"

She shook her head. "I ran here. Called Aunt Mabel and asked her to save me from my Asian Tiger parents. I never told you this?"

"You just told me that your parents were hard-asses. I didn't feel like intruding."

"I thought being nosy was a job requirement."

"I have this ability to turn myself off, you know."

She laughed.

19

Syakir looked like a young dude. Around Wesley's age, maybe. Today, he wore a hoodie, black skinny jeans and Birkenstocks. He had glasses on, but the lenses were darkened. Apparently, he'd spent so much time staring at the computer screen that he managed to fuck his eyes up nice and proper and now he had an excuse to wear sunglasses all day, every day.

Wesley wanted to say douche fashion, but that seemed a little too judgmental, even for him.

Syakir had a backpack and was suckling on a dark green vape device. He had his eyes down and was staring at the road, ears blocked off by a pair of earphones that would've made Dr Dre green with envy. They watched as he crossed the road and headed down the main street.

Delilah's source had mentioned something about Syakir hanging out at a spot near the bus station. Something about an empty lot behind the main building where he'd 'chill' – whatever that meant – before jumping into his car and heading home to Tawau.

Doing their best to look inconspicuous, they trailed Syakir, making sure there was a large chunk of space between them and him. He neared the Bus Station. He hung right, crossed the main entrance of the station and continued on by the shaded side of the building.

They'd both taken half-day leave from the store. Zara was there with Margie and Lucky. When asked, Wesley said something about going on a 'platonic' date, much to the delight of his aunt, who said, just as he left the store, that Delilah was good for him.

"I can see her in the Unduk Ngadau costume for your wedding reception," Zara had said.

The best Wesley could offer was a groan. But now, making his way towards the bus station, Delilah walking by his side, he felt a sense of comfort. Ask him to describe it, and he would've said (doing his best not to make the whole thing corny) that it was as if he'd found the missing piece in his life.

"Give him a few minutes," Delilah said as they neared the Bus Station's corner fence post. They waited. It had rained this morning, calmed a little in the afternoon, and now the sky was clear, but the coming dusk had a darker edge to it. The sky promised rain if it felt like it.

"Ready?" he asked.

She nodded. They went around the corner. A patch of trees sat on this side, followed by a trail that led down to the Station's parking lot. Next to it was the empty lot that had yet to be developed into another slice of modernity. The townspeople hoped it would be something subtle, say another block of shop lots. The more cynical mumbled about it being a shopping mall, or at least a shopping complex.

"Those colonizers are coming to snatch the last pieces of this town's dignity," they mumbled between sips of hot coffee.

Grass grew in patches around the lot. The rest of it was red earth that had the consistency of clay. Some sections were covered in gravel. At the far end was a parking shed made of zinc and wood, and a concrete floor that could fit two vehicles. At the moment, one lot was occupied by an ancient flatbed truck. Its tires were punctured and the windshield was gone.

The lot itself wasn't protected by fence or gate. It just sat there, open to anyone and everyone.

"Five ringgit says he's on the other side of the truck," Wesley said. He held out his hand, palm up.

She slapped it. "You're on."

They made their way towards the shed, doing their best to keep their feet on the dry and dusty ground rather than the sections of muddy, red earth.

"Ready?" Delilah asked.

He nodded.

As they neared the truck, they heard whistling. They moved slowly, one step at a time. When they reached the front end of the banged-up truck, the whistling had transformed into singing. The voice seemed to dip between falsetto and castrato. The song was Korean. The guy even added his version of Michael Jackson's 'hee-hee'. Wesley wondered if the guy was doing the crotch grab.

Delilah took a peek, pulled her head quickly back and said, "He's sitting with his back to us. And the headphones are still on."

She made way for Wesley to look. He could see the back of Syakir's head. He was on a lazy chair that was sagging at the bottom. In one hand was a joint. In the other was his phone. He seemed to be busy texting someone.

"What's the plan?" Delilah asked when they pulled back to safety behind the damaged truck.

Wesley shrugged. He set his phone to 'record' and walked towards Syakir.

20

"Who are you?" Syakir asked when he saw them, hands moving swiftly to rip off the headphones. His eyes, now free of the sunglasses, were red-rimmed from the weed, and bulged in worry and confusion. The almost-burnt joint dropped and lay forgotten on the ground.

Wesley didn't like how the guy's eyes lingered a little longer than necessary on Delilah.

"Friends," Wesley said.

"Tell me another joke."

"We knew Tommy," Delilah offered.

Syakir grinned. "If that was the case, he would've offered you to me *after* fucking you."

Wesley wanted to do something reckless, say punch the guy. But that would get them nowhere. He glanced at Delilah and saw she was biting her bottom lip. Her cheeks had turned scarlet. Her fists clenched.

"We're looking into his death," Wesley said.

"Death? You mean murder."

"Yeah. That."

"I got nothing to say," Syakir said. His eyes then moved to Delilah, and he ogled while saying, "However, if she gives me a lap dance, and a good one at that, you can ask me about Tommy again, and this time I might say 'boleh bah kalau kau'."

He opened his mouth to laugh.

Delilah moved.

Wesley had noticed the bulge in the back pocket of her shorts, and he had been inclined to ask, but the matter had slipped his mind, and now here it was: a can of pepper spray. She aimed it at Syakir's eyes and pressed.

A bit of a laugh came out. But that changed when the mist fired out and reached his eyes. Immediately he was screaming. His hands went to his eyes. A bit of the spray had entered his mouth as well, and he started gagging, which gave way to the sounds of choking. Then came the coughing and 'heh-heh-heh' noises as if he was about to sneeze.

"*I can't see!*" Syakir shrieked.

As he was putting on a show detailing the effects of pepper spray on a weed-addled mind, Delilah reached for his backpack against the side of the lazy chair.

Seeing some of what was happening, Syakir made a move for his bag. He was a little slower than Delilah, who pulled the bag out of his way and then, with both hands, smacked him on the side of the head with it.

Syakir groaned in pain. Delilah pulled open a zip, reached a hand in and pulled out a small Ziploc bag. It was packed to the brim with finely ground marijuana.

She then threw the bag to the side. It landed with a heavy *thunk.*

Syakir moaned, groaned and made retching noises. He asked for water. He scrambled on the ground in search of his bag. A lucky pivot and one free hand found a strap.

Wesley moved, going for the half-full water bottle. He pulled it out and began shaking it so Syakir knew he had the bottle in one hand.

"*My eyes,*" Syakir cried, gasping in pain, his palms rubbing frantically but not easing the pain. "Ya Allah, my eyes are on fire. Make it stop. Make it stop. Make it–"

"You tell us what you know about Tommy's murder and we'll help," Wesley said, doing his best to keep his voice calm. It was probably the first time he'd conducted an interview with someone who'd just been blasted with pepper spray. The results, he felt, might be a little skewered.

"If we get the stuff cleaned out from your eyes in about thirty minutes, you won't lose your sight. But we want answers," said Delilah.

As he writhed in pain on the ground, doing his worst to spread the chemicals all over his face, Syakir nodded and then began asking for water.

Wesley turned to Delilah. She nodded.

Wesley screwed the cap off the bottle and passed it to Syakir, who took it, moved his hand away from his eyes and doused the water over his face. His eyes and the skin around his eyes had turned a vicious shade of scarlet. Snot was running down his nose and drool was slowly ebbing down the corner of his mouth.

"You ... bitch!" Syakir said, pawing at the air and ground. "You fu–"

"Give us answers or I'm burning your weed."

"*NO*!" Syakir shrieked. He attempted a lunge.

Delilah moved. She tossed the Ziploc bag at Wesley, who fumbled but caught it. She made a fist, and as Syakir drew one knee up in a half-assed attempt to lunge at her, she threw her punch. Wesley watched as it connected squarely on Syakir's cheek.

He let out a comical "oof" that looked like it belonged in a comic book dialogue bubble and crumpled onto the ground, groaning.

"Do that shit again and I'll blast the whole can of pepper spray in your eyes," she growled while squeezing off a gentle mist of the stuff in the air.

Syakir lay there on the ground for a couple of minutes, groaning and moaning (crying had now joined the fray) before he mumbled something about complying with her wishes.

Delilah nodded at Wesley. The floor was his.

"Who killed Tommy?" Wesley asked.

"Mana saya tau," he said, sitting back up slowly. He poured water onto an open palm and began massaging the area around his eyes.

"What do you know?"

"Tommy did something stupid and smart," Syakir said. Before any more words come out of his mouth, he reached for his bag (Delilah tensed at this and readied a foot for what Wesley could only think of as a roundhouse kick) and pulled out a pack of cigarettes. Fired one up and said, "He was selling drugs."

"Everyone knows that. It's an open secret."

Syakir chuckled. "Nope. They know he sold drugs. What I meant is that Tommy was a drug kingpin."

"What?"

"Real shit. Or so he claims. See, he told me he spotted a 'gap in the market'. Can you believe that? Economics one-oh-one from the town junkie. He started keeping his supplier's pills then. Not selling everything, but claiming to have. Sold some, made some money, networked." Syakir paused to snort. The image of the town pariah making business connections seemed amusing to him. "Not long after, he had a ton of product. And he was selling it to anyone who wanted something to smoke, sniff or pop into their mouths."

"Everyone in town?" Wesley asked.

"You deaf or what? Yes. In town, at the casino ..." Syakir touched the area that Delilah had punched and winced. He threw a baleful look at her and continued: "He sold product at the resort to guests and workers. To the people who visited Palace Neptune, even though that's where his boss sells. Even sold a few grams here and there to the fishermen, though I'm very sure they'd all deny that on their mama's graves."

"Who was his supplier?"

"Beats me. I asked him so many times, but he never told me. I think it's out-of-towners."

"Why?" Delilah asked.

"Because the shit is good. No one overdosed, and I saw customers come back for more. Be it weed, syabu or ketamine."

"Where did he keep this stash?"

Syakir shrugged. "I don't know. He did mention that after he takes his own bit of candy, he hands it over to one of his partners."

"Is one of them a woman?"

He nodded. "And guess what, she works in the casino."

Wesley and Delilah shared a look. That confirmed the croupier that Tabitha told them about. "Did he have any more details about his plan?"

"Some of it. Look, we shared a couple beers and he told me some stuff cause he wanted to minta puji and show that he's this badass drug dealer. But he was smart enough not to reveal too much to me because if I knew, then loose lips sink ships and all that shit. But if it makes you feel any better, I can tell you what he did tell me. That sound good to you?"

21

Tommy Asandu was no Walter White, because where Walter White put in the effort to cook meth and had a strong reason for doing it, Tommy Asandu simply stole his supply of meth as he was greedy. Eventually, his supplier – someone powerful (as most drug barons were wont to be) – found out, decided he was a liability and ruled that for his trouble Tommy Asandu deserved more than a slap on the wrist.

Because Tommy Asandu had not just kept a little meth but then sold it, he'd managed to save enough money to start his own drug business in the small town of Darat Kumut. According to Syakir Hamzanuddin – perhaps the only person who'd called Tommy 'friend' – Tommy had persuaded three other souls into this mad venture.

Oddly, Tommy had enough acumen to know that he couldn't reveal who his three partners were. However, according to his sister, Tabitha, who was still mourning the death of a brother she'd loved, but had never loved her back, one of these partners might have just been revealed as

Wesley paused and pulled his hands away from the keyboard for fear that his right index finger would somehow hover up to the backspace key.

In fact, those 177 words were the most he had been able to write since he booted up his laptop, which had been tucked away for the last nine months. Hitting the power switch had felt like a tradition from another life.

And though it had been a while since he'd switched his laptop on, his fingers remembered the password, though he hadn't thought about said password in those nine months. His desktop was still the same: a mess of Word Documents containing some of his articles from when he was a reporter, pictures that he would have to slot into the Google Drive folders that the newspaper (online print, but the term was one of those forever things that just stuck) used as well as a myriad of notes and to-be checked-ASAP reminders.

He'd opened a new Word Document and stared at the blank white sheet and the cursor. The first 30 minutes had been hell. He'd type a couple of sentences and then hit backspace. Typed a few more things, didn't like what his brain shat out, and chopped those words away.

30 minutes later, he stepped out of his room, made for the backdoor of Zara's house and sat facing the clothes lines while smoking a couple of cigarettes. He stared at his fingers and asked *why?* Sure, nine months ago, he couldn't do it. But he'd gone to therapy. He had done his best to put that horrific incident away, to compartmentalize. Forgive himself. Accept that his ex-colleagues did not hate him for surviving. He had moved to Darat Kumut. Found peace. Fell in love. Found a way to slowly move on.

But he still couldn't write. Was it laziness? Had he been inactive for so long that he'd forgotten the simple basics of mixing and matching 26 letters into something coherent and maybe even lyrical?

After Zara and Margie had fallen asleep, he sat on the sofa and stared at the blank document and the blinking cursor that patiently (and without judgement) waited for him.

He placed the laptop on the glass and wooden coffee table, went to the kitchen and made green tea. As the water boiled, he thought of a man. Bald with a goatee and glasses. This man had been a chemistry teacher at a high school in New Mexico. He'd been diagnosed with lung cancer. He then teamed up with a former student to cook meth, and before long, he transformed from mild-mannered teacher into a drug kingpin.

Tommy Asandu was not that.

Wesley had rushed back to his laptop and typed out that first line, hit period and punched in a few more words. The kettle clicked. He quickly made the tea, sat back down and typed a few more words. Hit backspace a couple times. Frowned at a sentence that needed polishing. Went on Google to check synonyms. Drank some tea. Typed slowly. The old manner of typing with two forefingers. Spoke the words out the way he had done when he wrote his articles.

And now here he was. 177 words. It wasn't the best way to start a story (Wesley was more of the planning type with an entire skeleton and points laid out messily for him to follow), but it was better than not being able to write at all. Plus, he knew he could always come back and make changes.

He opened the notebook and looked at the notes he made after they were done questioning Syakir, who had given them the information on the second woman. Not the one who worked at the Chinese restaurant, but the croupier.

Connecting a pair of earphones to his phone, he played the recording from this evening.

"I saw her and Tommy meeting up a couple times. They saw me. They didn't see me, it doesn't matter." He'd paused here to shrug and continue smoking. By then, the irritation from Delilah's pepper spray had died down some, and he could mostly see again, though he'd opted to cover his eyes with his douche fashion sunglasses. "She has a stall at the kopitiam. Cooks noodles or something."

"What did they do?" Delilah asked.

"Passed stuff. Mostly it was Tommy passing her stuff."

"Did you know what it was?" Wesley asked.

"Nope. And he didn't volunteer any info either."

"What else do you know?"

"Well, once, during a dope spell, Tommy told me that he sold at the casino. Which is a big no-no."

"Why?" Wesley asked.

"Risky. But high return. He said that was his Palace Neptune. You see, his boss sells his drugs in two places. The Pearl-0 – that's the club in the resort. And Palace Neptune. Everyone parties there, so you've got a big pool, and you're the only dealer. But the boss takes … what, 70 percent of the profit? That leaves Tommy with 30, and he wasn't settling on that."

"So," Delilah's voice entered the recording, "he sells the stolen drugs at the casino?"

"High risk, high reward," Syakir said. "Just like gambling. And no, the drugs he sold at the casino were all his. The casino is open 24/7. You have the players who are itching for another go at the tables or the machines. Then you have the workers. Croupiers, waitresses, even the floor guards. These people might not be used to the night shift, but they need to show the CCTVs that they're working."

It made sense, Wesley thought as he paused the recording. Tommy's partner – the croupier lady – would sell her stuff, probably at a higher price, and Tommy would make some money. But they would need confirmation on that matter. At this point, it was just theory.

"Just the casino?" Wesley heard his own voice when he pressed 'play'.

"He sold to anyone who wanted a hit. Didn't matter if they were from the casino, the police station or the ferry terminal. Whoever needed a boost, Tommy would sell it to them. You could say he was a pillar of the community."

When he'd removed the earphones to give his ear canals a chance to listen to the breath of the night and the gentle hiss of wind from the sea, Ashini said to him, "I like that you're writing again."

The fine hairs on his arms rose. A lump formed in his throat. He turned to the right where the voice had come from, hoping to see her just the way she had been all those months ago before her death.

There was no one there, of course.

"I like that you're still constantly looking over my shoulder," he said.

He waited for her to say something. One of her famous quips, perhaps. Something that probably went: *The view could be better, though.*

But nothing came.

And so Wesley continued typing away at his laptop, hoping that before the lids of his eyes got too heavy, Ashini would tell him something else.

22

Wesley and Delilah had to work and babysit Margie, so their detective thing was put on hold for the rest of the day.

But one plus point was that since Zara wouldn't be available till the evening, they had to get their own food. And Delilah had a plan.

"While we're waiting for them to prepare our food, you want to look in her car?" Wesley asked.

"Do you have a better idea? And I don't think going up to her and asking if she's involved in drugs is such a good idea. Dumb shit like that normally gets you in a lot of trouble."

"But–"

"You're not looking into this as a news guy, remember? You're looking into this as …" she shrugged, "Singular Hardy Boy? Mr Marple Junior? Nancy Drew gone Gender Swapped?"

It was a serious moment, but he wanted to smile. In fact, a small smile creased the corner of his mouth. "Right, well, honestly, I was thinking about approaching her."

"And asking questions? Su Yen is a hardened lady. Have you seen how she handles customers?"

Su Yen, Tommy Asandu's alleged business partner, was one of the owners of the South Wind Bell Restaurant (no one called it that because calling it 'the Chinese kopitiam' was easier) and operated the kolo mee stall for the breakfast and lunch crowd. In the evening, she operated the till and, once in a while, if staff numbers were down, would turun padang and assist with menial tasks such as serving drinks and taking orders.

"If I find something, then we can make her talk. See if she knows anything about Tommy's murder," Delilah said.

"You're really enjoying this, aren't you?" Wesley asked, taking note of Delilah's excitement.

It was Delilah's turn to offer a somewhat sheepish smile. "Before I got into Virginia Woolf, Sylvia Plath and Margret Atwood, I was reading Enid Blyton and devouring Nancy Drew. Imagining it is fun. Doing it ... well, it's better than spending an entire day working and worrying about your literature review."

"It's a first for me, too," said Wesley.

"Ready to go over the plan again?" she asked, bouncing on the balls of her feet.

"Let's do it," he said.

X

Lucky made a sound and tugged on his leash, signaling that the road was clear and they could cross.

Delilah threw a quick glance behind her shoulder at the store. In the window, she could see Wesley standing by the counter. He looked concerned. One hand was curled into a fist, and the other rested on the binoculars by the cash register. The binoculars had been from Aunt Mabel from that one time she'd decided that she wanted to try bird watching but then gave it up when all it gave her were sweat-stained clothes and mosquito bites.

The Chinese kopitiam sat across the road and further down from the All-Convenience Store. It occupied a corner lot, so it had an open-air section where the stalls sat. The selection was limited, but South Wind Bell prided itself on quality over quantity, and this ranged from the chicken rice all the way to the bao and dumplings. A few of the stall owners who recognized Delilah called out and waved at her and Lucky. She smiled and waved back.

"Delilah," Su Yen said with a smile. She was a portly woman, hair tied into a short ponytail and covered with a hair net. She was dressed in a Man-U jersey, shorts and comfy running shoes. She held a massive pair of chopsticks which she used to pull and twirl steaming hot noodles from her pot. "And Lucky."

The dog grinned when his name was uttered, and because he liked putting on a show, sat down, opened his mouth and lolled his tongue out.

Su Yen clapped, looked around to make sure no one was looking, and tossed several slices of pork in the dog's direction. Lucky bolted up, caught them quickly and began munching. The dog grinned up at Su Yen, who was now wiping her hands on her stained apron to take Delilah's order.

"Might have to wait a while," she said, nodding in the general direction of the tables and chairs where people talked, stared at their phones, laughed and compared notes about their experience in Darat Kumut thus far. Many of the tables bore plastic cups with black numbers.

"All good," Delilah said, knowing that between 11:45 am and 12:30 pm was the worst time to order from the restaurant. "Lucky needs to go for a walk anyway."

"Sure he does," said Su Yen, and proceeded to make faces at the dog. Lucky panted happily at her and seemed to stall as Delilah tugged on his leash. Finally, he relented and followed her out.

Delilah made a left turn and headed for the parking lots, which occupied the side and the back of the shop-lot, forming a rough L-shape. Su Yen had parked her van (Delilah and Wesley had been observing since dawn because they wanted to know what car she drove) behind the shop-lot, which meant a pro and a con. The pro was that the location of her van – hidden away from Su Yen – would mean that Delilah had privacy. The con was that Wesley wouldn't be able to see Delilah, though he would be able to tell her if Su Yen had gotten suspicious that she was taking too long to collect her order.

As Lucky led her around the parking lot, stopping occasionally by the wheel of a car so he could raise a leg and spray the hose, she thought about the number of cups she'd seen on the tables. Half a dozen? Eight? Ten? Diu, lah. She hadn't been paying close enough attention. No … she had. It was just the excitement of all this got to her head.

The van in question was an ancient Ford Spectron that had once been a dull brown color and was now a rusted, peeling bucket of dog shit with several windows missing, a wiper torn clean off, half the driver's side rear view mirror shattered, and all four tires bald and clean of any treads. It looked unassuming, plain and somewhat depressing.

Only, to Delilah, it felt like the perfect vehicle to evade suspicion. Who would bother with a machine that was on its last legs and being held together by glue, duct tape and a couple of prayers?

Even Lucky didn't want to piss on this sorry excuse of a van. He did, however pause for several seconds to stare at the crummy pile of soon-to-be junk, with his head tilted on one side. His nose went up, and he began sniffing the air. Cautiously, he stepped forward and began with the passenger side wheel. Then to the rear wheel, and by the time he reached the back of the van, he was pawing at the rusted bumper (there was a sticker there depicting the MCA logo enshrouded with a red heart) and making low, whining noises.

Delilah pulled her phone out of her pocket and sent a quick voice message via WhatsApp to Wesley, telling him what the dog discovered. She glanced quickly to the side and saw she was alone. She brushed away the thick layer of dust over the rear window and looked into the back of the van. The back seats had been lowered (or removed), turning the rear of the van into a large space.

Delilah spotted an old pot. An electric kettle missing a lid. A large sack of flour, and a pile of something covered by a dark blue tarpaulin canvas.

No, not *something*. Boxes. One had tumbled down from its neat resting place. Probably Su Yen had been in a rush and just backed into the parking spot without thinking about the items she was carrying.

The van looked dark and dingy (one window had fucked off to the great beyond and been replaced with black plastic), and Delilah worried that the hinges of the van's tailgate would scream and whine as she pushed it open.

She placed her fingers on the hinge that would unlock the tailgate and pressed.

It wasn't locked.

"No way," Delilah said.

Next to her, Lucky was pressing his nose against the van, sniffing with abandon. The dog's behavior told her there was something in there she had to see. But to leave the van unlocked? Unguarded? It wasn't like this in the movies. In the movies – cheap thrillers that Delilah enjoyed as much as any Marvel superhero flick – the drugs (or drug money, or, in essence, anything related to drugs) would be triple guarded and kept under lock, key and a couple of armed guards with mean faces and meaner attitudes.

But to leave the van unlocked?

Well, one could always argue they weren't dealing with professional drug dealers, but people who were running a scam and gambling with their lives. Why bother keeping things tightly locked when you could store them in plain sight without arousing any suspicion? Especially when you were just the kolo mee lady, kan?

Makes some kind of sense, Delilah told herself as she pushed the tailgate up slowly. It didn't go all the way up, but offered enough space for her if she squatted. Seeing a gap, Lucky pushed his snout into the back of the van, panting excitedly. She placed one hand on his snout and gently pushed him away and was rewarded with a dog's version of an annoyed groan.

She reached for the box. It was a sneaker box. Gray and covered with the Nike swoosh logo at the top center, along with the words *Nike* and *Air Force*. The rest of the box was plain. She popped it open and–

Lucky got excited and went at the box with everything he had, forepaws in the van, snout pushed forward, eager as a beaver to sate his curiosity.

She undid the lid and pulled the box up. There was a pair of sneakers in there, wrapped in crinkly paper. She undid the paper to find ... a pair of sneakers. Nike Air Force 1s. A shoe that she and many other girls and boys had worn in lecture halls and walkways, covered and not, of John Harolds University College back in Kota Damansara.

Delilah looked at the other boxes. All of them were the same Nike box, offering the iconic chunky-soled, white sneaker. *These were shoes*, she thought to herself. Well, they could be fakes, but still. Just shoes, nothing too–

With a growl, Lucky grabbed hold of the sneaker and began ripping into it.

23

Her phone rang.

"Shit," she mumbled, realizing she had forgotten to put the damn thing on vibrate.

Below, Lucky was going cuckoo-bananas with his new chew toy. Like a puppy with his first shoe, he had his jaws locked on the sock liner, one paw on the toe area and was tugging for dear life.

"Lucky," she hissed, "stop it."

Lucky didn't seem to care and went on with his playfully violent ministrations.

Delilah grabbed her phone – it was Wesley calling – who else?

"Hey, you have a problem," he said, sounding breathless. "Su Yen's missing."

"What? And you couldn't tell me earlier?"

"I had a customer."

Delilah lowered the phone and took a peek from the side of the van.

Her heart shot up to her throat when she saw Su Yen, standing at the rear of the kopitiam beside the three young girls on stools washing the dishes in massive, circular buckets. She spoke quickly and, from what Delilah could see, looked like she was doing her best to placate whoever it was on the phone.

Delilah was still staring when Su Yen looked her way. She pulled back so quickly that she fell on her butt, wincing as the sharp stones on the asphalt bit through the seat of her shorts. Next to her, Lucky managed to rip a section of the leather (if it was real leather) from the sole.

"Lucky, *stop* it," she said. She grabbed the shoe from his mouth, which brought about another sad groan, shoved it into the still-open box ...

Her phone slipped out of her grip, Wesley still on the other end of the line, calling out to her.

She winced. The *clack* of phone on asphalt was as loud as a gunshot. She shushed Lucky, holding him close by the collar, the poor thing making soft whiny noises, sensing her panic, and waited, hearing Su Yen's footsteps on the ground, coming closer and closer and closer and closer and–

"Su Yen!" someone – a man – shouted out. "Someone here to see you," he continued in Mandarin.

The footsteps stopped.

"Who is it?" Su Yen asked.

"Looks like that new police guy who came a few days ago. You better come. He asked specifically for you. And I don't think he wants a bowl of kolo mee."

"Cibai," Su Yen muttered.

Delilah waited until the footsteps receded to the kopitiam before reaching for her phone. Wesley was still there.

"What happened?" she asked, panting. She let go of Lucky, who, in turn, looked mournfully up at her.

"Inspector Rabbil," Wesley said. "He and his partner stopped by. They spoke to the owner and he went out back, I think."

"Okay," she said, running the back of her hand against her forehead, cleaning away the layer of sweat that had built up there.

"You good?" Wesley asked.

"Better than good," she said, staring at the box, "I think we have some evidence."

24

"You barely ate," Aunt Zara said, shaking her head at Wesley's plate. "Was it the fish? I swear I followed the recipe and put enough paprika."

"It's not the food," Wesley said, doing his best to speak to her while he played a game of ball with Margie and Lucky. "I'm just excited. I've got–" *evidence to look at? a potential lead in solving a murder? ideas about why the dog went mad at a pair of knock-off Nikes?* "–a date … with Lilah."

Zara grinned. "Well, at least try and eat a bit, lah. You were so skinny when you got here and now you're still skinny. When they come down here, your parents, especially your mom is gonna pester me with why you're still a beanstalk. And I have a feeling she'll start making hints about my bad cooking."

"Your cooking is great," Wesley said as he stuffed his mouth with the grilled fish. But actually she had gone a little overboard with the paprika on this occasion. "I'm just … worried."

"You'll knock it out of the park," Zara said. "Now eat. *Slowly.*"

At night, the South Wind Bell Restaurant was still abuzz with people. The beer was cheap if you didn't mind the pounding music from the nightclub next door. The only place that was quiet was the parking lot behind the row of shop-lots, though they still spotted a couple from the club making out between two cars.

"Where did you leave it?" Wesley asked.

"The drain. Under some leaves. Let's hope no one spotted it."

"Looks like Su Yen is still at the station," Wesley said, nodding in the direction of the van. Inspector Rabbil and his second in command had come around and, in front of the customers, had exchanged words with Su Yen.

Based on her body language, Wesley theorized this was something big. The woman had been listening intently to the inspector until he said something that made her jump back and exclaim angrily in shock, giving the diners a show to go with their meals. Unfazed, the inspector spoke again, and this time, his second in command tapped the handcuffs on her utility belt. Seeing that, Su Yen nodded and followed, walking between the second in command and the inspector, the unlikely trio making their way towards the police outpost.

Delilah had stashed the box under some leaves and other detritus in the shallow drain bordering the parking lot. Squatting, she sighed and shifted the debris. She'd buried the box under a mound, but it should be here, right? So why wasn't she feeling the reassuring firmness of a cardboard box?

"Everything okay?" Wesley, who was squatting behind her, asked.

"Yeah," she said, trying not panic, knowing very well the box had been here. Right here. Under the brown leaves. Under a bag that smelled suspicious and wasn't leaking just yet. Under what might have once been a denim button shirt, torn and ripped in a few places, and a rubber boot that might've belonged to a cleaner. But where in the name of God was that fetid–

"Got it," she said, immensely relieved. It was under some more crap. She'd overdone the job of burying it, was all. There the box was. It still had heft, so no one else had found it.

"It's definitely drugs," she said as they stood up. "Why else would Lucky go crazy and try to rip it apart?"

"Maybe he's an Adidas guy," Wesley replied.

Delilah rolled her eyes. "Open it here?"

He glanced over his shoulder and saw another couple, tipsy, giggling and just about ready to Marvin Gaye and get it on over the hood of a very unlucky car. "Maybe somewhere else?"

"Not my place. Mabel thinks I'm out with you, so that means she's trying to write, so she'll want peace and quiet. Yours?"

"Zara's doing stuff in the kitchen. Margie and Lucky are watching cartoons. Won't be good."

"What about a third option?" said a new voice.

Wesley realized then that the giggling couple who'd been fooling around and several moves away from making a good mistake, had gone silent.

25

Inspector Rabbil leaned against Su Yen's van, arms crossed, with a mild look of annoyance.

This afternoon, he had noticed the gleam of light that came from the All-Convenience Store's window, and when he glanced at it, he saw the guy with a pair of binoculars looking directly at Su Yen.

"How did you know?" Delilah asked.

Rabbil said, "We managed to get a record of all calls and messages that Tommy sent from his phone. His constant calls sealed the deal. He was in contact with Su Yen. I spoke with a few other people in town before coming over to the restaurant, and they told me they didn't see any reason for Tommy and Su Yen to be talking to one another. He was the town pariah and she's a successful businesswoman. Two totally separate people who text and call each other every few days? Makes little sense, doesn't it?"

And so they had brought Su Yen in for questioning. Atiqah was still at the police station (he'd started calling it that instead of the very demeaning *outpost*) in its sole interview room, trying to get the woman to say something. The most Su Yen could come up with was that Tommy had called her to order noodles.

"Twice in one day?" Atiqah asked, standing there, hands on hips, looking very annoyed.

"My cooking's great."

And she had stayed with that narrative since the afternoon.

"I came back here in the evening. Made sure you two were doing your work," said Rabbil as he lit a cigarette. "I didn't know what I was looking for until I saw her van." To Delilah, he said, "You didn't close the tailgate properly."

"I did," she said.

"No, you didn't. The lock hadn't engaged, and as a police officer who was concerned for the safety of the vehicle as there could have been an attempted theft, I took a peek. Imagine my surprise when I saw a humble noodle seller had boxes of counterfeit shoes in her van. Weird, right? I also noticed the little pile you left in the drain. You were quick, but you didn't hide your evidence properly. The corner of the box was sticking out. So I checked it, took some photos and properly hid it. After all, there's no harm in someone stealing a pair of shoes that are fakes, right? It's like stealing from a thief."

At their shocked looks, Rabbil grinned in a way that took 10 years off his face, showing off the boyish good looks that his lovely wife Syafiqah had fallen for all those years ago at UM. He said, "You know the myth that *all* cops in the country are just there for the payout after retirement is not true. Some of us actually want to solve crimes. Some of us actually watched *Law & Order* and *CSI* and thought, 'shit, I could do that'. Did you know that?"

"We didn't think ..." Wesley began.

"That what?" he said, the bonhomie attitude still there. "That I didn't want to solve this crime? Kid, I'm not going to lie to you. It's been a while since I've been given a proper whodunit. And this," he waved both hands in the air, "is a proper murder-mystery. I'm glad I'm not the only one who sees it that way. Only I'm a cop and you two aren't."

"We're concerned citizens," said Delilah.

He laughed. "You two have seen too much *Scooby-Doo*."

"Are you gonna stop us?" Wesley asked.

Rabbil made a face like he was thinking about it. "I should. You guys got this far. Should I even ask how, by the way?"

"We asked the right questions."

If Rabbil's right eyebrow could go any higher, he'd probably make it in the modelling industry. "Sure. I believe that."

"You were going to offer up a third option?" Wesley said, pointing at the box.

"Right. We can't use the police outpost because this evidence wasn't seized using a warrant. I'd say my hotel, but since there's always eyes around and it's a small town, which means people are always talking, perhaps we could do it at the store?"

X

Delilah unlocked the back door and ushered them in.

Finding his way in the dark and doing his best not to bang into the racks and boxes of goods in the cramped space, Wesley found the light switch for the storage area, and soon the area was illuminated.

Delilah shut the door and placed the shoebox on the scarred rubber-wood roundtable they used for lunch.

"Is the cactus real?" Rabbil asked, pointing at the plant in its small pot in the middle of the table.

"Your powers of detection should be able to tell you," said Delilah. Rabbil snorted in return.

She opened the box, pulled the shoes out and placed them on the table. To Wesley, they looked like a regular pair of shoes. One had been torn up on the side, thanks to Lucky's excitement.

"The quality is shit," Rabbil said, placing a finger on the torn sock-lined area where the dogs' teeth had ripped and gnashed. "I have a couple pairs. Bought them with my own money. No bribes were taken."

"Lucky went crazy over them," Delilah said. "Maybe he smelled something?"

Picking up one shoe, Rabbil dug his hand into it and pulled out a block of cardboard that had been stuffed into it to maintain its shape. He dug his hand in once more but came up with nothing.

"Odd," he said.

Delilah picked up the other shoe and copied the inspector's movements, also coming up with nothing.

"It's just a shoe," she said, placing it back on the table.

Wesley picked that shoe up and, using his smartphone's flashlight, looked inside. Everything looked perfectly alright. There wasn't anything taped inside or along the sides of the shoe. He was about to place it back on the table when he noticed the edge of the insole was loose. Inspector Rabbil had said that the quality was shit ... but his instincts told him there was more here.

"Odd," said Rabbil, who was still looking at the shoe – now squinting at the leather stitching around it, focusing on the mudguard. "I could swear the stitches look fake ... like they just put it there to show it looks like the real thing." To display his prowess as an investigator, he brought the shoe close to his nose and sniffed. "The smell of glue is strong here."

From the pocket of his shorts, Wesley pulled out his disposable lighter, fired it up and placed it close to the section between the midsole and heel. He kept the flame far enough that it didn't damage the shoe, but near enough to warm up the glue holding the bottom and top together.

"I have an idea," he said.

"Are you gonna share?" Delilah asked.

"Uhh … try do what I'm doing."

Without a word, the inspector brought out his lighter and copied Wesley's act; occasionally, he'd move the flame along the heel, hoping to speed up the separation.

After a while, Wesley placed the lighter on the table. Next came the shoe. He had one hand clutched around the lining of the heel, his other hand around the midsole. With a deep breath, he pulled against the top and kept his hand firmly on the bottom.

The sections separated faster than he'd imagined. With it came the sound of the upper tearing from the midsole.

"Need help?" Delilah asked.

His hands were feeling a little drained, so he stepped aside and watched as she completed the separation in one savage move. The toe box and tip tore away, and what remained were the insole and midsole.

"What next?" Rabbil asked. He had torn off the top and now held the sole in his left hand.

"The insole," Wesley said. "Tear it up."

Delilah and Rabbil pulled. More sounds of tearing, but this went quicker than it had with the shoe's upper. What they were left with were the insole and outsole. With the removal of the insole, the three of them stared at the line extending from the heel to where the toes would rest.

"There's about an inch and a half of space between the outsole and the top of the shoe," Rabbil said. "A lot of real estate if you know what you're doing."

"Wanna look inside, inspector," said Wesley, "or do we need a warrant?"

"Let's have a look," said the inspector.

26

Inspector Rabbil had a big smile on his face when he got to the police outpo—

Station, he reminded himself. Police *Station*. Under one arm, he carried a shoe box – the same one he'd helped those two amateur detectives with. His other hand carried the bonus that Delilah had given him.

Most of the cops had called it a night and were heading off. The remaining three were Atiqah, who was aggressively vaping in front of the stained, mobile whiteboard where most of their facts were spelt out, Constable Rudolph and Sergeant Awang, who looked like he had aged 10 years since the start of the case.

Rabbil liked Sergeant Awang. The man had a folksy charm that made the locals respect him. He was friendly. No, he was *very* friendly. Pats on the back, fist-bumps, gregarious laughter, and an ability to constantly want to be part of the conversation.

What he wasn't, though, was prepared to handle a murder investigation like this one. Cops like Sergeant Awang were essential to the police in the way that cops like him were essential. Cops like Sergeant Awang knew how to tame an already tame beast. They carried with them a reminder that the law was still a thing, and even though the worst Darat Kumut had seen up to that point were a couple of drunks brawling, everyone felt safe with a cop like Sergeant Awang.

In a way, Rabbil envied the man because his life was so peaceful. All the man had to do was take care of the town. How hard could that be in a place like Darat Kumut?

"Bad news, boss," Atiqah said when she saw him. "Su Yen's lawyered up."

Rabbil pursed his lips. "What happened?"

"I … I pushed too hard, sir."

"Pundek," he said. "Is she still here?"

"Lock-up," Sergeant Awang offered.

"Room still wired?"

"No. We took the recording stuff out."

"Uh-huh." He checked his phone. Still enough juice for a quickie. There were a couple of miscalls from Syafiqah and a text message from her – a reminder to call as soon as he was free.

"Okay. Rudolph, get Su Yen into the interview room. Don't tell her anything. Don't bother answering her questions. Just get her in there and keep her there for a bit." Turning to Atiqah: "We can still hold her for questioning, kan?"

"Twenty-four hours, boss. Standard practice." Finally noticing the box under his arm, she added, "What's that for?"

"A prop," he said.

"Should I ask?"

He shook his head. "All in due time, Ticks. For now, just let me get into the box with Su Yen and pray that she finally sees the light of reason. You weren't too rough with her, were you?"

"I just annoyed her."

"She got any pressure points?"

"No."

"Which tells us …"

"That she has been arrested before."

"Did you dig?"

"I did. It's a little slow here." She nodded in the direction of her laptop. "The internet sucks."

"Well, find a way. We arrested her at …" he glanced at his watch, "eleven-forty-five this afternoon. It's five past ten. Time is ticking. Use the car if you have to. Drive somewhere that has decent internet and get me those results. ASAP."

"Yes, boss," she said, making her way to the laptop.

That left Sergeant Awang. Rabbil walked up to him, "Su Yen moved to town two years ago, right?"

He nodded. After the arrest, he had given Rabbil everything he knew about the noodle lady.

"Was she ever vetted?"

"For crime?" the man said, looking very flustered.

Rabbil nodded.

"No," Sergeant Awang said. Sputtering, his next words were, "There was no need. She looked like a regular person. Lived outside of town, sure, but I didn't see a reason to vet her."

Constable Rudolph stepped back into the main office area, a big smile on his face. "She's in the interview room."

"Good. Get me a coffee, constable and keep it warm. This shouldn't take too long."

"Is my lawyer here?" Su Yen asked. She looked bored. Her hands weren't cuffed. They were on the table, clasped together as if she was readying herself to pray.

"We'll get you your call soon enough. But before that …" Rabbil placed the box on the table, all the while looking at Su Yen for a reaction.

The woman stared at the box for several seconds, a little too long, in Rabbil' expert opinion. Readying herself, maybe, to spin the perfect lie for him.

"Never seen it," said Su Yen. "Now, where's my lawyer?"

"Sure about that?" Rabbil asked, nodding at the box. "We found it in the trunk of your van."

"That's an invasion of privacy," she snapped. "You can't do that."

Rabbil shook his head. "I didn't break into your van. Someone was trying to break into it." He paused, waited to see the look of curiosity on her face and then said, "This person got as far as removing one box out from the back of your van before I chased him away. He dropped the box. It opened and…" He opened the box and pulled out the shoes that had been torn apart. "The perpetrator had gotten as far as tearing up the shoe and removing the insole. Since I was in the midst of an active crime, I had to look and see why the thief had broken into your van." He paused. Watched her. You could just about see her lower jaw trembling at the sight of the soles and the exposed slit in the center. Su Yen knew. She was an active part of this.

"You could imagine my shock when I saw what was in these shoes," he said, turning the soles over.

Out came several tiny, tightly bundled packets of what looked like crystalized sugar. The plastic packets were smaller than the kind that restaurants used to pack cili padi. The sole could fit a dozen of these syabu packets. Then came the left sole.

He gave the sole a little tap, and out came bills. Tens, twenties, fifties and even hundred-ringgit bills, rolled up and held together with orange rubber hands, stuffed into the hollow of the sole.

Su Yen looked worried.

And now for the killer …

"And there's also this." He placed the cell phone on the interview table. "Tommy's second phone. There's one number in there. If I were to hit call, would your phone ring?"

Su Yen looked just about ready to panic. He had her at the precipice. Now for the gentle push.

"Can we talk now?" Rabbil asked.

27

The phone rang. And that screwed up his concentration.

Where moments before he'd been grunting, basking in the pleasure of the woman's moans (the moans always made him harder), now the only sound in his room came from the Bluetooth speaker by the side of the bed playing something from Sade. He didn't know the song because it came from one of those random Spotify playlists that some reddit subs swore were the best when having sex.

The sub-reddit had been correct, of course, but thanks to the phone call, he went limp, and the woman's moans of pleasure (which he knew were fake, *good*, but fake) had fizzled off to hisses as she suckled on her vape pen.

"What?" he asked, stepping out into the balcony and allowing a breeze from the Celebes Sea to whip against his nude form. He looked down and saw that he wasn't hard anymore. *Pundek.*

"News from town," another man reported. "The Bank's been caught."

"When?"

"This morning. Those cops investigating To—" the voice paused, realized that he'd been one syllable away from fucking up, then said, "those cops investigating the dead guy found some connection."

"What's the connection?"

"Don't know. All I know is that they tied the Bank to him."

"Hmm. What about the other two?"

"Don't know either. But the cops haven't got too far."

"Hmm."

"There's … another thing."

"Is there?"

"Two others are looking into it as well."

The naked man standing by the balcony rubbed his jaw. "Explain."

"Two civilians working at the convenience store are looking into the murder as well."

"Progress?"

"Unclear."

"Names?"

"I thought—"

"Names," the naked man said.

"Wesley Moysin and Delilah Loh."

"Get me everything on them. And keep a close eye on the Bank. Call me as soon as the cops let her out." He hung up but continued standing there, his flaccid penis pressed against the cool glass that made up the railing of the balcony. He turned right and looked out to the lights in the distance that made up the town of Darat Kumut.

Tommy's death was supposed to be easy. Tommy's death wasn't supposed to attract anyone's attention. And now, he didn't just have the cops on the scent. He had a couple of others who seemed to think they were in a murder-mystery story.

The man sighed. The night was ruined.

"Baby," his woman called from inside. "We're not done yet, right?"

Maybe he'd try choking her. Almost killed the last girl, sure, but she'd survived.

"Nope," he said, imagining her fragile neck in his hands and his coarse fingers gently squeezing. "We're not done just yet."

28

Wesley looked at his notebook, now updated with the info from their little adventure with the inspector. The official count from the one shoe with the money had totaled up to RM2,530. Not bad, especially if the rest of the shoes had about the same.

"Stop daydreaming. Those bags aren't gonna fill themselves up," Delilah said as she stepped in to grab a clean wiping cloth.

"Yeah, right. Sure," he said, closing up the notebook and quickly chucking it into his bag.

As he packed another paper bag with goods, Wesley thought about Su Yen and her connection to Tommy Asandu. Tommy was the dealer. Su Yen kept the money, but also some of the stash? Maybe she was holding the drugs temporarily.

"Okay," he mumbled to himself. "Makes sense."

Tommy had three other associates. They'd unmasked one: Su Yen, who probably kept some kind of financial record of how much the group was making. There was the croupier. And then there was the mystery guy. The fourth member. Had to be a reason to have him around, right?

Wesley placed the paper bags into a plastic basket and carried it with both hands. He pushed the door open with his hip and entered the store, which was abuzz with conversation. A few of the regulars called out to him. He greeted them back.

Delilah was at the cash register, smiling, accepting money, packing up purchases and returning change, doing her best to layan the customers that were there to pick, pay and leave.

As he was accepting payment from one of the customers who preferred the paper bag method of purchasing groceries, he spotted an older woman sitting at the last table, the one nearest to the doors. She was somewhere in her late 50s, gray hair tied into a thick ponytail that hung over one shoulder. Her cup of coffee was still full, but the steam had gone off. Her hands were in her lap, clutching what looked like some kind of cloth.

He accepted the cash from the customer, thanked the man and walked back into the store.

The customer nearest the little gap that led to the storeroom door was a familiar face. Salleh Arip, who'd been a boat captain for too long ("since I was in the womb," as he liked to tell and re-tell to anyone who'd bother listening) and now repaired fishing boats at the Terminal.

"Sal," he said, "that woman sitting at the last table. You kenal her?"

"Old lady?" the man whispered back, restlessly tapping the bottom of his Gudang Garam packet on the bar. "Long, gray hair? Starring into the distance? That lady?"

Wesley nodded. "I don't think she's one of the regulars."

"She's from Sandakan, I think. Or Semporna. Used to live here. Sad story tu. Her daughter works … no *worked* at the casino on the island. Went missing … six, seven months ago, ka? Just didn't come home. The resort security team went looking for her. Found nothing. Three days they searched the island. Poor girl. The mother comes around every few weeks or so, takes the ferry to the island and spends … I don't know, a day? Two days, just looking for her missing daughter."

"Did you know her?"

Salleh nodded. "It's a small town. Alisia Supian – that's her name, by the way – her daughter is – sorry, *was* – Abigail Martin Supian, I think … was a good girl. Loyal to her family. Hardworking. Wasn't smart enough like her siblings to leave this place, but she managed well. Worked as a waitress at the casino on the island. Some say she got into drugs and that's why she disappeared."

Story done, Salleh stood up and undid the top of the cigarette pack. He offered Wesley a sad smile and dropped some money on the counter for the coffee. Wesley grabbed the cash and passed it to Delilah, who in turn asked him to take over at the counter as she had to rush off to the toilet.

He took her place, continued to pour coffee for the customers, but focused on the lady at the last table, who still had her hands in her lap and her coffee on the table.

As customers poured into the store, the woman blended into the environment, and soon, Wesley found himself too busy to even glance in her direction. Only later, while he was delivering goods to another customer (the wife of a bigwig who worked at the resort) did he notice that the lady – Alisia – had gone off, leaving her still-full mug of coffee and some money on the table.

29

"The missing casino girl?" Syakir asked.

Wesley nodded. "Abigail Martin Supian. Do you know of her?"

They were sitting outside the ferry terminal, slightly away from the constant stream of people departing the ferry from the island. Wesley had made a call to the resort's IT Department, conning his way through by saying he was a relative of Syakir's and had some bad news for the stoner.

Syakir nodded. It had been a couple days since his accidental run-in with Delilah's pepper spray and her rapid fists.

To remedy his looks, Syakir wore a new pair of sunglasses, bigger than the last. Wesley noticed that the IT guy had been walking funny as he exited the terminal and felt a little bad for the stoner. Though the blame was on the guy for being a world-class prick when they'd first met.

Of course, Syakir had freaked out when Wesley approached him, saying something about sprinting off to the police outpost. Noting that Wesley was alone, he began looking around and muttered something about the scary-looking Amazonian that had sprayed fire into his eyes and given him an ass-kicking for the ages, before joining Wesley on one of the benches near the Ferry Terminal's entrance.

Wesley had told Delilah of his plan, which included speaking with Syakir. The hard part was telling her he'd didn't want her to come for the meeting with Syakir; the last thing he wanted was

Syakir running at the sight of her. She accepted his request and told him good luck, though he was sure that she wanted to be here for this.

"What does her going missing have to do with Tommy?" Syakir asked, lighting up a cigarette. He didn't bother fishing through his backpack for it, he'd simply reached over and grabbed Wesley's pack.

"Just a theory," Wesley said, irked by having his cigarettes taken without even being asked, but hey, tit for tat, right?

"That happened a long time ago," the stoner IT guy said. "Old news, bro."

"Did you know her?"

Syakir shrugged. "Maybe. Maybe not. Maybe go fuck yourself?"

"I can call Delilah if you don't feel like talking nicely."

Syakir snapped, "No need to get all emotional, lah, bro. I did know her, but we weren't besties. She worked at the casino as a waitress. One day she was there, one day she wasn't. The only thing I had in common with her was that she did drugs too. Not primo weed, but the real shake-and-bake shit."

He chuckled at Wesley's look of confusion.

"She was big on meth. Wasn't one of those addicts, though. Just did it because of the unstable schedule casino workers live on. A little speed, and you're up and running for a few hours."

"So there's a chance that she could be dead, lah? Like an overdose?"

Syakir made a hissing *psssst* sound and shook his head. "From what I hear, she's alive and well."

"Really?"

"Ran off with another colleague. Or so they say, lah."

"*They*?"

"Her colleagues. But it was weird."

"How?"

"Once everyone knew, they just stopped talking about her. Being respectful and all that." Syakir produced another shrug. "Life went on, and Abigail became another memory."

"What do you think?"

Syakir shrugged. "Don't know, bro. I didn't know her that well. We done here?"

"One last question," he said as Syakir looped one arm around his backpack. "Did Abigail have any friends?"

"I'll do you a solid. She has a fiancé. Or maybe it's ex-fiancé now?" Syakir's movements were slow and juddery, a sure sign of heavy cannabis intake. Wesley was jealous the guy seemed to live in a state of high. "Bah, I'll give you his details."

"He works at the resort?" Wesley asked as Syakir tore a page from a graffiti-ladened notebook and wrote something down with a shaky hand.

"Mm-hmm. Works as a security guard. Warning though," Syakir said, as Wesley took the scrap of paper from the stoner's hand, "the guy's a little … testy when it comes to Abigail. You ask me, I think she broke his heart. Poor bastard."

Wesley glanced at the paper, half expecting to see some gibberish interlaced with Stoner Hieroglyphics. What he got instead was legible cursive that didn't look like anything an IT guy would write. The name on the paper was Mark Anthony Jibril. Below the name, a phone number. Below the phone number was the block and lot number of the employees' quarters the man lived in.

"Try not to piss the guy off," Syakir said, finally getting up and leaving Wesley alone with the scrap of paper and his thoughts.

30

Su Yen angrily slammed the tailgate of her van shut.

Fired!

The old pig who ran the kopitiam had told her she was f-i-r-e-d.

"It's not good for the community, Su," he'd told her when he pulled her aside to give her The Talk. "The police dragged you away–"

"They didn't drag me–"

The owner rolled his eyes and said, "They brought you to the station – " Him stabbing the air with his forefinger in her direction wasn't making her feel better.

"For standard questioning. I–"

"If it was standard questioning, why did they keep you around for 24 hours? Why did a lawyer come? Sergeant Awang won't tell me anything."

"The lawyer was there because they made some allegations, and I had to answer–"

"Was it a crime?"

Su Yen had gotten stuck there. Of course, it was a crime. They'd found the stash in her van. Her idea to keep the drugs and money in plain sight – because of how far-fetched the idea was – had backfired. Now she was out of a job in the one lucrative place that she was beginning to look at as home.

She had to call the other two, convene a meeting and do something about the shit show they were facing after Tommy died. Things had to be done. Deals had been made. Promises had been brokered. KPIs needed to be hit. Money needed to be made. It was what Tommy wanted. He was smart, but he was also dumb. How could you be Pablo Escobar when you were high for at least 20 hours a day?

He had a good idea and he'd done a good job with Khairul to help negotiate the deal with those Kalashnikov-wielding Suluk drug dealers who cooked meth and grew marijuana on the islands and islets between Semporna and Zamboanga. Shit, even she'd been impressed when that first haul came in. Impressed enough to kiss her previous, less-than-legal side income of selling fake sneakers and clothes goodbye and go into the drug business. The money had been good, but the risk was always there, standing in one hidden corner and waiting for them to screw it all up.

She entered her van and checked the back. The boxes with the fake shoes (and all the goodies within the soles) had been removed. All that remained was the blue and orange tarp that had kept the boxes away from prying eyes, and even that was moved to one side to make space for the pots, strainers, pans, containers of spices and packets of noodles she'd packed up after being told to kindly fuck off from her only legitimate income source.

"That mangkuk Tommy," she mumbled. She pulled her hands away from the steering wheel, curled them up into fists and pounded angrily on the dashboard. The imbecile got caught.

He got reckless, ended up dead and now their entire operation here was compromised. As a group, they'd trusted each other. In a way, they were a good team because they complemented each other.

Khairul drove the truck that carried the goods, Cilla made the big bucks selling at the casino and hotel, and she balanced the books and made sure that they were making money and that Tommy, for all of his brilliance, wasn't taking too many of the proverbial cookies from the proverbial cookie jar.

There was also the matter of that poor girl on the island who'd taken a bad batch of mod-meth, (Modified-Meth was the term the Suluk meth chef had marketed), had a little accident and died at *in the casino. That* had been a true test of teamwork for the three of them. Getting rid of a dead body … if that wasn't the ultimate team-building activity to build trust among three people, she didn't know what was.

Cilla knew about Tommy. Khairul would be coming down tomorrow, so she'd update him. There would be a new batch of goods in his truck to be sold at Palace Neptune and the casino. All in due time, of course.

Su Yen started the van. She'd go home and think things through. She had money from her legal work and the haram drug cash, but … to stay at home and do what? Watch Netflix? A little porn with her vibrator? Appealing, yes, but not what she had in mind.

She needed to think, she needed …

She glanced over at the row of shops next to the Ferry Terminal and licked her lips at the sight of the Seaside Bar.

When was the last time she'd had a drink?

Maybe there'd even be a nice Korean oppa in there who'd be looking to try her pretty, pink Malaysian flesh.

Grinning, her mood a little better now, Su Yen killed the engine and stepped out of her van. Her hair didn't smell like soy sauce and roast pork. She closed the door and with a little pump in her step, made her way towards the bar.

31

Inspector Rabbil walked in when the crowd had thinned to the paltry few who were there to just pick, pay and leave, and settled on the stool. He reached for a rumpled copy of *The Borneo Post* someone had left earlier while Wesley and Delilah did their tasks.

Wesley and Delilah waited eagerly, fake smiles on their faces, while the last customer, an elderly lady who lived on the outskirts of town, paid for several cans of dogfood. Once she'd hobbled out of the store, Wesley told the inspector about Abigail Martin Supian.

The inspector listened. Then he was silent for some time before finally saying: "Good coffee."

Wesley looked at Delilah. Delilah looked at Wesley. They looked at Inspector Rabbil.

"That's all you have to say?" Wesley asked.

"I don't mean to sound dismissive," he said. "But what does a missing woman have to do with Tommy Asandu?"

"We think that Tommy had several partners in town, not just Su Yen. He was selling drugs at the casino – "

"And you know this how?"

"A source."

"Don't give me that."

"I can trust this source."

"Can you?"

"The source gave us Su Yen," Delilah said.

"Su Yen gave us nothing but a lawyer and a threat of police abuse."

"We got the evidence, don't we?"

"Inadmissible evidence. If it came to light that you guys broke into the van and I happily took it ..."

"No one will know."

The inspector snorted. "Of course they won't. Okay" – he pulled out his notebook and clicked his pen – "this source of yours claims that Su Yen wasn't the only person involved in this drug operation. There are two others?"

Wesley nodded.

"And this missing other lady?"

"Is leverage."

Rabbil pursed his lips. "Leverage for...?"

Wesley brought the inspector up to speed on what he'd learned from Syakir. "Our source claims that one of Tommy's partners works at the casino. Abigail worked at the casino as a waitress. And this source claims she used meth. Regularly."

"So *theoretically*, if I find the body or some trace of the body, then you can get this seller to cave in and tell you what they might know?"

Wesley and Delilah nodded.

"This source..." He said the word *source* as if just pronouncing it left a bad taste in his mouth. What is it with reporters (or has-beens) and their love for their sources? "...Didn't say that this Abigail girl is dead."

"That's the belief."

"And you want to find her?"

Wesley nodded.

"And I'm involved because?"

"If she's alive, we can talk to her. *You* can talk to her."

"*If* she's alive," Rabbil repeated. "That's some very weak sauce."

"Worth a try. You can say that it came from an anonymous *source*."

There's that word again, Rabbil thought. The Darat Kumut Amateur Detective Agency (it was a term he had labelled these two) had a point. So far, they had nothing. Another avenue didn't hurt.

No one could give them any new leads. Same shit from everyone. They'd checked alibis, quietly brought people in for interviews and pored over the facts of the case again and again and again. And the results: nothing.

"Alright," he said. "I'll bite. What's the girl's full name?"

"Abigail Martin Supian. Age 29."

"That's it?"

Wesley pulled out his phone and showed a picture of Abigail he'd taken from her Facebook page. In it, she stood leaning against a coconut tree on a beach, in a low-cut dress whose hem reached her mid-thigh, sleeves short. Her hair danced in the breeze. One hand was held over her eyes to block the glare of the sun. She was pretty, and Wesley failed to see how it was she'd ended up a meth addict.

Using his phone, Rabbil snapped a picture of the missing woman. He downed the rest of his coffee and said, "I'll keep you guys updated, then. And remember, no more dicking around, okay?"

32

Two days later (with the vague notion of 'fucking around'), they were on the noon ferry bound for Pulau Kumut. And they weren't alone. Margie and Lucky had managed to talk their way into joining Wesley and Delilah to the island. Aunt Zara was taking care of the shop, and she said it would be great if Margie could go with them if that wasn't a problem.

Wesley gave in.

Delilah was surprised to see the three of them instead of just him.

"I couldn't tell her no, right?" Wesley said. As they had a live animal (on a leash, of course) they had to wait with the vehicles, which was perfectly fine for them. Delilah was in the driver's seat of Mabel's ancient Volvo. Wesley stood by the door. Margie was sitting on the hood, waving a Dora the Explorer flag and giggling as Lucky tried his best to paw it out of the air.

"We're going to interview someone," Delilah said. "You can't just bring her along. Things could get dangerous."

"What was I supposed to do?" he asked, "tell Zara no?"

Doing that would've been devastating for Margie. Wesley would've felt bad, too, because he rarely spent time with his 5-year-old cousin.

"Make something up, maybe? Wes, it's dangerous."

"I didn't do it on purpose."

Margie squealed loudly. Lucky had been close. He was growling playfully at the flag now and making Margie giggle.

A few tourists looked their way and acted all oohs and ahhs. Little chubby girl and her very adorable dog. Some even whipped out their phones for a little Instagram story action.

As for Mark Anthony, Wesley had managed to reach the man, but when he introduced himself, all he got in return was the sound of someone breathing heavily into the phone. That was at midnight. He sent a couple WhatsApp messages, but all he got back were blue ticks.

"Let's just hope that this Mark Anthony guy isn't some violent prick," Delilah said, eyeing Margie to make sure some rando stranger didn't come over and offer her candy.

The best Wesley could do was nod and agree.

X

Margie clapped when the captain announced they were minutes away from docking.

The tiny speck of land mass that was Pulau Kumut had been growing bigger and bigger in the last 30 minutes, and now here it was in all its glory. Pulau Kumut Town, even smaller than Darat Kumut, occupied the northwestern section. At the center and gently rising up was Bukit Kumut, from which the brochures promised some of the most majestic views of the Celebes Sea and its surroundings. The resort sat on the northeast side. The employee quarters were along the way.

How? was the question. They knew Mark Anthony worked at the resort and lived in the quarters, but how would they get in touch with him? You couldn't just go to the quarters and start asking around, kan?

The ferry continued on, gently cutting through still waters as it made for the smaller terminal. Passengers had stepped back into their cars or were getting ready by the walkway.

People seemed excited. Some wondered why things weren't moving faster. Parents calmed children down. A baby was howling some three cars behind them, cranky because he didn't get enough sleep or formula.

The ferry came to a stop. The walkway doors opened, and the foot traffic out of the ferry began. The large ramp that cars used to get in and out of the ferry was still locked up. Once the passengers on foot were taken care of, the ramp was lowered, and cars slowly poured down and into the tiny town – though *village* was a better term – of Pulau Kumut.

The buildings here clung close to the sea. As Delilah drove, Wesley saw that the shops hugged the coast.

The ferry terminal here was smaller, just a simple, single-floor building with a roof that looked like it needed some maintenance and walls that were begging for a fresh coat of paint.

And yet the shops, small and smaller still, were crowded with tourists, both foreign and domestic. If they weren't invading the shops, they were on bicycles or walking or hopping on the vans with the resort's logo stamped on both sides. They were groups that went around taking photos of each other. Selfies. Cool aesthetic shots for Instagram. They ate ice cream. Sipped on inexpensive drinks. One stall had a crowd just gobbling up tarap.

"There are so many people," Margie said. She had both hands on the window and was staring out in wonder. Next to her, Lucky poked his head out the window and was looking at everyone with some curiosity. People looked back. Some smiled, some waved, others pulled out their phones.

Pulau Kumut's one road was a single-lane affair which looped around the island, starting in town (or the *village*) and ending back in town (or the *village*). At the turn, they saw a sign. Right would lead to the southern side of the island. Left took you north towards the resort.

Delilah turned left.

She drove just below the 50 km/h mark, and occasionally the trees on both sides would give way to stunning vistas of green grass, golden sand and the light blue and emerald of the sea. There were also houses. Some on stilts. Others on concrete pads. Some houses were clustered together in small groups of five or six. In some spots, there were only two houses or just one.

As they drove, the road inclined. You wouldn't notice it at first, but there were warning signs telling drivers to watch out, fast cars could come screeching down from the top of the hill.

Finally, they came to a break in the road. Preceding that, a sign telling anyone that down this road was the employee hostels. The sign never said it was 'employees only', so they had some excuse to enter.

The road wasn't long. Round a bend, past a couple of trees, and they arrived. The hostel took up a large, open space filled with six buildings, single-floor units which stretched out towards the beach. The one amenity they could see was a faded futsal court on one end, right next to the parking lots, where two mixed teams of five players each were trying to score goals.

At the sidelines were others, torn between watching the game (whose players were now looking in their direction) and the arrival of these folks.

One of the players, a tall, attractive woman with short, curly hair dressed in a training top, Lycra shorts and battered sneakers, approached them. She looked confused at the sight of these four who obviously didn't belong in the employees' hostel.

"The resort is just up the road," she said, lowering her hand to pat Lucky on the head as he was the only one who'd decided to approach her head-on. Margie had gone off towards a little garden of colorful flowers near the futsal court.

"Thanks," said Wesley, "but we're looking for someone here."

"Sure you're in the right place?" a shirtless guy with a surfer's bod asked. A couple of people laughed.

"We are," said Wesley, "we're looking for Mark Anthony Jibril. He works security at the resort?"

The woman turned to her friends, who turned to each other. After several seconds of just looking and not speaking, she said, "Why are you looking for him?"

"We want to ask him about Abigail," Delilah said.

That sent murmurs among the group.

The woman turned to her group and called out to one of her friends to take her place.

"Come on," she said, "walk with me."

The group walked away from the game – which resumed the moment they were gone – with the woman leading.

"Who are you guys, and why do you want to ask him about Abigail?"

"I'm Wesley, that's Delilah. This is Lucky." Lucky reached up to the lady again for pats and was handsomely rewarded. "And that's Margie, my cousin."

Margie bounced towards them and was also rewarded with a high-five.

"I'm Isabella Majeng. But I prefer Bella."

"You heard about that guy dying back on the mainland?" Wesley asked.

She nodded. "Word gets around here. He was the town troublemaker, kan?"

Delilah and Wesley nodded.

Wesley said, "We think Abigail's disappearance might be connected to that guy's death."

"Really?"

Delilah gave Wesley a look. How much could they tell her? How much were they willing to share with this woman they'd just met?

"Did you know her?" Delilah asked.

"I do. I work security at the casino."

"Were you close with her?"

"How about you tell me something and I tell you something?"

This time, it was Wesley's turn to look at Delilah.

"Is there some kind of NDA here?" she asked.

"No ..."

"And I can see you aren't cops. But you've got some information."

"We're just looking for the truth."

"Is that so? Bah. How bout this. I tell you everything I know, and you tell me what you know. No secrets."

"Can we trust you?"

"Can I trust *you*?"

Faith, Wesley told himself. This was all a game of faith and if he'd survive the leap into it.

"We're looking into the death."

"Are you guys detectives or something?"

"Or something," said Delilah.

Bella just nodded. Maybe she'd heard worse, maybe she didn't care. She motioned at them to continue.

Taking the proverbial baton, Wesley said, "We know Abigail was a drug addict."

Bella nodded. "She was a high-functioning one. You guys know what that means, kan?"

Wesley said, "They're addicts, but they're smart enough to keep a normal façade, show the entire world that they're okay."

"A-okay," Bella said. "I'm pretty new around here. Started what … eighteen months ago? They put me in the casino because there's a high turnover there. No one wants to work the casino because of the odd hours. I thought to myself, hey I wanna prove the boys wrong, right, so why not do it? Show them who's got the pants. Been there since. It was also there that I met Abigail. By then she was strung out, but doing her best to look like she was fine. She'd been on the casino floor for almost three years by then. It was supposed to be a short-term thing, but the drugs and the big tips got her hooked."

"Did she offer you some?" Delilah asked.

"Didn't offer me her stash but offered to intro me to her seller. This was when I first started. The constant late nights and early morning jumps were doing a number on me. Abigail noticed and offered. I declined. She continued trying to sell it to me, but I politely declined each time."

"Did she tell you who sold the stuff to her?"

"She didn't. All she told me was that this person was selling to everyone. Customers, the croupiers, the bartenders, the cleaners, even security. I didn't want her to think I was going to rat her out, so I didn't ask her to name names."

"Do you think she disappeared?" Wesley asked as they neared the beach. Margie had found a branch and was playing fetch with Lucky.

"I can't say," Bella said. "One day she was there, and the next she wasn't. Her supervisor tried calling, but she never answered. Did a welfare check at her place, and the team that went said her room was a mess. Like she went back, scrambled through her drawers and closet, packed a bag and just left."

"No note?"

Bella shook her head.

"And Mark?"

"That's where things stop making sense. Mark and her … well, when I did see them, they were inseparable. Lovebirds. Stuck to each other like Siamese twins. When you're that in love, would you just leave without telling your partner? No note, no text. Everyone said the same thing. It didn't make sense.

"It crushed Mark. He wasn't the same after she left. He came to work, left work, spent time in town and locked himself away in his room. Developed a drinking habit. Hasn't got himself fired. Yet."

The concrete path that cut through the cropped green grass ended with a turn to the right. In front of them was the beach. At the end of the beach, inches away from where the waves broke on the sand, a shirtless man sat under the sun.

Even from that distance, they could see the bottle half-buried in the sand next to him.

"Mark's right there," Bella said. "I don't know his mood today, so be careful, okay?"

33

The man was drunk.

Which could be a good or a bad thing.

Wesley was a happy drunk who'd butcher The 1975 and CHVRCHES, or do his best to screech out some Celine Dion. And maybe if you were lucky, he'd shoot out a dirty joke which the PC crowd would cancel him for. That wasn't too bad because he had friends who, when drunk, turned into absolute monsters. One guy, after too much Southern Comfort on the rocks, had turned from a chillaxed, life-of-the-party who knew just what to say and when to say it, into a raging drunk who'd sworn on his mother's grave that he would find his ex-girlfriend's new beau and cave the guy's skull in with his foot. Plot twist was that he had cheated first, so …

"Who … who're you?" Mark Anthony slurred, staring up at them with some form of reverence.

Wesley squatted down. "Mark Anthony?"

"Mm … that's my name," the man slurred.

"I'm Wes and this is Lilah."

"Hi Wes and Lilah," said Mark. "Nice day, isn't it?"

"Sure is," Wesley said.

"I swear I heard a dog and a … a uhm…" The man's mouth pursed as his brain fought the fog of booze in search of the right word. "Girl," he said, pronouncing the word slowly. *Guhh-erl.* "Somewhere." He paused, blinked his red eyes slowly, and the blinking seemed to unlock a thought which came out of his mouth as: "Abigail wanted a girl."

And once the words came out, the next things to move were his hands. They went for his bottle. One held it in place as the other unscrewed the cap. Up went the bottle. Down sloshed the liquid.

"Who's that?" Delilah asked.

"Who?"

"Abigail," Wesley said.

"Abigail ..." Mark Anthony said, doing his best to pronounce the name, "she was ... no, she *is* my best friend. The love of my life. And my fiancé."

"Why did you say 'was'?" Wesley asked.

"Sorry." The fingers of one hand tapped the neck of the half-empty bottle.

"Where is she?"

"I don't think she's coming back."

Behind them, not too far away, Lucky barked. Margie giggled.

"I like that sound," Mark Anthony said.

"Mark," Wesley said, "what happened to Abigail? Why isn't she here?"

Delilah put a hand on Wesley's wrist. *Slow down*, her look said.

"One day, I came back from work, and she'd packed her bag and left. Didn't say a single thing. And the state of the room we shared ... it was like she was ... she was ... she was ... she ..."

And all the emotions that Mark Anthony Jibril had been keeping in for the last few months, kept dammed away by booze of varying qualities and types, broke. He sobbed, loudly at first, one hand going up to cover his eyes. Then it lowered so that his crying wouldn't alert his colleagues to come down and see what all the fuss was about.

Wesley almost sighed with relief. He was worried about coming here. And those worries hadn't abated when he saw that the man they wanted to speak to was drunk. For a moment there, just before the tears had come pouring out, he was sure Mark Anthony would lose his shit and come at them screaming.

When the crying had subsided to weak mewls, Mark Anthony reached for the bottle of alcohol once more, but this time, Delilah reached over and placed a hand over his. "Maybe it'd be better if you talked about it," she said.

He nodded. Wiping away the tears with the back of his hand and sniffing back the twin trails of snot which were threatening to run down his nose, he said, "I thought she was happy. I knew she wasn't doing well. That she took … *supplements* so that she could function at work."

"You knew about her addiction?" Wesley ventured.

"We tried not to call it that," Mark Anthony said, sounding hurt. "It was the only way she could maintain working long-term at the casino, and I didn't want to make her feel like she couldn't do her job. I let her do it and … now she's gone."

"Where?"

"I don't know," he sputtered. "Her mother thinks she's dead … but she isn't."

"How do you know that?" Delilah asked.

"Because she isn't," he said, staring at them, looking anything but drunk.

34

Wesley was sure he and Delilah would make terrible parents (counting your chickens before they hatched at *this* stage of the relationship was never good) because only after they'd calmed Mark Anthony down did they realize Lucky and Margie were missing.

Mark had gone back to gazing at the horizon, holding comfortably onto his bottle of tequila, as if he was looking for another reason to take a swig.

"Where's Margie?" Wesley said. Looking around, all he saw were the pretty golden sands, the green verdant bushes and brown bark of coconut trees. No dog. No 5-year-old girl. Nothing. No point in reaching for his phone either. Aunt Zara had decided: Margie would only get her phone when she was 12 at the earliest.

The sudden silence seemed eerie. The voices of the hotel staff playing futsal or just hanging around the grounds of the quarters seemed distant and far off, doing little to ease the anxiousness spreading over him.

Wesley's right hand, the enabler of so many bad habits, was trembling.

His feet were glued to the sand.

Delilah was looking around too. Her eyes scanned each part of the beach. She shot a quick glance at Wesley. Beads of sweat had formed on his temples. The faster ones were already sliding down the side of his face.

"We need to find her," Wesley said softly. Lucky going missing was one thing; the dog would find his way back to them soon enough. Margie just going off like that, when she knew better … oh, who was he kidding. He'd never spent any time with Margie alone at all, except when they'd been at home. He didn't know shit about taking care of her, and here they were, missing a child.

With a deep breath, he called out for his cousin.

"Margie!" Delilah echoed back.

"Lucky!" Wesley called. *Don't panic, don't panic, don't panic,.* He licked his parched lips, turned back and for a moment there, wanted to run over to Mark Anthony, grab the bottle of tequila and take a long swig. Alcohol was the first thing he'd drowned himself in not too long after Ashini had died.

"Wesley," Delilah said, "look. Footprints."

"I …" Wesley bit his lower lip when he saw Margie's sandals, abandoned beside a bark of wood that had spent a little too long in the ocean. Parallel to her footprints were Lucky's pawprints.

He grabbed the sandals, and they continued down the beach, walking as quickly as possible on either side of the prints, doing their best to ensure they didn't brush them or stray too far.

The prints continued further down the beach. In the distance, they could see the roof of the resort. Go further, and soon they would encounter hordes of tourists sunbathing and relaxing by the beach.

Delilah grabbed his wrist in a vice-like grip that told him how concerned she was.

Is she beating herself up the way I am? Wesley wondered. She'd known Margie longer, had babysat her before came around in a bus, full of baggage and needing a fresh start. Was she as terrified as he was? If so, she was doing a good job of not showing it.

"They went into the jungle," Delilah said.

The tracks took a sharp right turn. Once upon a time, long ago, a path had been cut from the beach to wherever the endpoint of this place was. Now there was a path made from grass that had been stepped on. On both sides were a mix of brown and greens. The coconut trees had given way to bakau trees, which in turn had offered the land to the dipterocarps. Their buttress roots were layered in shrubs. From the upper canopy, birds sang, cried and called to one another.

Wesley led the way. The trail ended with the grass, but in some patches of wet earth, he noticed Margie's tiny footprints.

"Margie!" Delilah called out.

"*MARGIE!*" Wesley roared out. "*MARGIE!*"

They paused in the middle of the track to listen.

Wesley wiped away sweat from the side of his face. What if he couldn't find Margie? He could already see it: Inspector Rabbil looking worriedly at him, Aunt Zara doing her level best not to lose her shit right then and there, and probably mad at him. Her screw-up of a nephew, who'd gotten a colleague killed because nothing said 'a moment of immortality' like being featured on the front page of the next day's edition. The wily reporter and his photographer chasing bank robbers. And now he'd gotten her only daughter missing

What would he do? Walk into the ocean with a weight tied around his ankle maybe.

"Wes."

He'd heard it too. His ears weren't playing tricks with him, right? He wasn't on the verge of losing his shit. No … no, he was sure that a voice, the voice of a child, had been calling him.

Or maybe …

"No," he mumbled to himself.

There was an old folk's tale that any child of Darat Kumut and Pulau Kumut knew. It involved the orang halus, or orang bunian, depending on where you came from. The seas were bountiful because the elders had ordered that a parent surrender a child to these benevolent creatures every year, ensuring prosperity for the town. Some say that if you hear the sounds of children in the forests, you'd do well to turn and walk the other way.

He banished the thought, took a deep breath, ignored the grating feeling that was plaguing his throat and shouted once more for his cousin.

And this time, someone shouted back at him.

It came from down the trail.

35

When Rabbil stepped back into the police outpost (*station*!), his headache – it was a real brain-buster of a thumper – worsened at Atiqah's curt shake of her head.

"Nothing from Tawau?" he said.

His second in command said, "They had her landlord unlock her door. They went in and checked. Nothing. Anything from the van?"

"No," he said. He dug into his pockets and found the Uphamol that he'd packed. Those things were shit. Nothing beat a headache like Panadol. Not the regular stuff, Actifast. They could kill a headache in minutes. And he felt like half of the usual 10 pieces they gave wouldn't be enough to fix this growing shit storm.

See, this morning – while he was still comfortably dreaming about lying in bed with his beautiful wife, inhaling the soft scent of Head & Shoulders (hers was always the Lemon Fresh one) which left its wonderful scent over the pillows and the bed and the strawberry watermelon from her body gel – Atiqah had called.

The news had been brief: the surveillance team that Tawau CID had loaned out hadn't spotted Su Yen at all. In fact, the team of four doubted she'd returned to the low-cost flat she rented.

Rabbil thought that his second was being a little paranoid. He'd told her to ask Tawau to check on Su Yen's friends, see if she'd had a little too much to drink and was spending the night on a couch.

He wanted to drift back into sleep and take away the edge from last night's bucket of Guinness, but of course, he wasn't some corporate, paper-pushing, ladder-climbing hack. He was a cop. And Su Yen not coming back home made him worry.

He'd called Atiqah and told her to put the word out. Got Sergeant Awang and his merry band of uniformed officers to poke around the haystacks with a magnet and see if the needle would magically appear. That had been at 8:27 am. An hour later, one of the uniformed bumpkins delivered the news. Su Yen was last seen at the Seaside Pub right after she was fired from the kopitiam. Later at around midnight, an hour before closing time, she was seen leaving with a man. She entered a car, but no one knew the make and model. Looked like a burgundy-purple-brown Proton Saga – the 2021 model – but it could've been a darker color or even black. License plate? None available. Bumpkin cops, remember?

And so they had started the search. Whoever was available that morning went out asking questions. Rabbil chose the All-Convenience Store. Zara, the pretty lady who ran the place, was there, layaning customers, pouring coffee, exchanging jokes, listening attentively to locals and tourists alike. The two amateur detectives? Not available. Where were they?

"Oh, they took my daughter to pick seashells on the island."

He'd wanted a coffee then, but settled for a whole papan of Panadol. Those jackass detective-wannabes. Didn't they promise not to mess around? Sial lah.

Days had passed, and they were no closer to finding the person responsible for Tommy Asandu's death. Now parked right next to that little whodunit was Su Yen. Missing. Feared dead? Here's *not* hoping.

"What's the word, boss?" Atiqah asked.

Rabbil stared at the stained whiteboard they were using for their diagram. It was in moments like this that he lamented the job of a murder detective. Those damn movies and TV shows made it fun. Even in *Se7en*, Morgan Freeman and Brad Pitt didn't actually catch the killer. The weirdo had just walked in and turned himself in because he had a point to make.

Most murders were simple. This wasn't simple at all. He'd been doing amateur CSI on Su Yen's van earlier. The counterfeit shoes and the passengers they held were no longer there.

"Boss?"

"What about that financial check on Su Yen, Ticks?" he said. "Turn up anything?"

"I'm still waiting for the results … I'll rush it."

"That's what I wanted to hear. Tell whoever's doing it that I want the results in 30 minutes. If not, I'm willing to pull rank and start making threats."

He turned to Sergeant Awang and said, "Send out patrols. Rudolph, go too. Search the sides of the roads. She might be alive. She might not. Be prepared for the worst."

The worst came later, just around lunch, when one of the two amateur detectives called. By then, the rain was falling, and the winds were roaring at the windows.

36

Wesley heard his cousin just as the first drop of rainwater fell on his hair.

"*WESLEEEEEEEEEEE!*" Margie screamed at him from some undetermined location deep inside the jungle.

How can it be so dark in here? he wondered as he put one foot ahead of the other. He glanced back once to see how far they'd come. The way out was a tiny portal that looked far away. It made every step forward one step away from escape.

Delilah was several paces away, following Margie's cries.

"Wes, come on," she said.

As he soldiered on down the path, he felt the weight of the jungle pressing against him. *One foot in front of the other*, he told himself. Their path was straight ahead and narrow. The thick upper canopy of trees blocked the sunlight, though in gaps they flared down to give the shrubs on the ground some form of illumination.

Margie's cries were nearer this time.

His heart pounding, Wesley moved faster, Delilah matching his pace.

Margie's cries got louder as the sky darkened. Up there, the dark clouds roared and groaned. Thunder boomed. In the gaps, they saw the crackle of lightning. It wasn't just rain, a thunderstorm was brewing and just about ready to fall. And the idea of the roar of rain drowning out his cousin's cries filled Wesley with dread.

"There!" Delilah cried.

Wesley saw a gap in the foliage. His steps were quicker, moving without any care for himself. A branch slapped his face. Something scratched his bare legs. His right foot left its selipar. His breathing didn't feel right. His mind projected images of little Margie lying on the ground, her ankle broken. Her face bloodied after a bad fall. Unable to move. Terrified. He imagined her face, always cheerful with her ever-swinging ponytails, this time pale with worry and fear because he wasn't there for her, he—

Stumbled out of the jungle and into a clearing.

"Wesley!" Margie cried out at him.

He stood there for a moment, not realizing Delilah had bumped into him. His limbs were frozen stiff and numb, his tongue felt glued to the roof of his mouth. His legs were on the verge of losing function. Wesley was reminded of when they had pulled him out of the wreck that had once been Ashini's dark blue Axia. As the medics checked him for any signs of concussion and physical damage, he'd been able to say one thing: "My friend. My friend … please," he'd coughed somewhere around this point because his chest hurt, his head hurt, his limbs hurt, (fuck it, at that point everything was a flare of pain and burst of agony), but the paramedics were telling him to breathe, breathe, breathe, breathe, breathe, *BREATHE*!

And yet the words had still come tumbling out: "Boss, my friend. How is she?"

The paramedics had looked at each other. There were two of them. An older woman and a younger man. The way they shared that moment said it all. You didn't have to put it into words, and his brain, still processing the pain, still making sense of what just happened, realized it. Ashini was dead.

"Wes?"

It wasn't Delilah. It was Margie. She was standing right in front of him, one chubby hand wrapped around the bottom of his shirt, looking up at him, eyes wide in worry. *Worry!* When he'd been the one inch away from shitting his pants.

Wesley fell to his knees and wrapped his arms around her, much to her shock.

"Wes? You okey-dokes?" Margie asked.

"Don't *ever* do that again, Marjorie Augustina!" Wesley said, surprised that his voice went several octaves higher than he was used to.

Margie blinked several times, surprised that her cousin, often soft-spoken and jolly, could be this angry with her.

"I'm sorry," she said in a small voice.

Wesley wanted to cry. He'd been frustrated, scared and angry that he'd lost her. A child he'd promised to take care of.

"Lucky went first. He tugged at his leash," said Margie, "and I couldn't hold on. He just ran away." She nodded towards the dog.

Who in turn was busy digging a hole. The dog's clean, tan fur was now mud-spattered and filthy. Lucky might be a lot of things, but his act of tearing away from Margie and charging into the jungle to dig a hole sent a cold shiver down Wesley's back. Did the dog know something that eluded them? Lucky had, after all, sniffed out the drugs in the fake shoes.

"Lucky," Wesley said, letting go of his cousin and standing up.

The dog managed to dig up a shallow pit. He was still visible, but his head and front paws were lost in the midst of wet soil, now turning muddy.

Wesley took two steps forward to see what Lucky was going cuckoo-bananas about … And recoiled as if he'd been slapped in the face. He turned, walked back to Margie, got on one knee and asked, "Did you see it?"

Delilah raised an eyebrow. "What's going on?"

"Don't look," Wesley quickly told her.

"No," Margie said to Wesley. "I just waited. I tried pulling on Lucky's leash, but he didn't wanna go."

Delilah, who saw what Lucky was up to, gasped and cursed. To Wesley she said, "Is that …"

He nodded gravely. "It is. We need to call the police. Could you …"

"Yeah, sure." She turned and made for the way out, tracing their steps.

Wesley told his cousin to wait right there, far away from the hole the dog was digging. This time he got close and squatted down. He could see most of it. And it didn't look pretty at all. In fact …

"What the…" Wesley mumbled. He crept a little closer, aware that the rain was in its cats and dogs phase; all out and unrelenting. In the mud, close to where the left arm lay, was a piece of metal that, even after sitting in the earth for God knew how long (though Wesley was sure that six months was *the* answer), was still bright enough to stand out.

He reached out and grabbed it.

It wasn't just a piece of metal.

Rubbing away the mud, Wesley saw it was a nametag. Gold in color. The pin was lightly rusted, but it was still in good shape. The black ink that the hotel used to print out the name was still there.

"Jackpot," Wesley said, his voice drowned out as thunder roared in the skies, and the rain continued to fall, fall, fall.

37

"And you're sure the dog didn't ..." Rabbil glanced back at the body. "You know ... chew it?"

Wesley shook his head.

"So it—"

"*He*," Margie corrected, her teeth chattering, a thick towel wrapped around her. "Lucky's a *he*."

"Of course, take note of that, Ticks," he said to his second in command, who was busy jotting things down while the inspector held an umbrella. Back to Wesley: "He did not damage the body in any way?"

"No," Wesley said for probably the third time. "Once Lucky exposed the body's upper torso, he just stopped and walked away."

He glanced down at the dog, who was sniffing Margie's shins. He had one hand in the pocket of his shorts, turning the nametag in his fingers.

"And that's all there was in there?" Rabbil asked. It was the third time the inspector asked that question. As if ... as if ... as if he knew Wesley was hiding something.

Or maybe you're just overthinking, Wesley told himself. To the police inspector, he nodded. "Yeah. I had one look too long and that's it. I wasn't gonna get down on my knees and poke and prod it."

Rabbil's left eyebrow went up an inch. "*Did* you poke or prod it?"

"Very funny, Inspector."

Rabbil shrugged and offered a smile that – to Wesley – didn't look genuine at all. "Had to ask."

Delilah said, "Do you think it's …"

Rabbil raised a hand to cut her off. "We don't know anything except for the fact the cadaver was once a person. At the moment …" He turned around once more. Three uniformed officers were busy trying to secure the crime scene. Two were trying to erect a plastic sheet above the body. The other was doing his best to clear out any water to ensure any evidence wasn't washed away.

Though since the rain had been pouring for some time, Wesley doubted there was much evidence left.

Evidence like the nametag in his pocket …

"ME on the way?" Wesley asked.

The inspector's eyebrow went up once more. "She is. So is your aunt. You know, the last time we spoke, you two promised there wouldn't be any more …" he stopped when he realized that there was a child between them, "*messing* around. And now …" he waved a hand over to where the three uniformed officers were doing their best.

"We just wanted a day trip," Wesley said. "There was no intention for this to happen."

Rabbil's lips pursed. His headache had eased some on the ferry over, but it was coming back now with a vengeance, gently thumping the sides of his head. He bit his lower lip and moved close to Wesley, lowering his voice so Delilah and Margie wouldn't hear this next part.

"You already have one murder linked to you. And not too long after, here you are with a body not five feet away. You used to be a journalist, so you can see how this doesn't work in your favor, kan?"

"Like I said, Inspector, we were on a day trip when this happened."

"Right," he said, pulling away from Wesley. "Well, I guess that's it then. When Miss Zara comes along, you guys can leave. But we might still have questions."

Wesley nodded. In his pocket, his hand continued twirling and rubbing the nametag. They'd have to plan the next trip to the island soon.

X

Dr. Nitta Siddhu didn't look unhappy with the weather condition. In fact, when Rabbil finally caught a glimpse of her face, he saw that under the hood of her raincoat she had a big grin. *Are medical examiners always weird?* he wondered.

"I never thought I'd be examining a body during a storm," she called out to him.

"Expect the unexpected," he said back to her.

"Who found the body?"

"A dog."

The grin faded some. "For real?"

"The dog caught the scent and dragged a five-year-old after it right to this spot." He nodded at the small mound of earth, the shallow grave and the tent that the three officers (now soaking wet and warming up as best they could in the Land Cruiser) had managed to erect. To their credit, they also managed to set up a series of waterproof floodlights on tripods around the crime scene to illuminate the area.

Atiqah had driven to town to check in on forensics, which would be a necessity once Dr. Siddhu determined whether the victim belonged in the foul play category.

Rabbil followed closely behind, glancing down miserably at his leather shoes which would be ruined by rain and mud come tomorrow. He'd managed a raincoat but not a proper pair of shoes to go gallivanting in the mud.

Dr. Siddhu pushed open the flap of the tent and stepped in. There was barely any space in there for two people, as the tent had been placed over the hole the dog carved out.

"A dog smelled this?" she asked again, squatting and looking at the thing that had once been a living, breathing person, lying there on its side in a shallow grave.

"Yeah."

"Amazing. And he's not a cadaver dog? Retired, maybe?"

"I wouldn't know," Rabbil said.

"He should try out for the team," she said, snapping open her backpack and extracting a pair of nitrile gloves. "Heard the news report on the radio?"

Rabbil, who wanted a cigarette, shook his head. "Breaking news?"

"Storm. Some kinda early monsoon thing. Blowing over from Southern Philippines." The nitrile gloves made a quick snapping sound against her thin wrists. With one hand, she reached into her bag and pulled out a zippered pouch. She unzipped it to reveal a set of items that would look at home on a metal tray in a sanitized and clean autopsy room.

"I thought MEs carried metal suitcases," Rabbil commented.

"Imagine lugging one around in this weather," Dr. Siddhu said. "Now, inspector, I know this is the fun part of any investigation: looking over my shoulder at everything I do and then making notes in your head until I can give you the prelim, but maybe you can wait outside? I like to work in peace." She reached into the bag, and this time, what came out was an ancient-looking iPod, the earphones wrapped around it.

"Sure thing, Doc," he said, knowing what she said was the truth and as the wind blew and ice-cold droplets of water drenched him, a cigarette was not just welcoming; it would be a necessity.

38

Zara clambered out of her Myvi and dashed towards her daughter.

Wesley stood next to Delilah, holding her hand. He felt bad. He'd let Margie out of his sight and for a moment there, he almost lost her … or thought he had, anyway.

"You silly, silly girl," Zara said, breathing in her daughter's mop of shoulder-length hair. "You gave mommy such a fright."

Margie sounded like she was on the verge of breaking down. "Sorry, Mumma," she said. "Lucky just dragged me and I … well, I had to follow."

Zara's shoulders hitched as her breathing got ragged.

Wesley let go of Delilah's hand and pulled away from her. He took several steps forward, ready for his lashing. Would she say that she regretted having him around? Why had he bothered to come to Darat Kumut? Why had she bothered to take him in? Why had she so stupidly allowed him to take her only child out? He could imagine all these things said angrily, words cruel yet honest.

"Zara," he said, throat dry, tongue numb and brain empty.

Zara let go of her daughter, stood up and …

Wesley inched back, ready for a slap.

It didn't come.

Zara hugged him.

"Thank you, Wesley, thank you so much," Aunt Zara said, quietly sobbing into his left shoulder. "I thought I would lose her. When Inspector Rabbil came over, I thought, I seriously thought that something bad happened to her … or you. Or Delilah. I wouldn't know what to do if … if Margie … if she … if …" This time, she sobbed into her hands.

Wesley wrapped an arm around her. Next came Margie, who glued herself to her mother's hip. Lucky came over, sniffed, and tried to join in by jumping up. It didn't work, so he settled on pressing himself into the little circle they made.

"Lilah, get in here," Wesley said. And Delilah did. She stood next to him, and he felt one of her arms pressing into his lower back.

Earlier, as they waited for the cops, they had worked out a cover story. The three of them went on a little trip away from the mainland so Margie could pick up seashells on the beach. Margie, liking the idea, had sprung into action and went off to fill her kid-sized nylon bag. Wesley and Delilah had pitched in, helping Margie by collecting an assortment of shells: bonnets and cones, figs and drupes, a couple of limpets and an odd assortment of sundial and moon shells. Her pride and joy was a harp shell the size of her fist.

"Well," said Zara, pulling away from the hug and smiling at the lot of them, "that's enough of that, I guess."

Wesley reached into his pocket and pulled out the nametag. He placed it on the table and sat down, grabbing his mug of hot coffee as he did so.

Delilah, who was sitting next to Mabel, got up and took the nametag and held it up so her aunt could inspect it. Mabel pulled out a pair of circular reading glasses, which made her look a bit like a plump owl, and mouthed the name on the tag.

"While you were making the call to the cops, I found this," he said. "I wanted to see what Lucky unearthed, I got too close and …" he shivered. The rain was falling long and hard. The wind roared at times and screamed when it wanted a respite for its vocal cords. Thunder joined the chorus a couple of times. Lightning flashed when it felt the scene needed some stage lighting.

When they'd returned, Mabel was knitting something strange and shapeless, her writing pad on one side and a bottle of Jameson whiskey on the other. The entire living room smelled pleasant, making Wesley a little sleepy.

Once they told her about what had happened on the island, Mabel instructed Lester to get the table on the verandah upstairs ready. Wesley had asked for coffee, extra strong.

"The name is 'Priscilla'," said Mabel, "but you're certain the body in there belongs to Abigail?"

"I think it is."

"Well…" Mabel took a long pull from her pipe. "Is there a chance the body could be someone else?"

"Could be," said Wesley, wrapping his hands around the hot cup, feeling grateful for the warmth it brought, even though that warmth was slowly dissipating.

"So if the body in the grave belongs to Abigail, who's Priscilla?" Delilah wondered.

Silence. Wesley downed his coffee and made for the coffee pot. It was five minutes to 11, but he needed the next four or five cups because he wasn't going to sleep later, no. He had a date with his laptop and a Microsoft Word document that was now entering its 50th page. And he was excited to see if he could make it to page 60.

"Let's look at what we have," said Mabel. "Su Yen has the money and some of the drugs. Tommy was the supplier, I suppose? And your source from the resort said that someone was selling drugs in the casino. So that person is their contact there. Priscilla could be that person, but we don't have any proof of that."

Delilah filled her own mug and after a sip, said, "Could the nametag have fallen when the body was placed into the grave?"

"Priscilla's nametag?" her aunt asked back. "Seems like a stretch, doesn't it? If something like that happened, I would have noticed it. But then again, I think I'd be a bit of a wreck if I were trying to get rid of the body. It's easier when you're writing it."

"What happens now?" Delilah asked.

"Do you still want to keep the story going?" Mabel asked. "You two have a very good lead here." She pointed the stem of her pipe to the nametag on the table. "Would be a shame to see that a key piece of evidence—"

"Or leverage," Lester interrupted from his seat behind Wesley close to the French doors. "I mean, if this Priscilla chick is real and is connected to what Tommy Asandu was up to, you could use this to get her to talk, am I right?"

Wesley agreed.

The man had a point.

39

X

After the morning crowd had dissipated, a black SUV pulled up and parked in Aunt Zara's parking lot, right in front of the All-Convenience Store.

Wesley and Delilah watched as the rear doors opened, and two very unlikely men and a very scantily clad woman stepped out. The two men were complete contrasts of each other. One was tall, just a hair over six feet. Wide shoulders, muscles held together in a tight-fitting shirt with Hawaiian prints. He wore chinos and loafers. A gold chain gleamed in the sunlight, protruding from a very hairy chest. A large gold-plated watch dominated one wrist. The other was encircled by a silver bracelet.

The other man was short; his Hawaiian shirt billowed in the breeze, its bright colors shouting 'Look, very fat man over here!' He also wore chinos (they flapped with every step, Wesley noticed). He wore no watch or necklace, although Wesley did notice a gold earring in the man's left earlobe.

The woman was young. Looked to be in her mid-twenties or younger – Wesley really couldn't tell, and wasn't there some social rule where you weren't supposed to ask a woman her age? She had on a colorful top that did little to cover her torso, and a pair of shorts that had been designed with the expressed purpose of showing off as much ass as publicly allowed. She had on fancy selipars (the slide-in kind with the brand name over the strap), a very expensive-looking watch, earrings, a pearl necklace and a silver bracelet that matched the one Mr. Hunk was wearing.

Just as they were leaving the asphalt of the parking lot for the concrete of the sidewalk, a gaggle of tourists – an entire Korean family by the look of it – passed by, noisily chattering away.

Mr. Hunk threw the group a very distasteful look. Wesley continued watching and noticed Mr. Hunk gave the last person in the group, a young girl barely out of her teens, a very appraising look.

Mr. Hunk said something to Mr. Fat, and the man began laughing obscenely. Mr. Hunk just looked at his friend with something akin to amusement. It reminded Wesley of how one would look fondly at a pet that had just done a very clever trick.

The woman – Wesley would have to refer to her as Ms. Top – turned and said something to Mr. Fat. He nodded thoughtfully and said something back to her that had Mr. Hunk in stitches. His words had the opposite effect on Ms. Top, who then said something that killed the laughter.

Mr. Hunk barked something at her, and Wesley saw the woman wince at his words, whatever they were. In fact, she even shrank away from him when he neared her. Mr. Hunk tried to play it off by giving her a little pat on the bum as she entered the store.

As the door opened, they caught a whiff of the man's words.

"… why don't you go in there and find something useful, Sugar. There, try the magazine racks. Try *National Geographic* or *Reader's Digest*, it's not *Teen Beat* or *Vogue*, but who knows, your little brain might know something about what's going on in the world outside ours, not just who Justin Bieber is sucking off these days."

Mr. Fat, who had been waddling behind him, let loose a very loud and high-pitched cackle that didn't belong to a frame as big and wide as his. As the two men neared, Mr. Hunk pulled off his Aviator shades and proffered a massive grin, showing off his pearly whites to the only two people in the store.

"Hi, guys," he said; the smile had widened, his arms had flared out, palms out. Mr. Friendly he was. "This is the All-Convenience Store, kan."

The voice was deep, but it didn't boom. It had, Wesley would later describe in the Microsoft Word document that had cleared 60 pages and was making steady progress to 70, a gentleness to it that could ease any situation. *See that John Steinbeck novel over there, the one you pretend to have read and wrote essays about, that's the kind of voice you want narrating the trials and tribulations of the Hamilton and Trask families.*

"Sorry to barge in without making a reservation—" Behind him, Mr. Fat was cackling, and behind him, Ms. Top had discovered something in a 2005 issue of *Reader's Digest* that fascinated her.

"Jude, really," said Mr. Hunk in that clipped tone that belonged to some English boarding school, "this is a serious matter."

"My apologies," said Mr. Fat, now introduced as Jude. He wheezed out one more cackle.

"My name is Raul Krishnan." He paused to allow that fact to sink in, then added, "Arthur Krishnan's son, you know the owner of the Pearl Below the Wind Resort?"

Wesley and Delilah nodded.

"Nice, so..." He got on one of the stools, smile still on, and said, "We heard about what happened yesterday. Sounds very bad."

"Very bad," Jude said. He assessed the stool, decided that maybe some mountains weren't meant to be climbed, and remained standing just behind Raul Krishnan. "I'm Jude Ambrose, by the way. Lawyer to the Krishnan estate."

"Nice to meet you," said Wesley. "I'm Wesley and this is Delilah."

As this exchange was happening, Raul Krishnan threw a quick glance over at Delilah. For a moment there, Wesley could swear (on a stack of Bibles, no less) that the man's charming facade dissipated and in its place was the look of a very ravenous predator.

"And your friend over there?" Delilah said. Wesley fought the urge to glance at her and wondered if she had seen Raul's look.

"That's Sugar," said Raul. "She doesn't matter that much in this conversation. She's … well I guess the proper term would be 'candy'. Am I right, Judy-Boy?"

The fat lawyer giggled disconcertingly. "Indeed, boss."

"Anyway. We're here because of what happened yesterday. The body you found? Caused quite a stir back at the resort. Management is fumbling around and acting like those chickens with their heads chopped off. So I thought, you know, being the kind to grab the bull by the balls–"

Though he was shifting uncomfortably from foot to foot, the fat lawyer managed to squeeze out a quick giggle.

"—and dealing with the situation head-on. There's no easy way to put this to the two of you," – his eyes moved from Wesley to Delilah, where they lingered a moment too long, then back to Wesley again – "but management is worried about what could happen if you guys … you know, *talked*."

"Talked?" Wesley said, feigning curiosity.

Raul smiled at him.

Wesley resisted the urge to take a step back. The man's friendly, aww-shucks look dissipated. In its place was something that seemed to be pretending to be human. It leered at Wesley. Teeth out in a menacing grin. Raul let that look stay on his face a moment longer, then transformed (it was the only word Wesley could use to describe what was happening) back, saying, "Well, I know you used to be a journalist, Wes. Can I call you that? Your friends call you that, kan?"

"Yeah."

"Nice. Nice. So, Wes, the thing is, the resort doesn't need a bad name." Hands on the table, Raul leaned in. "Dead body found on the grounds of a place that has thousands of people visiting it daily? Bad rep, bro, bad rep. Do you guys know the term 'trickle-down effect'?"

Before they could answer, Raul was already speaking. "Same thing could happen here. Bad resort means fewer people. Which in turn means a reduced number of visitors to the town. You know, less tourists. Less money going around. Especially to those who need it."

"Happened during the pandemic," Jude added.

Raul nodded. "It did. And who do you think helped the town when it was at its lowest? When people were owing the banks left, right and center? The K-Corporation, of course. Look, this didn't come from me, but even your Aunt Zara had some debts. Shit, the bank was threatening to take back the store. And not just this lot. The others as well. The K-Corporation took care of it. What was the name the marketing boys came up with, Judy-Boy?"

"K-Cares," Jude Ambrose dutifully said.

"Right. K-Cares. Every single business in town, especially the struggling ones, were given loans so they didn't have to worry about the big and scary bank as it came down and started shuttering businesses. We stopped it. We helped. Loans with zero interest. That's what we gave to this town to make sure everything stayed afloat."

"But–" Wesley began.

"So," Raul said, raising his voice to drown Wesley out, "if you guys blabbed to the wrong person, someone with reach, say, people would be afraid to come to the town. A bunch of hillbillies killing each other and burying the dead in shallow graves? Nope, not coming. Board the ferry? One of these filthy locals might push me into the sea because I smell better than them. Come to Darat Kumut town? Those hicks who live there might offer my five-year-old meth.

"What do you think happens then? The money dries up. And then on top of their bank loans, they have the K-Care loan to pay off. Zero interest, but still, money is money. And the resort has to be taken care of, which means that zero interest promise might undo itself."

"Are you threatening us?" Delilah asked.

"Am I?" Raul asked, feigning shock. "You guys don't own a business, nor do you owe me money. The rest of the town though … I mean, when they find out that you two are the reason why the interest rates suddenly shot up and with the threat of losing their business over their heads … I shudder to think about what might – no – what *could* happen."

This time, Wesley turned to Delilah. She looked back at him with concern.

"So, I guess what I'm trying to say here is take it easy. And make some right decisions. I really think you guys make a great addition to the town, and it wouldn't be nice if the town treated you with anything less than the respect you both deserve. Uh, Judy-Boy."

"Oh, right," the lawyer said. He reached into the back pocket of his pants and pulled out an envelope.

Raul looked at it with disgust. Not only was it crumpled, the corners looked damp.

"This here is a little letter from the office saying that you guys get a complimentary five-day stay at the resort. If I'm not mistaken, you'll also have all access to The Casino of Pearls. And don't you worry about spending money. The casino has been instructed to give both of you one thousand chips. Which translates to ..."

"One thousand ringgit," Jude Ambrose said.

"Smart man, Judy-Boy," said Raul. "Of course, I give this to you with the knowledge that you understand what I just told you. You know, about the importance of discretion?"

When they didn't reply, he said, "Think about it. Okay? Might be a good thing for you and Zara. Heard she's been burning the wick at both ends? An hour at our spa ... a slice of paradise."

Next to him, the lawyer was nodding vigorously.

"Well, I guess that's that."

Raul Krishnan slipped off the chair, stretched his back and called out for Sugar.

"Enough acting smart, darling," he said. "Come on over here and let's go. We have reservations. Judy-Boy, you can call one of the drivers from the resort, kan?"

The fat man sputtered an answer in the affirmative, but Raul couldn't be bothered. He had one hand clasped firmly on Sugar's bum and was leading her out. Just as the door was closing behind him, he turned and winked in their direction. No genial, friendly Mr. Aww-Shucks now. Just a pale imitation of something that was playing at being human.

40

"Okay, can you see me now?" Rabbil asked.

"Hold on, I don't think the problem is on your side, I think it's coming from me ... government-funded buildings don't exactly get the best internet. Sometimes, it's better if I just use my ... voila, we have perfect connection. Hold on, lemme just get the camera on and ..."

The image that came out was grainy and elevated because he could see only Dr. Siddhu's head and shoulders. He could also see the rest of her 'office', which had the trimmings of the standard autopsy room. The floors were a muted green, the walls were some kind of aqua-blue that looked stale, and around the place were metal autopsy tables, lab tables, charts on the walls, and at one far side, a corpse lay on the autopsy table close to where the medical examiner stood, its form covered with a white cloth.

"Good to see you, Inspector," Dr. Siddhu said, her voice tinny. Her big smile didn't mask the dark bags under her eyes, and he felt bad for her. It had been two days since the body in the shallow grave was found, and Dr. Siddhu had been adamant that the results would be ready for him as soon as possible.

"I suspected foul play at first," she said, "on account of the massive wound to the side of the victim's skull during the first examination."

"Is it murder?" Rabbil asked. Two feelings were building in him. One was excitement and the other was dread because once he told Syafiqah, she would realize that her husband, who should be back in KK and at her beck and call as their first child was coming, wouldn't be back soon.

"I doubt it," Dr. Siddhu said. "Especially given the broken tibia and fibula. Those are the leg bones. Don't quote me on this, but I suspect the victim had a nasty fall and bashed the side of the head against something very hard. At the moment, I am ruling the cause of death as blunt force trauma to the head, followed by blood loss and shock. I doubt the victim was even aware of dying."

Rabbil took note and said, "So an accident?"

"Most likely. I doubt it was at the area where the body was found. Lack of evidence is the biggest culprit here. What I think happened – and this is just my two sens, Inspector – is that she died and someone decided to bury her in the jungle in the middle of nowhere."

"She?"

"Yes. This victim was a woman. In her ..." the good doctor paused to consult her notes which were off-screen, "late-twenties to mid-thirties. This one's a guesstimate, so let's just wait for the final results, okay?"

"Sure thing, doc."

"We've sent samples for toxicology, and I know you're hoping that I bless you with some kind of warp-speed answer, right?"

"Toxicology can take some time. I know this song and dance routine, doc."

"It's a wait-and-see game."

"Just like politics."

She smiled. "Praise–"

The good doctor was cut off. Her screen had gone dark, and a red box in the center told him the call had been disconnected and Zoom was doing its level best to reconnect.

"Sial," he mumbled.

Then, Dr. Siddhu's screen came back online. "Can you hear me, inspector?"

"Loud and clear, doc."

"Sorry about that. Anyway, as I was saying, I could be guessing, but based on my findings, the victim had been in that grave for just over six months. We also don't have any ID on her, we're a little shit on prints because of decomp, and her face is too … well any chance of identifying her via facial features have gone down the drain. Also because of decomp."

"But you can still do it via dental work, right?"

Prior to answering, the doctor looked down at what Rabbil assumed was her notes and then said, "I can, yes."

"Great, look ,there's a dentist in Tawau who is waiting patiently for those records."

When Dr. Siddhu raised a questioning eyebrow, Rabbil said, "Six months ago, a woman who worked at the casino on the island went missing. I checked with the cops here, and everyone believed she had run off with another man despite there being no evidence to support such a belief. The woman's age matches the age range you presented earlier. This is no confirmation, of course. If it isn't her, then it seems we have another mystery on our hands."

More like another problem for him, but he didn't feel like voicing *that* issue out.

"You think this is the girl who went missing all those months ago?"

"It's a theory I'm pursuing," Rabbil said.

"Right. Send me the number and I'll be in touch with the dentist."

He reached for his phone …

Just then the front door of the outpost banged open. In stepped Atiqah, and she had a very peculiar look on her face. Rabbil knew this look. Trouble was afoot.

"Boss," Atiqah said, "it's one of the patrols. They found Su Yen."

"Is she …"

Atiqah shook her head.

"Everything okay over there?" Dr. Siddhu asked.

Rabbil turned back to the screen of his laptop and shook his head.

"Looks like we're going for a hattrick here, doc," he said, feeling grim and very tired.

His phone buzzed. A message from Syafiqah. Call her. He would, but he had a feeling she wouldn't like the news he was gonna tell her.

41

Zara placed Raul Krishnan's letter on the counter.

"A bribe?" she said, rubbing her temples. "That's what finding a body was worth? A weeklong stay at daddy's resort?"

Delilah nodded.

Wesley, who was stocking up the selection of candy, chocolate bars and lozenges nodded too. "And one thousand ringgit for each of us."

"One thou ..." Zara picked up the letter once more.

"Item number thirteen," Delilah said.

Zara groaned. It seemed like the vice around her head had tightened just a little more. "This is madness."

"Apparently, we can spend as much of it as we want in the casino or we can just cash out ..."

"I should've never taken that damn K-Care insurance," Zara said. "It was too good to be true. I thought it was an act of goodwill, you know, charity? I didn't know Raul Krishnan would use it to own the town."

Wesley felt bad for his aunt. The last three days had done a number on her. On the first night, after he'd returned from Mabel's, he sat at the dining table, laptop open, adding words and words to his growing manuscript when Zara stepped out of Margie's room, sobbing quietly. He sat there and watched as she stood by Margie's open door, looking into the room at her still-sleeping daughter, who was curled up on the bed with Lucky sleeping at her feet.

He watched as his aunt wiped away her tears 30 minutes later and retreated into her room. The next morning, she was her cheerful self. Margie and Lucky acted as if the events of the day before had been their own little adventure, something fun, and now that it was over, it was business as usual.

But when Margie made to step out of the house, Zara shouted for her in a voice that didn't belong to her at all. Her voice was shrill and scary, filled with fear and desperation.

"Sorry, mommy," Margie said.

Zara had hugged her daughter once more and said that she was sorry, and that Margie could go out, but please stay within the confines of their cozy home. Margie told her mommy that she would.

The whole episode with Zara standing outside Margie's door had happened that same night, though this time it was 20 minutes and not 30.

Wesley wondered if his aunt was getting any sleep at all. Between her part-time lawyer job in Tawau and managing the store's books, she didn't seem to be well-rested. The incident on the island had made things worse. The bags under her eyes became more prominent, and she developed something of a slouch.

Now, seeing her with her hands on her head, bent over and slouched, Wesley felt sad for his aunt. Her glow had dimmed, and in the last three days, she looked 10 years older than her 37 years.

"We should take it," Wesley said, standing up as he put in the last Cadbury bar.

Delilah stared at him. Zara's head snapped up. She had a frown. "We should accept the bribe?"

He nodded. "Why not? You could use the break. One week away from everything. It's not so bad, right?"

"But Wes, this is a *bribe*," his aunt said. And Wesley was taken aback by how she said the words. No shrill tone here, ladies and gents, just resignation and defeat.

"What's the alternative?" he asked calmly. "We don't take it, Raul Krishnan gets suspicious and comes back. He might not even be too gracious then." He flashed back to the reptilian look over Raul Krishnan's face. The man had been playing at being a normal person when he stepped into the store. When he left, what he'd been, his original form, had taken over, and Wesley had seen that. The thought of it sent a shiver down his spine. Just thinking about it now reminded him of how Raul's eyes had lingered on Delilah. What if Raul came back and this time, he wouldn't be friendly, he would actually …

"Plus, you need a break," he said to Zara. "Maybe this is it."

"The store …"

"Can close for a few days," Wesley said.

Zara sighed. Her hands went to the letter once more, and this time, she played with it for several minutes, aimlessly flipping it around. "Maybe you're right, Wes. Maybe this is just what the doctor ordered. The office has been giving me too much paperwork and clients, and I'm sure they're trying to tempt me with a full-time position. And the accounts here to deal with, and Margie and …" Zara sighed, rubbed her temples again and slid the letter to Wesley, "The number's here. Why don't you call it and make the arrangement? We'll go on Saturday. Lilah, I want you to come as well. Think of it as your bonus."

Delilah grinned. "It'll be a pleasure, boss."

42

Rabbil glanced at his watch and saw that the meeting with the Head of KK CID would begin in precisely 5 minutes.

He glanced at the front door, wanting desperately to sneak out and get a quick nicotine fix. He made to stand up, but as he did, his eyes fell on the folder in front of him. Slowly he sat back down. There would be no nicotine for … maybe an hour? Superintendent Aznil Nisbawi, veteran of the Criminal Investigation Division, wanted many answers.

For example, how did a suspect in an ongoing murder turn up dead days after speaking to the police? Could Rabbil, a seasoned investigator with an impressive case closing rate, explain why he allowed Su Yen to go back without an out-of-sight escort? How did a single suspicious death turn into two homicides and one concealment of a corpse? And now half (if not the whole) town knew about Su Yen's brutal murder and was happily discussing the very morbid details.

Aznil would probably start with Su Yen first.

Damn it, Su Yen, Rabbil thought as he flipped open the file and began looking through the initial report, which had cost him three phone calls from Syafiqah and a very long WhatsApp message – also from her – regarding the importance of calling your wife when she's in the last stages of pregnancy.

Her body had been discovered by children creating content for TikTok. The place was a palm oil estate 10 minutes from town. The rows and rows of dark brown trunks and green fronds kept anyone curious enough away. There was nothing to see in a palm oil estate, right?

Wrong.

The kids were smart enough to call the cops and wait. When Rabbil arrived, one of the quartet that had been copying and showing off the latest viral dance was still bent over, upchucking his lunch into the drain parallel to the guardrail.

Tawau CID dispatched a team, the team identified the woman based on the ID found on her, and they, in turn, gave Atiqah a call. And now the team was waiting for Forensics. Rabbil didn't feel like standing about with his thumbs tucked into the belt loops of his pants. He wanted to see the crime scene.

"How far?" he asked the young sergeant, who looked about ready to join the TikTok kids in their new Vomit into The Drain Challenge.

"Follow that path," the young cop said, pulling out a packet of Era cigarettes and lighting one up with a trembling hand. "Keep on the path. Don't turn left or right or whatever. About five minutes in. You'll … you'll see it."

"That bad?" Atiqah asked.

"Worst crime scene I've ever seen," the young sergeant said, shaking his head.

Rabbil led the way. Atiqah followed closely. Rotten palm oil fruit littered the ground.

"Who owns this plot of land?" he asked Atiqah.

"I didn't check," she said. "Some big corpo that lost money during the pandemic, I think."

Rabbil grunted something in reply. His leather shoes were now muddy (again), and his shirt wet with sweat. The day was hot and humid. In the distant west, the clouds were already darkening, and rain, or a storm, seemed promised for Sabah's East Coast. His mood was growing foul, matching the sudden stench in the air.

"Remember that case we did? The husband-and-wife murder in Telupid?" Atiqah said.

"Wife and *lover*," Rabbil corrected. He remembered that case clearly. The bodies had been rotting for days. And the murders had been in April, at the zenith of the hot season. The duo had their heads bashed in. The husband had run off to Miri. A neighbor had caught the scent. Rabbil almost puked at the entrance of the house. A couple of the first responders had already marked a spot some distance away from their patrol vehicle.

These days, Rabbil was getting used to that rotting scent of human meat.

The smell in the still, warm air reminded him of that hot day in April. The young sergeant was right. This one was gonna be gnarly.

"Ya Allah," Atiqah said.

"Stay behind the yellow tape," Rabbil muttered.

The path opened into a clearing with a couple of rotten old tree stumps at the center.

Right in front of them, the path would have continued if not for the dead body hanging between two trees.

"Stay behind the tape," Rabbil said once more as he reached into his back pocket and took out his notebook.

X

The superintendent looked like a bit of sleep would do him some good.

"Medical examiner?"

"Rushing it," Rabbil said.

"Three dead bodies," Aznil said, running a hand through his short crop of white hair. "And it's not even been a month."

"Feels like it," Rabbil mumbled. His eyes strayed to the front door. The craving for a cigarette was strong now.

"What was that, Inspector?"

"I said it does feel like a month, tuan."

"Funny. Walk me through the crime scene, Inspector."

Rabbil took a deep breath, glanced down at his notes (pointless because he had been going through them ever since the message had come in at 7 am, saying his boss wanted a briefing on the Darat Kumut mess at 10am sharp) and began.

"The victim has been identified as one Yoh Su Yen. Aged thirty-five."

"You say identified, Inspector, but her face is … well …"

It was a mess.

At one point, Dr. Siddhu stood up and paced away from the body, joining Rabbil at the border between the crime scene and the rest of the palm oil estate. "I need a break," she said. "Her face. Her head … it's just … bad."

The eyes were puffed up with bruises. The nose was smashed to bits. The cheeks looked enlarged – *almost like a hamster with its mouth full,* Rabbil had thought to himself when Tawau's Forensics team had e-mailed him the crime scene pictures.

"And the nails in her head?" Aznil asked.

"Post-mortem," Rabbil replied. "A total of six nails fired into her skull."

"*Fired*?"

"Nail gun."

"Hmm."

"Cause of death was blood loss due to the wound on the victim's jugular measured from left to right. She bled out. ME said it was a slow death. And she speculates that as the victim was bleeding out, her tongue was removed."

His boss grunted. "Go on."

"We think she was tortured. Kept somewhere else for a time and then brought to the palm oil estate to be interrogated. Once the interrogation was completed, she was executed."

"Motive?"

"We're pursuing one at the moment."

Superintendent Aznil pursed his lips. "I'd like something firm, Inspector."

"Well, the going theory is that Su Yen and the first victim, Tommy Asandu, were involved in a drug operation along with several other figures."

"Proof?"

"We're still looking."

"I see. So they killed her because she blabbed to the cops?"

"Could be."

"Hmmm. What else can you tell me about the crime scene?"

What else was there to tell except for the terrible tableau that greeted them? Su Yen had been on her knees. Her arms raised up and tied to a pair of palm oil trees on either side of her. She was naked from the waist up. Her head was down, and you could've thought this was all a little kinky S & M action gone wrong had it not been for the trail of dried blood down her chest until her knees, or the crown of nails that dotted her scalp.

"Tawau Forensics managed to identify three sets of footprints between the sizes of seven to ten. They're readying a report for me."

Aznil grunted, so Rabbil continued.

"There were also a couple of cigarette butts. Saliva might be found, but one of the Forensic officers said that the person had grounded the butts into the mud."

"Any viable suspects?"

"We're looking through her bank accounts, her phone, speaking with her friends in Tawau and in town. We'll get something."

"This theory that connects her to the first victim, tell me more about it."

"We believe that Tommy Asandu and Yoh Su Yen were involved in the sale of drugs in Darat Kumut. They and two or more individuals were selling drugs in town as well as on the island resort."

"We believe Tommy Asandu and Yoh Su Yen were involved in the sale of drugs in Darat Kumut. They and two or more individuals were selling drugs in town as well as on the island resort."

Aznil chewed on that information for some time. Finally, he said, "Did you look at crime stats for Darat Kumut?"

"I did." He hadn't. Atiqah or Rudolph had been working that angle. They'd told him that outside of petty theft and the occasional drunk tourist, the town was a peaceful little place. "No cases of drugs have been logged in." Of course, one could say the cops here had been paid to look the other way. Keep the peace and think of the greater good, right?

"I won't comment until you get me some evidence. So I suggest getting to it, Inspector."

43

Wesley stood up and walked around the dining area and living room, banishing the pins and needles in his feet. He glanced at the clock on the corner of the laptop screen. 1:49 am. What had once been planned as an article had gone beyond that and was now over 150 pages long. He was surprised at what it had become, hadn't expected to actually maintain the story's momentum.

He yawned, but he wasn't exactly tired. His brain was still running on gear five after looking through the many documents – both online and offline – regarding K-Cares, the interest-free loan scheme that the K-Corporation had come up with to help businesses when everyone realized that the Movement Control Order would be a little longer than the 2 weeks that the government first announced.

He'd asked Zara about it, and she'd gone off to her bedroom and found some documents that representatives from K-Corporation gave her after she called and enquired about the loan. They were the standard-issue promotional brochures that talked about the benefits of signing up. Wesley Googled and saw that the website for K-Care was more or less the same: word-salad and promises of ensuring the sustainability of your business.

He'd pored over all of it through dinner and later on after helping Zara with the dishes.

Then, when his aunt and cousin had retired to their bedrooms, he sat at the dining table, a mug of tea at the ready, and began typing, recalling everything Raul Krishnan and his stooge-slash-lawyer had told them. They'd be heading off to the resort tomorrow, and the person on the other end of the line had been very excited to hear they would be coming over to enjoy a 'slice of paradise'.

Wesley yawned. He grabbed his mug and took a sip of lukewarm tea, grimacing at the taste. He placed the mug back down and stretched, making a few bones click and clack.

He was about to sit back down and continue when his stomach rumbled. Dinner had been light and at 7 pm, which was ... seven hours ago.

Wesley decided he'd done enough writing tonight. He saved the Word document and then shut his laptop down. He stepped out of Zara's house, locked the door and made his way out.

The night was cool. It was quiet, the only sounds coming from the beach where the waves lapped. Up above, the palm fronds rustled. He made his way down the Beach Path towards town. He had one place in mind. And the gnawing hunger made him move faster.

At one point, the quiet of the night gave way to the gentle thumps from Palace Neptune. Even though it was 10 minutes away, Wesley could still hear the club music that poured out of the place.

He spared the place a glance. At this hour, it was the only place that was still crowded, though some tourists were finally balking from the strain of too many cocktails and too many sweat-soaked hours on the dance floor. He was sure that the need for something oily and salty would bring them to Abu Bakar's Burger Bakar.

But as he was human, he erred – for at this time, Abu Bakar sat alone at his one square plastic table. Normally, boys from the Ferry Terminal would come by with a couple of beers and a lot of stories, most of them funny and involving townsfolk or dumb tourists. The only proof that someone had been by was the beer cans all crumpled up and tossed into plastic bags against the burger stall.

"Owen closed up shop and left," Abu Bakar said, smiling at Wesley, indicating the Seaside Bar.

"I'm here for food, actually."

Abu Bakar grinned. "Well, thankfully, I'm not closed." He stood up and made his way towards the skillet. "What'll it be?"

"A juicy cheeseburger? I'm craving one."

"One juicy cheeseburger with all the trimmings coming right up."

X

Wesley groaned as he sank his teeth into the burger. A part of him wished that he was in the throes of the munchies so that his herbal-enhanced tastebuds would welcome Abu Bakar's joyous creation, but this was good enough. He didn't even mind that the grease and fat from the juicy patty, as well as a combination of melted cheese, mayo and ketchup was rolling down his chin, an unsightly view it must be.

"I didn't think Zara was *that* bad a cook, truth be told," Abu Bakar said, settling down in his chair and placing a Gudang Garam between his teeth.

"She isn't," Wesley said defensively. "It's just been a while since I've had a burger this good. Compliments to the chef."

"Who accepts such kind words as well as payment," Abu Bakar said.

"Quiet night?"

"Tonight's one of those nights." The old man poured himself some coffee from a thermos and downed the beverage with a smack of his lips. "If it's quiet after 2, then it'll probably be quiet for the rest of … oh, we have a guest artist tonight."

Wesley turned and looked. A skinny little cat padded cautiously towards them, sniffing the air, interested perhaps in the smells that emanated from the old man's skillet.

"I met this poor child the night Tommy died," Abu Bakar said, urging the cat to come closer.

"You saw him?" Wesley asked after swallowing another bite.

"We did. I was here with Sergeant Awang and a couple workers from the Ferry Terminal. He came by, made a few silly remarks and off he went. Along came this poor little thing." Abu Bakar bent down and scratched at the area between the cat's ears. "Poor thing was limping. I had a feeling that little shit must've done something to her. Either him or the person who came a little after."

Wesley paused. He lowered the burger – down to its last morsel by then – on the paper plate and wiped his chin with the tissue.

"There was another person?"

Abu Bakar nodded. "Looked like it. I didn't see much of the man. Rosdi – one of the guys from the terminal – did. I was making Sergeant Awang's breakfast McMuffin." He scoffed at that, sending out a sharp plume of kretek-scented smoke. "If it looks like a burger, and smells like a burger, then it's a burger lah bah. Why call it a muffin?"

"Boss," Wesley said, trying not to sound too excited, "this other man, what did he look like?"

"Eh? I don't really know. Like I said, I was working the grill."

Wesley's heart sank.

"But Rosdi did say he liked the man's shirt, lah."

"Shirt?"

Abu Bakar nodded. "Well, it was mostly black, but Rosdi said he saw something on the back of the shirt. A skull with hair? I swear lah, kids these days are really into some weird things."

44

The moment their names were mentioned, the pleasant smile on the receptionist's face became wider. Her voice, from that friendly tone of any hotel receptionist in any five-star resort, also transformed. She was genial. She made jokes, she was more animated, she even asked if they needed a refreshing mocktail while she settled the details of their week-long stay.

"In the meantime," she said, "here are some brochures that you might find exciting." And she passed them five different brochures detailing what treasures you could find at the Pearl Below the Wind Resort. You had diving. Snorkeling. Parasailing. Not good enough? Maybe rent an ATV and blast down the trails around the hotel. Still not feeling it? In the evening, the beach area was transformed into an open-air bar where if you were lucky, someone might start a volleyball match on the beach. Socializing, especially among strangers, was highly encouraged. Still not feeling the love, brother? Well why don't you …

The mocktails arrived. And with it came cold towels, served on a rattan tray, smelling of lemongrass, jasmine and a light touch of mixed fruits.

As Wesley sipped his drink, he took in the hotel lobby. It was open-air. When you walked up the short flight of steps, the first thing you saw wasn't the lobby, the fancy chairs or the smartly dressed staff, but the beach. And beyond that, the sea.

After you soaked all that in, the rest of the lobby was spread out for you. The massive reception desk to the right was where a constant stream of guests checked in, checked out and asked for directions. In the central area, which was surrounded by a ring of lush greenery, light streamed in from a high vaulted ceiling. To the left was the lounge that extended towards a massive balcony and sitting area with plush views of the swimming pool and beach and sea.

Extravagance was the middle name of the Pearl Below the Wind, and Wesley did his best to capture all this for his book.

X

"We've been told not to accept any tips. Especially from you," the bellboy said smilingly. "You and your family are to be given special treatment. Express orders from Raul Krishnan."

"Thank you," Zara said.

The bellboy bowed and swiftly left.

Once the door closed, Margie and Lucky made a dash for one of the two bedrooms in the suite, she giggling happily away like this was the biggest adventure of a lifetime.

When he'd called, Wesley had expected the hotel to tell him that no, dogs weren't allowed. But somehow, the person who answered had been more than happy to allow an animal into the resort. Wesley had assured her that the dog was potty-trained and had asked if they were willing to give a ground-floor room. The receptionist had told him that when it came to their comfort, anything and everything would be done.

And so, they were given an Executive Suite on the ground floor with direct access to the hotel gardens where the dog could "relieve himself as much as he wanted to," the woman had stated.

Wesley bent down and grabbed his and Delilah's bags. He stepped into the living room, heard Zara's and Margie's voices from the room to his left and turned right into the second room.

"Ah," he said, taking note of the queen-sized bed.

"What's wrong?" Delilah asked.

"Should've asked for twin beds."

Delilah looked at him. "Twin beds?"

"Yeah. Never mind, lah. I'll take the couch. Mind if I take a pillow or two?"

"Yes, Wes. I do."

He turned to face her. "What–"

Delilah grabbed his arm and pulled him into her orbit. Her lips touched his, and he shuddered as her tongue slid into his mouth. Instinctively, his hand went to the small of her back (he was reminded gently of how Delilah stood about two inches taller than him), and he pressed himself against her. He could feel one hand against his waist, the other on his neck.

Delilah pulled away from the kiss. She was smiling. "Do you know how long I've been waiting for that?"

"What does it say when it's the girl who has to make the first move?" Wesley said. His legs felt weak and rubbery. It had been a long time since a girl had kissed him like that. Shit, it had been the first time a girl had initiated the kiss.

"Says a lot," she said.

"I almost wanted to. The other day when ... when we found Margie," he said.

"Why didn't you?"

"I … I was scared you wouldn't want to."

"You shouldn't have been scared, Wes. I've always had a soft spot for you. Ever since you walked into the store. And everything that's happened since … well, I guess I really wanna take a chance with you."

Wesley looked at her for a couple of seconds. What do you say to that?

Instead of trying for words, he shrugged and kissed her. Delilah didn't seem to be interested in words, either.

Delilah pushed him and he fell, tumbling onto the bed.

Is the door closed? Wesley wondered as Delilah straddled him, her hands slipping under his T-shirt.

45

Margie and Lucky were in the garden. Wesley had bought Margie a kite at the Ferry Terminal's tourist store, and she was now running back and forth to get it in the air.

Zara was sitting on one of the lounge chairs, ankles crossed, a Michael Connelly paperback resting on her lap. She had ordered white wine while he'd been taking care of perfunctory matters in the shower (and bathtub) with Delilah, and had downed half the bottle.

"You guys finally got it on," Zara said, smiling knowingly.

Wesley grinned sheepishly. "We weren't too loud, were we?"

"I had to let those two out before Margie could ask why Delilah was laughing-screaming from the other room."

"Sorry."

"Don't be. She likes you, and I've seen you giving her the side look every five seconds or so. It's so obvious you wanna be with her. I couldn't think of a better place to finally set it in stone."

Wesley couldn't either. He'd enjoyed every moment of the last hour or so with Delilah, but part of him knew that there was more at stake here than a romantic getaway. They were here because they had to look for Priscilla. They needed answers. It didn't help that Rabbil had texted him this morning with the news: Su Yen was dead. Murdered.

"Can I have some?" Wesley asked, nodding at the glass.

"Go crazy," Zara said. "The waiter brought three goblets. The tray is by the entrance."

As Wesley poured the wine, he reminded himself once more why they were here. Priscilla. She could be around, and maybe the right person to get information from. He would let Zara, Margie and Lucky have their little fun in the sun. He and Delilah would go looking.

"Pour me one, sugar," Delilah whispered into his ear.

Wesley shuddered and let out a mild yelp, the golden liquid sloshing up to the rim.

Behind him, Delilah had one hand over her mouth and was laughing. Her hair was still damp and wrapped in a towel, but the rest of her, exposed through the sleeves of her bathrobe, glowed, and the smell of the hotel soap seemed like a pleasant distraction from their actual mission here.

Wesley bit his lower lip. Tempted he was to reach over and kiss her, but Zara was there, and while she had given her blessing, wouldn't she contemplate the lack of manners amongst the youth if he started eating Delilah's face right in front of her?

"Fancy," Delilah said, adopting a faux British accent, holding the goblet by its stem and swirling the liquid.

"You're glowing," he said.

"Tell that to your ears," Delilah replied.

They felt warm. He was flushing. He surprised himself by giggling. "Sorry. It's been a while."

"At least try and be a little discreet about your feelings, Wes."

He just smiled.

"And let's not forget why we're here," she said in a lowered voice. "You brought the nametag, right?"

He nodded. "Yeah."

"Cool. I'll get ready and then we'll check out the casino?"

X

It was Delilah who noticed the tail.

They were taking the scenic route (it was the *only* route to the casino) when she pulled him off the shaded path and dragged him to a little Japanese-inspired garden, complete with a koi pond, tall fronds and lush, green bushes before planting a kiss on his lips.

"Isn't it a little too early for exhibitionism?"

Delilah pinched his arm, pulled away from him and whispered into his ear: "Someone's following us."

"Wha…"

"Security guy. Short and beefy. Short hair. Mean look."

"How …"

"He's been on us since we left the lobby," she said quietly. "Close enough to keep us in his sight, but far enough that we wouldn't notice."

"How did you notice?"

"Remember when I stopped to take a picture of the vines along the roof of the path?"

"Yeah."

"I saw that he stepped away to one side. When he saw me looking, he pulled out his phone and acted like he had some message he had to read. Then when we got to that stone with the plaque, I saw him again. He smiled at me, Wes. *Smiled*."

"Shit," he mumbled.

"Feel free to say that again."

"Okay, so we just continue and act like everything's hunky-dory?"

"Wanna try?"

They stepped away from the garden and went back to the path. The casino was right in front of them. It was separated from the hotel and located next to the nightclub which was shaped like an amphitheatre.

At the front door of the casino, standing by the attendant, was a short and stocky man wearing a dark green polo T-shirt with the resort's logo on the left breast pocket. Under the logo was a single word: SECURITY. He had a cigarette tucked in the corner of his mouth, and while he chatted amicably with the attendant, Wesley saw that the man kept glancing in their direction.

Delilah's elbow poked him in the ribs. Hard.

So Raul Krishnan had sent someone to spy on them. To keep him apprised of their movements. He could also be using them to flush out the other culprit who was selling drugs in his fiefdom.

The entrance had marble floors and walls, with faux Roman pillars holding the ceiling up. The windows were massive and made of stained glass. To their left was a little lounge where the losers drank in solitary silence and the winners reveled by shouting into phones and throwing booze down gullets, keen on spending the prize money. A little waterfall and some greenery livened the place up, but the mini chandeliers from the ceiling, as well as the gaudy faux gold ornaments and furniture, reminded everyone this was a mini-Vegas on a tiny island lounging in the Celebes Sea.

The casino lay behind a double door painted gold from top to bottom. Its surface was inlaid with a plethora of carvings. Animals and men and mythical beasts, flora and vegetation along the sides and corners.

As they neared, the doors opened and an ageing couple stepped out. Leading was the man who looked very cross. His fists were bunched at his sides. Sweat rolled down from his temple, and his jaw looked about ready to implode and crush his teeth. The woman was red in the face, had one finger pointed at his back and seemed to be shouting obscenities at him in Cantonese.

"Apparently, he burned half their life savings," Delilah whispered, as they gave the very angry duo a wide berth.

"The house always wins, right?" Wesley replied.

The casino was as massive as it was impressive. The double doors opened to a viewing balcony which offered any first-time visitors a peek at the obscene extravagance.

The first thing they saw were the slot machines, arranged in five rows and firing out many odd little jingles. More than half of the machines were occupied by the just-got-here crowd (you knew who they were based on their massive smiles even when they didn't win a thing) or the one-more-roll committee – people who had spent everything and were banking on the machine's Random Number Generator to gift them a set of 7s that would justify the money they had lost.

Beyond the slot machines was where the real money was: table games. These had five different categories, everything a budding gambler would need for a subsequent trip to the high court in Tawau to declare bankruptcy.

The first row of tables were for the poker players. Quiet at first, barely a word by anyone, but then an eruption of noise once the winner made everyone else fold.

Past the poker pit were the blackjack tables. Also quiet until the right number was found, and everyone sounded off their frustrations or happiness.

Then came baccarat. Steady hands, steady eyes and slow movements here, nothing fancy. Unlike the previous two tables, most of the players here were older. They smiled and chatted as they played, but you couldn't miss the predatory gleam of the avid gambler in their eyes.

And lastly, towards the end of the casino were the noisy twins: the craps and roulette games. Here the games were fast-paced. People laughed. They shouted. Cursed one another (in good spirit, of course). Smacked shoulders as much as grabbed them. And a few kisses were traded as well among the winning parties.

At the center of the casino floor, between the poker and baccarat tables, was a massive fountain made of gold (or metal painted gold) in a bowl of marble, inlaid with colorful tiles. It depicted a mermaid. In one hand, she held a die, and in the other, a pearl. Water fired off from the holes in each item, and the mermaid wore a pleasant smile. She seemed to be saying to anyone who gazed upon her: "This is a place of relaxation, a sanctuary from all your troubles".

Sashaying among the tables were women in one-piece cocktail dresses designed to show as much cleavage and leg as possible without turning the casino into a sex den. Gracefully, these women balanced trays in one hand and moved around the floor, handing out drinks and taking orders from thirsty gamblers.

Also among the players were men in suits and aqua-green ties. Their posture, rigid and firm, along with crewcuts, proclaimed them as security. Wesley noticed a few were talking into microphones attached to their wrists. All also had earpieces. And looked stoic.

"There," Delilah said, nodding at the cashier's table – which, like almost everything else inside The Casino of Pearls, was gaudy. It was built to look like the bottom half of an oyster. There, cashiers worked together greeting and verifying customer identification before allowing another group to change money into chips – for the newly-arrived – and cashing out chips – for the ones who had decided that a hard day's work of gambling was done and money needed to be spent elsewhere.

"We'll use mine first," Wesley said.

The cashier smiled at them. "Executive Suite, under Mr. Krishnan?"

Wesley nodded. "Wesley Moysin and Delilah Loh. We don't need to show the letter, do we?"

The woman's smile never faltered, even as she shook her head. "No, you don't. How much would you like to withdraw?"

"Is five hundred enough?" Wesley asked. "I've never actually been in a casino."

"Well," the woman said, "I guess that depends on the kind of gambler you are."

"I don't gamble," he said. "I don't even know how to play poker."

"I only gamble during CNY. And that's out of obligation," Delilah said.

The cashier said, "Then five hundred in chips should be enough for some laughs."

Her laughter wavered some when she saw something beyond Wesley's right shoulder.

He turned for a glance, and came face-to-face with a stern-looking member of the casino security.

Wesley knew her. Bella from the employee's quarters.

46

When they had first met Bella, she was in a skin-tight training top and Lycra shorts. But in her suit and heels, she towered over Wesley and Delilah. Her hair was now scraped back and tied into a short and severe ponytail.

"I remember you two," she said, smiling. "The Darat Kumut Amateur Detective Agency. Wes and Delilah. Lucky and Margie here?"

"They're at the swimming pool with Margie's mom."

The trio began moving, Bella between them.

"You know we were told about you two. Actually, you four, but we were specifically asked to look out for both of you."

"Any reason why?" Wesley asked.

"You guys are VIPs. Strict and direct orders from upstairs. Specifically, Raul Krishnan. We heard about what happened the other day. The … body you guys found."

"There's more to it," Wesley said.

"Oh?"

"We can … you know, trust you, right?"

"What an odd question," she said. "Any reason why you'd be asking such an odd question?"

"Well, we saw someone following us," Delilah said. She then described the guy they'd seen earlier.

"Hmm. That sounds like one of Raul Krishnan's boys." Seeing their confused looks, she added, "Raul has his own security team. Not like an army of men, but three or four who report directly to him."

"Are they dangerous?" Delilah asked.

Bella moved her head to one side, as if she was going to shake in the negative, but paused and said, "No one knows. They lepak around Raul and follow his every order. There's a rumor that they don't have any background in security work, but you didn't hear that from me. In other words," she turned to Wesley, "it's off the record."

At his look, she added, "I read up about you. About what happened in Bukit Bintang," Bella placed a hand on his shoulder. "I'm sorry about what happened. I really am."

"Thank you," he said, doing his best not to wince at the memory that suddenly exploded in his head and the gentle throbbing that followed suit. In the days after the incident, any thought of what had happened would send him reaching for the nearest bottle of booze. These days maybe half an Actifast would do the trick.

"Anyway, about the body we found the other day …" – he reached into his pocket and pulled out the nametag – "we found this in … well, it was near the body."

Bella took it and stared at the mildly rusted nametag and the name still etched onto it. "I knew it," she said. Her eyes went bright with understanding. "It was so obvious, right in my face!"

"Knew it?"

"Priscilla is one of the best croupiers on the floor. She does not have a single infraction. She doesn't drink anything but water and coffee. She doesn't smoke. At the end of every shift, her uniform is still spotless. Her hair is never a mess, and she's friendly to *every*one."

"So she's a perfectionist?" Delilah asked.

"Anal," Bella said. "Every other card-fucker – that's what we call the croupiers here, by the way – has a little problem. No one is perfect. But Cilla, that's what everyone calls her, is a little angel."

"And you don't buy it?" Wesley asked.

They had stopped at a circular standing table where gamblers who needed a quick break to sip drinks and re-strategize would go and huddle for a little wisdom from God or the internet. Wesley could see a few of them. Some were bunched together and discussing strategies. Others were frowning and scowling at the tables they had just come from, mentally forcing some kind of luck to appear and save them from the financial hole they were digging.

"I don't at all," Bella said. "No one's perfect. No one is willing to take another person's shift because they are 'nice'. But here's Cilla, willing to do that, regardless of the time. She's right there, by the way," Bella nodded.

Sitting at the baccarat tables, Priscilla was neat and immaculate. Her hair was braided into two long ponytails that fell down her shoulders and to her chest. She wore glasses, the round kind with thick lenses. Her hands were clean, no nail color or polish. Yet her hands moved swiftly. A new game was being played, and she deftly moved chips from the pot and to the players, snatched cards from the automatic shuffler and slipped them to the player. Her face was plain, the kind you'd most likely forget after one look. *A forgettable face*, Wesley noted to himself.

"She doesn't look like she belongs in a casino," Delilah said. "Give her a cardigan, a blouse and flats, and she'd belong in a library."

"Kan," Bella said. "At least you've managed to figure out who's been supplying drugs in the casino. Abigail was very vague about who was slipping her the drugs. I could probably guess a couple names. Probably even point them out from where we're standing."

The three of them stared at Priscilla as she herself watched the players.

"How are you two gonna play it?" Bella asked.

Wesley looked at Delilah. "Wanna try good cop, bad cop?"

"I can do the whole silent and scary routine," Bella said.

"Think you can bring her to a quiet place?" Wesley asked. He felt a little uncomfortable here, even with the many, many people who dotted around the tables and flitted between poker and the slot machines. He rubbed his arm and felt his hairs standing. He looked around again and saw … nothing that'd raise his suspicions.

And yet …

"Bella," he said, "we really need your help."

The casino security officer looked back at him and nodded. "Just tell me what I need to do."

47

Inspector Rabbil went ballistic once Wesley was done talking.

"YOU WANT WHAT?"

Wesley brought the phone closer to his ear and said, "Su Yen's pictures. As many as you can spare?"

"What you playing at, Wesley?" Rabbil barked into the phone. "If you have a lead, show it to me right now. You found something in that shallow grave and–"

"You approaching her and asking your questions is gonna get her clammed up," Wesley said. "We gave you Su Yen, and now she's dead."

"And you think you can do better?" Rabbil asked. "You and Delilah are not police officers. You don't solve crimes. That's my job. So please, give up this lead and I'll make sure you guys get some of the credit later when the reporters start asking questions."

Wesley took a deep breath. He was doing his best not to lose his temper. After counting backwards from three, he said, "Inspector, let's make a deal."

"I don't'–"

"You give us the pictures," Wesley said, talking over the government official and hoping to God the man wouldn't take it to heart, "I'll get her to agree to talk to you. There's a chance that whatever happened to Su Yen has reached her, and she wouldn't want to meet the same fate. She probably knows that Su Yen was killed *after* being interrogated by you guys. I'll convince her to talk, and then you can … I don't know, protect her."

"That's not your call to make, Wesley. This is a police matter …"

"What a bang-up job you're doing, bossku."

"You …"

"I'm trying to help you here," Wesley snapped. For a moment, he forgot that he was speaking to a police officer. The gaudy painting in front of him – a team of horses running along a field of gold – disappeared. It was replaced with a field of red. Wesley burned with rage. His grip tightened around his phone. He wanted to tear the painting out from its faux-gold frame and rip into it. A white guy in a massive floppy hat bumped into him and mumbled an apology. Wesley wanted to jump on him and just bash the man's brain in. He could hear Rabbil saying something about following protocols, but by God, did he want the man to shut the up and just help him here.

When Rabbil stopped to catch his breath, Wesley said, "You talk to her, bring her to the station, she's finished. She won't say a thing, and you're left with a potential lead asking for her lawyer. And pray tell, inspector, what happens when you don't find a single thing to leverage against her? You cut her loose, and two days later, she ends up dead. Is that what you want?"

"No …"

"You can't even guarantee that she'll talk if you bring her in."

"Can *you* do that?"

"Give me the pictures and I will. If I can't convince her to tell me something by the time you get here, you can have her."

Rabbil went silent. Mentally, Wesley began counting back from 10 to one in the hope the inspector would say something. When he reached four, Rabbil said: "Okay. Fine. I'll send you some of the shots. But they aren't pretty."

"I don't need them to be pretty, inspector. I need them to work."

"They better, Wesley. For your sake."

And with that, the inspector hung up.

X

Wesley stared at the pictures. The inspector had been right. They weren't pretty at all.

Along with the pictures was a short and quick message from Rabbil: *Her tongue was removed while she was bleeding to death. Maybe you can use that to get your lead talking.*

Appreciating the inspector's less-than-subtle jab, Wesley pocketed his phone and made for the smoking room. He touched the pack of cigarettes in his back pocket. He'd noticed earlier, while putting on his clothes, that his cigarette intake had been decreasing. And even before that, while he'd been in the bathtub with Delilah, she'd leaned back into him, kissed him and then made a comment about his smoking.

"I won't kiss you if you've just smoked," she said.

"It can't be that bad."

"It is."

"I'll think of quitting."

"Don't just *think*," she said. "Do."

As he fired up a cigarette in the casino's smoking room (the ashtrays were balanced upon the shoulders of faux-gold plated female angels with massive chests), he felt a little bad about making what could be an empty promise.

And yet …

He stared at his phone with its dead screen, and knew that his promise to Inspector Rabbil could be one made of empty clouds that might dissipate with one blow. Could he actually get Priscilla to talk?

His phone buzzed. He looked at it. A message from Delilah. Bella was ready. She was on her way to bring Priscilla to a little spot that some of the staff used as a smoking area.

Wesley looked at his cigarette. Half-gone. He took another long pull, killed it, and stepped out of the smoking room.

48

The little spot was located past the employees' toilet. Two heavy doors led them out into a little patch of space with a clear view of the beach and sea. There were a couple of plastic chairs on one side and a faded Milo tin between them filled to the brim with cigarette butts.

"You got the pictures?" Delilah asked.

Wesley nodded.

The door opened behind them. Out stepped Bella. Trailing behind her was Priscilla, who looked calm and composed. Her eyes widened a little when she saw Wesley and Delilah.

"I thought you said someone in management wanted to see me," she said to Bella.

"I lied about the management part," Bella said. "But these two do want to see you."

"No thanks," Priscilla replied, still unfazed. She turned. Bella grabbed her wrist. "I'd like to listen to their questions and your answers, Priscilla."

"Let go of me."

"No," Bella said flatly. "Sit down and listen to them."

"I'll scream," Priscilla snarled as she struggled to release herself from Bella, who in turn looked mildly bored as she kept Priscilla from getting free. "I'll call the cops. I'll make a scene."

"You can do that," Wesley said. "And then I'll tell Raul Krishnan that you've been selling drugs in his casino."

At this, Priscilla stopped struggling. She fixed Wesley with a look that oozed hate and fear. Gone was the calm and emotionally-empty woman.

"You don't know what you're talking about," she breathed.

"I do," he said calmly. "Took me a while to figure the whole thing out, but I think I have most of the story already. There could be gaps, but I'm sure you'll help fill them."

"I'm not telling you shit."

"Okay," he said, digging his phone out and accessing the pictures Rabbil had sent to him. "One call is all it takes. And then ..." He passed her his phone.

Priscilla stared at the device as if it was some sort of evil machine that would harm her, but after a few seconds of hesitation, she took the phone from him.

The moment her eyes landed on the picture, she dropped his phone. He bent down and picked it up.

At which point Priscilla kicked him.

The tip of her loafer caught him on the side of his head.

Wesley cried out in pain and lost his balance. Delilah reached out for him.

Bella's grip loosened.

Priscilla pulled free and made for the double doors.

Bella was already moving. Her long arm reached out, caught one of Priscilla's braided ponytails and yanked.

Priscilla screamed. It went an octave louder when Bella tugged at her ponytail and then let go. In her pain, she stumbled back and fell on her ass.

Priscilla made to get up. She managed one knee on the ground before Bella was all over her. She dragged Priscilla up by the same ponytail she had wrenched on earlier, and as Priscilla got ready for a very loud scream, Bella wrapped one hand around the woman's mouth and used her right arm to twist and press Priscilla's arm against her back. Priscilla screamed as Bella added a little pressure to her joints.

"Shut up," Bella said, "sit down, and comply. Or I will snap your arm. Do you understand?"

Through her gurgled whimpering, Priscilla nodded vigorously.

"You okay?" Delilah asked Wesley.

Wesley touched the corner of his right eyebrow. It was wet with blood. There was a cut there, but it wasn't too deep. Superficial. Might not even leave a scar. "I'll live. Chicks dig scars, right?"

Delilah rolled her eyes, "I don't."

"You'll learn to love it."

"Ass." But even as she said it, he noticed how a handkerchief had magically appeared in her hand. He took it from her and dabbed at the wound. It didn't feel too bad.

He got up, held the phone to Priscilla, saying: "We're trying to help you, Priscilla. We know about Abigail." He reached into his pocket, found the nametag and presented it to her.

Seeing it, her eyes widened.

"I won't even tell the cops about this," he said, touching the cut across his eyebrow. "I'll just say that the door slammed into me."

"They're notorious for having bad springs," Bella said. To Priscilla: "I'm going to let you go now. You won't scream, kan?"

Priscilla nodded again.

Bella looked to Wesley and Delilah for confirmation. Wesley nodded.

Bella removed her hand from Priscilla's mouth. And she, in turn, just glared at Wesley and Delilah.

"Sit down," Wesley said, nodding at one of the chairs.

Priscilla, demure now, flashed him an annoyed glance as she sat down. Wesley took the other chair. He offered her his cigarettes. She declined.

"How do you know?" she asked him. "About the drugs?"

Wesley's heart rate was starting to pick up. He told it that this was no different than the many editorial meetings he'd sat in where he had to propose front-page stories while every single member of the editorial team – there were over 30 – watched. But he'd survived their onslaught of questions, which sometimes made him wonder if they thought his ideas were stupid. This would be like that. It was just a matter of presenting the facts. And wasn't that what he'd done since graduating from university three years ago?

"Well," he started, doing his best not to stutter, "it's a little complicated. But ... it sort of makes sense." He took a deep breath, readied the mess of facts swimming in his brain, and began speaking.

49

The facts of the case were as follows:

Tommy Asandu, the town rascal, was killed. Only, Tommy Asandu wasn't some dumbass with a need to roll a fat joint every 30 minutes or so. No. Tommy Asandu had business acumen. He had dreams. Using money saved from all of Raul Krishnan's drugs that he'd kept and then re-sold, he'd found a way to source drugs and sell them to everyone who had the money. Somehow, Raul Krishnan got wind of this little operation, and he decided that names needed to be named and punishments needed to be meted out. Only, the punishments didn't have anything to do with maintaining the reputation of the hotel.

"Delilah, can you give me the bag I passed to you earlier?" Wesley said.

Delilah reached into her rattan bag and passed him the little black plastic bag that was tied into a knot at the top.

Wesley undid the knot and pulled out a little baggie that was ziplocked at the top. He leaned in towards Priscilla. Bella and Delilah moved closer to have a look. The little baggie contained a few specks of crystals with an aqua-green tint.

"Raul Krishnan killed, or had Tommy killed, because he was encroaching on his business. Poaching his customers."

"How did you get this?" Bella asked.

"There's this guy on the mainland who sells burgers. With some help, he managed to get one of the addicts to spill some tea. That guy, a dock worker, told me everything. Raul Krishnan has locals in town who he trusts to peddle his stuff. His stomping grounds are Palace Neptune on the mainland and the Pearl-0 on the island, which doesn't surprise me at all. He sells exclusively to the tourists, foreign and local. But he only sold his drugs in the clubs.

"Tommy, on the other hand, was selling to everyone on the island and the mainland for a fraction of the price and making a killing of it, correct?"

Priscilla didn't answer. She had her eyes on the concrete between her penny loafers.

"The town couldn't do anything. Almost everyone owes Raul Krishnan money thanks to the business loan he provided during the pandemic. Say something and he immediately takes over your business. They practically signed over their lives to him when they signed up for the K-Care loan.

"No one said a thing. Just closed one eye. Some tourists buy his stuff at the club. But most of them buy from the casino. Am I right, Priscilla? Has business been booming?"

When she realized they were all waiting patiently for an answer, Priscilla mumbled: "It has."

"So Tommy was making money. Money that he had Su Yen keep. Along with some of the drugs for … well, I'm sure you'll be able to enlighten us. Which makes her the banker? Accounts keeper? Tommy … for all his faults as a human being, excelled in the wrong kind of entrepreneurial spirit. You sold the goods in the casino. And I'm guessing there's a fourth guy who brings the drugs in, right?"

Priscilla's stare reverted back to calm and leveled. She allowed the silence to hold for a few seconds before she nodded in the affirmative.

Finally, after a very dramatic sigh, Priscilla said, "Tommy made money selling for Raul Krishnan. He was good at it. Getting people curious enough. Giving them a little pinch. A *taster,* he called it. And when they wanted more, he'd up the prices a little. Not too much. Extra ten ringgit. Extra fifteen. Sometimes even upwards of fifty. Especially for the guys who liked their girls to cosplay as zombies.

"I don't know when it came to him, but he realized there was an untapped market. He proposed to Raul to sell in the casino and to the locals. But Raul ... well, he has a bangsawan mentality. He looks down on everyone in town. He told Tommy to stay in his lane and sell only to tourists. Tourists come and go. And should there be a problem, the local cops could be convinced to shut the hell up."

Wesley fired up a cigarette and said, "But that wasn't enough for Tommy, kan?"

"Nope. He wanted to sell his shit to *everyone*. Didn't take him long to form a 'proper business strategy'. Darat Kumut," Priscilla said haughtily, "is a town full of drug addicts. The fishermen. The cops. No one reported Tommy, because his prices were lower than Raul's. If anyone reported him, there would be a lot of unhappy customers."

"How much money did he make?" Delilah asked.

"A lot. With a supplier willing to sell in bulk, and with demand, he had the perfect money maker."

Wesley glanced at Delilah, who in turn glanced at Bella. Something cold was creeping up the small of his back. She had taken note of something Priscilla said earlier.

"Tommy was selling to the cops?"

Priscilla shrugged, calm and nonchalant. As if they were discussing the fluctuating price of oil. "You know, Tommy was so full of shit. But he was pretty honest when it came to the kinds of people who bought from him. Tommy didn't discriminate. He sold to anyone. Anyway, I started selling and well, the kinds of people you see who need a little pick-me-up? You'd be surprised.

"Anyway," Priscilla continued, "Tommy managed to broker a deal with a group of former Abu Sayyaf kidnappers who had left the people business for the drug business. I don't know how much of it is bullshit, but he swore they occupied one of the many little islets between here and the Southern Philippines to cook and grow their shit. And let me tell you something. That stuff that he sold, it's the shit."

"And how did Raul find out about this?" Wesley asked.

"Abigail. The silly little bitch who died."

"She was murdered?"

Priscilla shook her head.

"Suicide? Overdose?"

"A stupid accident. Abigail was … well, a real go-getter. Like, she would kill for tips. So she worked her ass off. Took every shift available and *whored* herself if the group at the table had a big chunk of moolah. But to reach that level, she'd have to be energized. Boys don't wanna see a saggy or moody act. To do that, she needed to have her daily dose of vitamins."

"And you obliged?"

"It's a free country, baby. One day we had a new batch in. The Abu Sayyaf boys had screwed up, but they didn't tell Tommy. He asked, though. Really did. Wanted to know why the batch didn't have the crystal-clear touch that the usual stock had. One of the guys told Tommy that this batch had been cooked with a 'little' fentanyl. How much exactly? They didn't say. But we learned about it the hard way. Give me one of those first, bah." Priscilla nodded at the pack of cigarettes Wesley had. He passed it over to her. She looked at the ten soldiers who stood at attention inside the box, picked one, and fired it up.

"Prior to her shift, she'd park herself in the staff toilet and consume the stuff. No needle work, no marks, no problems. Only … this time she took a little too much. I was waiting for her to come out, get some feedback on the stuff. When she didn't, I got worried. I walked into the bathroom and …" she paused and continued taking long pulls from her cigarette. Once the last bit of smoke was pulled in and expelled, leaving a long blue trail, she dropped the butt, crushed it under her loafer and continued with her story.

"I don't know what happened in there, but I have a theory. That shit those Abu Fuck-ups put in there gave her a bad trip. She slipped, fell and hit her head on the edge of the toilet. Cracked her skull open because when I found her, she was lying on her back and bleeding out. I checked her pulse. She … she … she never made it."

"What happened then?" Delilah asked. They were captivated. Wesley couldn't understand how calmly she was telling all this. None of what happened seemed to faze the woman sitting in front of him, with one leg over the other and her hands clasped together on her thigh.

"I called Su Yen and Tommy. Tommy wasn't in town. But Khairul was."

Delilah said, "Khairul is …"

"The guy who drives the stuff around. He delivers vegetables, fruits and meat to the hotel. I recommended him for the driving job. He and Su Yen came over. We got the body into his truck, cleaned the toilet up and finally gave Abigail a burial."

"Which was where you dropped this?" Wesley said, reaching into his pocket and pulling out Priscilla's nametag.

Priscilla sighed. "I guess so."

"Since her fiancé or whatever was busy at work, we managed to enter their hostel, pack up some clothes and make it look like she'd had a change of heart and decided married life wasn't for her. Khairul and I then spread the rumor that she was alive and well in Sandakan, or KK, depending on who asked."

Priscilla asked for another cigarette. Wesley indulged her. When half the thing was burned, she said, "We don't really know what happened next, but a couple months after the whole Abigail thing, Tommy told us he was being followed. We didn't believe him. Told him that all that shit he was snorting finally caught up with him. He said no, and we left it at that. Not too long after, he snapped a picture of what he believed was his stalker. But his phone camera was shit, and we couldn't really see anything." She took a pull from her cigarette and then added, "I mean, you could see the shape of a man in the dark. But that's about it."

"And then he died?"

"*Murdered.*"

"Who did it?"

Priscilla looked at Delilah. Wesley watched as the calm façade faded and out bloomed indignation.

50

"You fucking kidding me?" Priscilla said. "Do I look like ChatGPT? No, I don't know. But maybe try asking Raul Krishnan? I'm sure he found out about Tommy's entrepreneurial spirit and decided that it needed to be shut down ASAP. Because you know what the real kicker of the whole thing is? While he was buying and selling and making all of us a lot of money, Tommy was still selling for Raul. Wouldn't you be pissed if you found out?"

"You need to tell the cops this," Wesley said.

"Yeah, right. That'll be a solid 'no' for me, *dawg*."

Wesley unlocked his phone and accessed the pictures Rabbil sent him earlier. He chose the worst one. It was a close-up of Su Yen. You could see the nails implanted in her head, how her mouth was open, the red and pink chunk in her mouth that used to be attached to her tongue. You could even see the blood trail from her mouth down to her even bloodier neck.

He swung the phone to Priscilla. "*This* is what they did to the person who held the cash. The banker. What do you think they'll do to the person who was actually selling on the casino floor?"

It only took one look. Priscilla looked away from the picture and hissed a curse.

"If you don't go the police with what you know," Wesley said, "they'll find you, and there's nothing that anyone can do to help you."

What he didn't tell her was that Delilah was recording away on her phone. Insurance, in case Priscilla tried to wriggle away from the truth.

"I can't do prison," Priscilla said.

"Can't do the time ..." Bella said.

"Fuck off!" Priscilla snapped back at her.

"Right now, the man investigating Tommy's and Su Yen's murders as well as the discovery of Abigail's body, is on the way here. I told him I'd get you to agree to protective custody as soon as they find the person responsible for the killings, so I really need you to be a team player here."

"*Team player*?" Priscilla's voice went up a full octave. "I don't want to go to jail!"

"You don't have a choice in the matter, Cilla," Bella said. "It's either they get you for the drugs or for hiding a dead body."

"No. No. No. No. No. To both. I–"

Wesley had a sudden thought. He said, "What if they can't prove the hiding of a dead body?"

All eyes were on him.

"What are you talking about?" Priscilla asked.

"The only proof they'll have regarding your whereabouts and connection to hiding Abigail's body is this." He showed her the gold nametag. "Would be a bit of a bummer if they didn't have it, right?"

"You're not serious," said Bella.

"I am," he said. To Priscilla: "Tell the cops everything. Tommy, the drugs, Raul Krishnan. Except what happened to Abigail, of course. Tell them that and this," he waved the nametag in her face, "is gone."

"How do I know you won't sell me out?"

"I won't. Abigail's body has been found. Her mother and her fiancé can finally mourn, and that's … well, good enough, I guess."

"You're not serious," Bella said again.

Wesley ignored her and kept his eyes on Priscilla. His heart was going at top speed and he was worried she might just back out right there and decide to take her chances with Raul Krishnan.

But what chances were those? Raul Krishnan would punish her the same way he'd punished Su Yen. Priscilla would beat her crime of hiding a dead body, but she'd still pay for the drugs, and to Wesley, that seemed like a good enough win.

"We'll tell the cops that you were helpful," he added, hoping that, as flimsy as the words sounded, she'd agree and decide to work with them.

Priscilla pursed her lips and was eyeing the ground in front of her, the gears of her brain clicking away in hopes that she could find an out to all this.

"What if I say no?"

"We leave you. Raul finds you and you're screwed. And guess what, he has one of his goons following me and Delilah around. He probably knows that we know about the drugs, and he's using us to flush you out. You're not exactly up to your neck in choices here. We leave, and there goes your chances of being alive beyond the next few days."

A red flush was slowly creeping up Priscilla's neck. You didn't have to be a genius to know the right choice.

When her brain finally came to the right conclusion, Priscilla sobbed angrily. "Fine," she said, her lower lip stuck out in petulance. "I'll take the deal. I'll go to the cops. Whatever."

Wesley leaned back, the tensed and coiled muscles of his body loosening. It was a win of sorts, but there were still questions.

Chief among which being: Who killed Tommy?

51

“I’m not going to cuff her,” Rabbil said. “Although I need you to promise that you won’t run,” he said to Priscilla.

“I won’t,” she said, her lower lip still sticking out.

When Rabbil called Wesley for an update, he was told the good news: Priscilla was willing to tell the inspector a rather long story about what was happening on the island and in Darat Kumut. However, he had to come alone because the police force was compromised.

“Compromised?”

“Yeah,” Wesley said. If Raul Krishnan knew that even one of the cops in town was a fiend for crystal meth, he’d have twisted the guy’s arm for information on the case. Even if he didn’t, Wesley wasn’t taking chances. Bella told him that one of her friends at the workers’ quarters would pick Rabbil up, take him to the quarters and then they’d make their way – on foot – to where they were.

The trip took 30 minutes. Wesley paced. Delilah and Bella talked about bath bombs. Priscilla shamelessly nicked his cigarettes and puffed away.

When Rabbil arrived, he looked unhappy. His leather shoes were caked in sand. His tie was askew, and he was sweating. His guide looked cheerful and happy – and had a fist bump ready for Bella.

“What if she doesn’t speak?” Rabbil asked Wesley after the latter had given him a summary of what they’d found out.

"We recorded her."

"Smart. You still don't have a name for the guy who killed Tommy."

"Do you?"

Rabbil didn't say anything to that. The truth was that the small team of cops was split between Tommy, Abigail and Su Yen. They had found nothing on Tommy, nothing on Abigail, and the only thing they had for Su Yen were the cigarettes and the shoe prints.

"I'm not supposed to share this with you," Rabbil said, "but we're thinking that all three incidents involve separate culprits. The person who killed Tommy didn't leave any evidence, but suddenly he, or they, are leaving cigarette butts and footprints everywhere? It doesn't compute."

"And the dead body Lucky found?"

"Well, we've confirmed it's Abigail. Dental. The ME is convinced her death was an accident. They found minute traces of methamphetamine in her. Going theory is that she had some, it screwed her up, she got into a mishap that killed her. Her body was then stored away because … well, who wants to find a dead body in their resort, right?"

"You think it was someone in the hotel?"

"That sounds like a good motive," Rabbil said. "Unless you got an alternative?"

Wesley shook his head. "I don't have one, boss."

"Okay then. You holiday here and I'll try get her to speak. Good job, Wesley. It's a shame you left the newspaper business."

"I was … I …" He paused to catch his breath and then said, "I didn't want to go back."

Rabbil nodded. "I know. Good thing you didn't."

X

"You're not gonna get into trouble?" Delilah asked.

Bella shook her head. "I told my super I had period pains. He was almost fired not too long ago because he was making tampon jokes. These days I use it just to escape from work."

Wesley and Delilah laughed. They bid farewell to the security officer and followed the thickly carpeted path back to the casino.

The casino was still in full swing when they got there. People still hoping for a little love from Lady Luck, at the tables or the slot machines.

They were almost at the exit when Wesley felt something crunch under his shoes. He pulled his foot away and saw that someone had dropped a receipt. Because seeing discarded trash was a peeve, and there was no harm in just depositing it into a nearby bin, Wesley bent down and picked it up. Out of curiosity, he smoothed out the crumpled bit of paper and saw that the person who'd tossed it had managed to salvage some of the money they'd transformed into chips. Maybe in their haste they'd dropped it. Or maybe salvaging that small amount was not worth the person's time.

Receipt still in hand, Wesley swiveled in search of the nearest dustbin.

Meanwhile, Delilah was answering a call from Mabel. By the sound of it (they were firing away in Cantonese), Delilah seemed to be confused about something Mabel was telling her. Wesley looked at Delilah and mouthed, "Everything okay?"

Delilah's confused look turned into a smile, and she nodded before raising her free hand up, index finger and thumb in a circle, middle, ring and pinkie up. Everything was okay.

Out the casino they went, and there, by the waterfall, was a dustbin. Wesley made for it and–

"Wes, wait!"

He turned to Delilah. Her voice had just the faintest trace of worry.

"All good?"

"Aunty, hold on, ah," she said. She lowered the phone and said, "The receipt?"

"This?" he asked.

She nodded.

Wesley passed it to her, standing by the phone so he could listen.

"Aunty, Wes is also listening in case you're wondering why I'm speaking in English."

"Ah, okay," Mabel said."Can you describe the receipt to me, Lilah?"

"Okay, uhh ... white paper. At the top, center is a pearl—"

"*Clam*," Wesley corrected.

"Right, a clam opened up with a pearl in its bed. The pearl has a pair of dollar signs on it. The whole thing is in some kinda aqua green scheme. Below that is the casino name – Casino of Pearls."

"That's the chit I have in my hands, but it's not a receipt," Mabel said. "You know, I don't gamble if it isn't CNY."

"And I've never entered a casino before," Delilah said. "Where did you find the chit?"

"It was behind the dryer."

"So," Wesley said, "If it isn't you or Mabel, then it's got to be Lester, right?"

"Is he there now?" Delilah asked.

"No, I sent him out to the pharmacy in Tawau. My gout is acting up again. Too much beer, I think."

"Mabel," said Wesley, "what does it say on the chit?"

"Well, some of the writing is faded, um, hold on, I'm going into the study for my glasses and ... okay, so on the left column are words, but all I'm seeing here are the letters U, C and M. Then a date from two weeks back and on the right column are some numbers. It's mostly faded, but I think a little over thirty thousand?"

Wesley and Delilah looked at each other.

"Can you see anything else?" Wesley asked.

"I don't think so. There's a short sentence at the bottom. Something that could be *honored* and *immediate pay*. But I could be wrong."

Wesley shrugged at Delilah's questioning look. She then told Mabel that she would call back in a few minutes.

"Be quick about it. I'm worried," Mabel said.

Once her phone was in her bag, Delilah said, "What do you think?"

"Other than the fact that Lester has a bad gambling problem, nothing much. On the flip side, the chit wasn't like this one," he said, showing her the one he'd found a few minutes before. "But then again, I don't know a lot about the casino industry. Maybe we could ask someone about it?"

Delilah smiled. "I think we'll need to use your phone now."

52

"UCM. Are you sure those are the words on the chit?" Priscilla asked.

"As sure as the Pope is Catholic," Wesley said.

"Funny. UCM is short for Unpaid Casino Markers. Those are short-term, interest-free lines of credit that the casino offers. But at the Pearl, Markers are rare because they're only given to 'trusted' customers."

"Meaning ..."

"People who've spent a lot of money. Normally, the pit bosses – they're the managers – will give each croupier a list of people who have markers. These are people who are trusted and have good standing at the casino. This guy who has a UCM, is he wealthy?"

"He works as an assistant."

"I guess he isn't making over 200,000 ringgit a year, then?"

"If he is, then I'm a cricket who talks a big game about conscience, has a tailcoat and a top hat," Wesley said.

On the other end, Priscilla emitted something that sounded like a strangled cough. Wesley guessed he'd just made her chuckle.

"This chit, was it a piece of A4 paper?"

"No, it's just a small slip of paper, the size of a receipt ..."

"Are you sure?"

He made a mental note to ask Mabel that later if Delilah called her again, but confirmed it with Priscilla.

"Odd."

"What's wrong?"

"Well, you ask your police friend to shave a few years from my sentence, and I'll tell you."

"I'll talk to him about how you cooperated. Make sure that the prosecutor knows that before they propose a sentence, should you plead guilty."

"Not good enough."

"Come on, Priscilla. I thought you were being proactive."

"I'm being realistic."

"I'll talk to Rabbil about it later, okay? Just tell me what I need to know and I'll convince Rabbil. Have you told him about Khairul yet?"

"No. I'm sweating him out."

"The more helpful you are, the better your chances."

Priscilla grumbled. "Fine. Whatever."

"You were saying something about the chit?"

"Yeah. UCMs aren't printed on a chit or receipt paper. They're printed on the company letterhead. On thick paper. To make it more … exclusive? That your friend has a UCM is odd. Can you give me his name? I memorized the names of the people who have credit with the casino."

"Lester."

"Describe him?"

"Taller than me. Shoulder-length hair. Has a goatee. Occasionally he wears glasses. Wide-bodied."

… but Rosdi said that he saw something on the back of the shirt. A skull with hair? Abu Bakar said, kretek cigarette popping with every puff and drag.

Wesley bit his lower lip. It couldn't be, or … could it?

"I … don't think I've seen him at my table. And the name isn't familiar at all. UCM lists aren't easily given out."

"Okay. Thanks for your help. Could you pass the phone back to Rabbil now?"

×

"Second time seeing you around and not at the machines or tables. One could get suspicious," Bella said. She had a tablet under one arm and her smile seemed a little strained.

"Sorry, but we have one last favor."

"Delilah told me. You guys are looking for someone who's been to the casino before."

"Who *could've* been to the casino before," Wesley clarified.

Bella raised an eyebrow. "So … you're going on a fifty-fifty chance kinda thing?"

"This person had a UCM chit."

The eyebrow went up a little higher. "A UCM *letter*, you mean."

"Chit, the size of a receipt. Like one of these." Wesley showed her the crumpled thing he'd accidentally stepped on.

"Now you've got my undivided attention," Bella said with a grin. "Come on. Let's find a table and crack this case."

Did it surprise Wesley at all that there was a café in the casino? At this point, if Bella brought him to a petting zoo within the casino that allowed the gamblers to ride the elephants in hopes that it would put a little pump in their step when they were heading back to the pit, he would've probably said, "Just as well, I guess."

The casino served the same stuff as the hotel, but the drinks here were a little cheaper. Quantity, not quality, had to be the motto of the place.

They chose a table next to a man who was watching a YouTube tutorial on how to perfect the poker-face.

"What would you guys ever do without me," Bella said. "I mean, would the plot even move forward if I didn't say hi the other day and ask what you two were up to at the worker's quarters?"

"You should put 'Deus ex machina' in your resume," Wesley said.

Bella laughed. "I like to think it's a little thing called fate. If you believe in such things."

Delilah nodded. "I was raised Buddhist, so fate's a big thing for us."

"Atheist bordering on Agnostic," Wesley chimed in.

Bella grinned. "When did you lose your faith?"

"When my parents asked me to do my own research. You?"

"When I realized I was a raging dyke."

Laughing, Bella set up the tablet and said, "So when Delilah came looking for me, I thought she'd lost you to the blackjack table. It's one of the more popular ones. Then she told me you needed access to the CCTVs. And since you guys are amateur detectives ..."

"And we don't have warrants," added Delilah.

"Or authority," said Wesley.

"And that's why you two will owe me dinner. Like a really expensive one. Not Abu Bakar's Burger Bakar. But the real deal."

"The pub on the island any good?" Wesley asked.

"Free flow?"

"I guess."

"Not guess, handsome," she said. "*Know*. Because I agreed to go on a date with this incel who works in the video rooms to get the footage. Anyway, who are we looking for?"

"Here." Delilah tapped and slid her finger across the screen of her phone. She angled the phone toward Bella to show her a picture of Lester. It was from a wefie that Delilah had taken on her phone. Mabel's last book launch party.

"Oh … I know this guy."

"You do?" Wesley asked, surprised.

Bella nodded. "But the detectives need proof, right? So …" She accessed an app on the tablet, then chose a video overlooking a poker table. The angle showed the players, and sitting on the far left was Lester. The game had just started. The dealer laid out three cards on the green felt. Lester took one look at the cards and there went his poker face. He winced in pain for a second and then rearranged his features in an attempt to appear calm.

Only, one of the other players at the table, a calm and collected older lady, had spotted Lester's tell and had a sly grin on her face.

They watched as the baton was passed around and the bet raised. The guy next to Lester, seeing that the temperature did not match what he was packing, threw in the towel. Lester tapped some chips on the table and then tossed them into the growing pot at the center of the table.

"Risky," Wesley said.

"He's, you know, taking a *gamble*." Bella's joke was received with very little fanfare.

The round continued. The cash was raised. More chips into the pot, but no one was throwing in their cards. As the game at hand was Texas Hold'em, the dealer proceeded to flip out the fourth card. This time, Lester didn't bother keeping a straight face. It sagged a little, and he proceeded to cover this up by running a hand across his forehead.

"He's jittery," said Wesley.

"I think he knows he doesn't stand a chance," Delilah said. The other players seemed to be weaving and bobbing with the current. The baton was passed once more. Call or raise. Sweet or sour. The first person raised. Three chips.

"Three hundred," Bella reported, "I think."

The next player peeled up his cards to stare at numbers. There was no reaction on his face as he tossed the cards onto the table with a quick shake of the head. So far, two of the five players had decided this wasn't up to their speed. The player next to Mr. Just-Folded matched the previous three chips. Lester licked his lips. They could see that his small pile of chips had shrunk. He had enough for one more raise.

And so he decided to fuck everything up by going all in.

Only now did the other two players react. The one further from Lester pursed her lips. She took a peek at her cards, decided there was a better round waiting for her and called it quits with a swift flick of her wrist. The next player simply nodded and called it.

Lester was licking his lips now and doing a good job of looking strenuously constipated.

The fifth card was revealed.

The remaining player smiled. It was a short one, a curl at the corner of his lips. But it was enough to tell the trio that he had this game in the bag.

The dealer asked for a show of hands.

Lester went first. His cards were a crying shame and a fart in the wind. The other guy had a straight flush.

Lester sagged, picked himself up and left the poker table.

"When was this taken?" Wesley asked.

Bella fiddled with the tablet and said, "End of last month."

"Can you track him with this?" Delilah asked.

"Sure. Let's see here ..."

She switched between cameras nearest to the poker table, and they watched as Lester made his way towards the bar to join the congregation of the broke, depressed and delusional few who were most probably checking their bank statements to see if they could power through to the next round. He had a drink, and then decided that maybe the best course of action was to return to the cashier's table and change some more money for chips.

Bella switched to another camera (one of many) which was focused on the cashier's table. He dug through his pockets, found some money (crumpled but usable) and slapped it on the table.

The lady said something. Lester didn't take well to the muted words that exited her mouth and smacked his palm down on the desk. A couple of civilians in the vicinity looked but shrugged. Just another loser lashing out, they probably told themselves.

"Wanna bet on the why?" Bella asked.

"Didn't have enough money to play," Delilah said, not taking her eyes off what was happening on the screen: Lester waving his arms in the air and looking very unhappy with the service they were providing.

A short stocky figure in an aqua-green polo T-shirt came over and tapped Lester on the shoulder.

Lester turned – ready, it seemed, to let loose some vitriol. But at the sight of the man, he slumped. Like a balloon that had its knot undone, he sagged and began apologizing to Mr. Short & Stocky, who pushed Lester aside and said something to the cashier before turning his attention back to him. Then, money woes forgotten, the two men left the bar.

Bella switched cameras as she continued to track Lester and Mr. Short & Stocky.

They walked back towards the pit, but changed direction, making for the side hallways that led to the private offices. The last camera that caught them was at the end of the hallway.

"Where did they go?" Delilah asked.

Bella leaned back against her chair. She blew out a sigh.

"Bella?" Wesley pressed.

"Raul Krishnan's office," she said.

53

The ferry bounced gently against the sea, rocking it as it made slow progress towards the mainland. The sun was setting. The sky had turned a shade of indigo as the night shook itself awake to take over the shift. A breeze, pungent with the salty scent of the sea, ruffled Wesley's hair. A bird squawked.

"You sleeping?" Delilah asked.

"Just resting my eyes," he said. His body felt like it could do with the soft sheets, duvet and pillow of the bed he'd shared with Delilah, but his mind seemed to be creating scenario after scenario as he pieced together a theory from everything they had so far. Far off, somewhere in the real world, somewhere Wesley didn't want to be, Delilah was saying something. He opened his eyes and snuck a peek at her. She had backed the driver's seat and was painting her toenails. She had a diligent look on her face as she concentrated. It looked mundane, but Wesley took a mental snapshot of her. A cliched line (found in so many romance movies and novels) ran through his mind: she looked perfect. *What a brain fart*, he told himself and chuckled.

"That's your answer?"

"Hmm?"

"I said, do you think Lester did it?"

"Do you?" he asked back. "Do I?" he asked himself. "Well ... if you apply a little logic and some of Occam's lessons to the situation at hand, Lester seems to be the most likely suspect as he has a motive bigger than my ... vocabulary."

Delilah laughed, and Wesley felt his ears go warm as he flushed.

The meeting in Raul Krishnan's private office had taken over 30 minutes. When Lester exited, he was carrying a bulging tote bag with the resort logo on it. With Bella's help, they managed to find out that Lester owed the Casino of Pearls just over RM278,000. Their source – a cashier – then told Bella that Raul Krishnan had ordered that they allow Lester to continue gambling there. In fact, every time the man came in, he was given an allowance of RM1,000 in chips. He rarely cashed out. Another dealer told them Lester was a terrible gambler.

"Comes here regularly, he's the most well-known face in the pit because of how often he's in here and …" said one dealer, a pretty woman with a dyed fringe, who managed an excellent overhand shuffle on her deck of cards without taking her eyes off them, "I see him like what … two, three times a week?"

"All he does is lose money," another dealer, a slim guy with a perfect combover and massive square-shaped glasses told them with a shrug.

Which meant he was using, and losing, about three or four thousand ringgit per week. That was a lot of money.

"My guess," Wesley said slowly as he climbed out of the car and popped a cigarette in the corner of his mouth, "is that Raul chose Lester. He spotted a guy, a constant gambler, invited him into his private office and then began giving him small allowances. Here's a little money, why don't you play some more. Oh, you're out of cash, we got this thing here at the casino where you can owe the house and pay later when you make it big."

"And instead of actually making it big, Lester ends up owing big to the casino. To Raul Krishnan," Delilah said.

Wesley nodded. "And when he realizes he's in too deep, Raul decided to drive the fangs in. First, it's the tote bag with drugs. Here, Lesty–"

"Lesty?"

"He called his lawyer Judy-boy. So why not do the same for Lester?"

She shrugged. "You were saying?"

"Bring the drugs to Palace Neptune. Drop them off. Start with that. Gives Lester more incentives. Innocent work to convince him this isn't as bad as it actually is. Don't ask too many questions about what you're carrying. Do the job and we'll up your credits at this place."

"You know what I don't understand," Delilah said as Wesley deposited the butt of the cigarette into an almost empty mineral water bottle. "Doesn't this idiot know he's digging himself a massive hole? You know, of debt?"

"That," Wesley said, plucking out another cigarette, "is just like asking me why I love smoking. Or why an alcoholic can't stop after the first drink."

"It's the brain, then?" Delilah asked.

Wesley nodded. "A fascinating organ."

"So," Delilah picked up the baton and said, "Lester's debt grows and grows, and at one point, when Raul realizes that the debt is big enough to push Lester over the edge, he calls Lester over and offers him something big like a discount."

"Discount?"

"Or a clean slate."

"Now you're speaking my language."

"All he has to do is kill Raul's competition. But that … well, begs a bigger question. Would he actually do it?"

"That would depend on how desperate he was. You lived in the same house as him, right? Did you see anything that would … I don't know, tell you he had a problem?"

She shook her head. "No. He was perfectly normal. Everything was all hunky-dory, which is why him going to the casino is such a shock."

"But you would've noticed him going missing. He's Mabel's assistant, after all."

"During the day. He does research for her and types the pages she's handwritten. Normally his duties would be completed after lunch. And if she doesn't have anything for him to do, he's free to just wander around."

All of this was conjecture, of course. There was no proof (*A skull with hair?*), nothing solid tying Lester to Tommy except for Raul Krishnan. And Lester had appeared to be a calm and easygoing presence at the house.

Wesley killed the cigarette, threw the bottle away and sat back down in the car. He hoped they would get their answers when they reached the mainland.

54

"Finally," Mabel said when they walked into the house. "You two need to give me some answers."

"In due time, aunty," Delilah said. "Do you have the ..."

"It's there," Mabel said, pointing towards the coffee table in the center of the massive expanse of a living room.

They made their way cautiously towards it.

The little slip of paper didn't bite or bark at them, and Wesley felt a little foolish at how careful he was being. Delilah picked up the chit and looked at it. She passed it to Wesley. There it was, a piece of paper stating that the customer had been given the privilege to owe the casino money.

"We need proof," Wesley said.

"Room?" Delilah asked.

"What are you two going on about?"

"Well," Wesley said, "we think Lester might have killed Tommy Asandu."

Mabel's jaw dropped.

The three of them stood there looking at each other.

"We'll bring you up to speed as we search his room," Delilah said.

"I think I'll need some gin so I can absorb all this," Mabel said, as she sank into her favorite armchair.

To their surprise, the room was clean. The bed was made, the desk was clear of any clutter, and all documents or papers had been carefully shuffled and kept in the book rack. Also on the desk was a slim black laptop.

"Where do you wanna start?" Delilah asked.

"I'll check the desk, you go through the book rack, see if there are any letters or incriminating documents. We'll save the laptop for last."

They got to it.

On the table, the sheaf of paper by the laptop was for Mabel's latest novel. Wesley put that aside and looked at the storage box where Lester kept his stationery. He found several USB drives and placed them by the laptop. He looked through a notebook and saw that it was a series of things Mabel had asked Lester to research. Nothing nefarious or mysterious. Just notes written in a tiny and tidy scrawl.

"Anything?" Delilah asked.

"Maybe, maybe not. You?"

She shook her head.

"You do the bed, I'll do the wardrobe?"

"Bah."

Delilah checked in the little bit of space under the box spring. She had her phone out and switched on the flashlight.

Wesley approached the wardrobe and opened the double doors. He was greeted with shirts and T-shirts of varying colors, as well as shorts, jeans and slacks. One thing of import stood out, though. It hung slightly away from the other clothes. A black T-shirt. BSF on the front, the skull with the hair and forked tongue at the back.

It has to be, Wesley thought to himself.

He tried the first of two drawers. Socks, boxers, underwear and some handkerchiefs, but nothing. The second drawer was empty. He pushed the drawer back, but instead of going all the way in, it caught on something and refused to close fully.

He pulled the drawer out all the way and pushed it in. Same result.

"What's going on here?" he mumbled as he tried for a third time. Same result. After the fourth time, he pulled the drawer out of its rails and looked into the empty spot.

There, on the ground, a bit of tape still attached to the upper edge, was a notebook. This was a smaller, pocket-sized version of the one that sat on the desk. He reached in and grabbed it.

"Found something," he said.

"Ditto," Delilah replied.

They met up back at the desk. Delilah had found a book entitled *A Dummy's Guide to Gambling and Beating the System.*

"He highlighted passages, marked pages and even wrote notes in the margins," she said.

Wesley waved his find at her. He opened the first page and frowned.

"What is it?" Delilah asked.

Numbers. He showed her.

The numbers were arranged into neatly written columns with letters at the top. The first was the letter J, followed by a series of numbers. The next column started with an F, and below that, more numbers. The third column was M, followed by more numbers. They both noticed that the value of numbers in the first column was smaller compared to the numbers on the third column.

"J, F and M," Wesley said. "Sound familiar to you?"

Delilah pursed her lips. Her brain seemed to be functioning at a higher level than Wesley's because she immediately said, "January, February and March."

Wesley looked at the rest of the letters above the other columns. After M came A, M, J, J, A. Delilah was right.

"The numbers here must be …"

"How much he's lost to the casino?"

"It can't be how much he's making from his part-time job as a property agent, right?"

Delilah elbowed him playfully. "Sarcasm isn't helping."

"It's my coping mechanism," he said, using his thumb to flick through the pages. "By the way, how long has Lester been working for Mabel?"

"Uh … since before the pandemic. 2019, I think? Late 2018, maybe?"

"2018 for sure," Wesley said. "Look here, top right corner of the page: *'18*. And if we flip here …" he flipped a couple of pages. Same set-up. Months, total amount lost, as well as *'19* on the top right corner. Between Lester's gambling records were calculations: where he was overspending; where he was only occasionally earning back what he was tossing into the casino.

Things only got worse when they reached 2021. For most of 2020, the casino was closed due to the COVID-19 pandemic, and perhaps during that time, Lester had saved some money, because come 2021 (in the month of April), he'd gone on a binge, losing RM5,448 on the first day. The following months saw the daily number decrease, but the spending power was there. Lester was throwing almost everything at the casino.

"It's–" Wesley had been thumbing through the rest of the notebook (the pages were blank) when he saw there were some notes in the last few pages.

"Looks like we've found the proverbial smoking gun," Wesley said softly.

55

Minutes before Lester came back from the errand in Tawau that Mabel had sent him on, Wesley stood in the backyard enjoying one final cigarette as he readied himself for this little bit of theater.

He took a long drag from the cigarette, closed his eyes, and saw the story in front of him. Sure, it looked convoluted at first: a big mess of death, drugs and devilry. But now he had a clear sense of the whole thing. He'd waded through the shit and was ready to tell the story in a clear and concise way.

"And I'm glad you managed it, Wes," she whispered into his ear.

Wesley's eyes snapped open. He jumped in surprise and turned around. He was in the backyard, looking at the neatly trimmed grass, the hedges that had overtaken the wall, the bed of flowers that Mabel worked on as she ruminated each chapter of her young-adult mystery novels. There was no one behind him. But when he turned, he saw Ashini.

She stood there wearing the same clothes she'd been wearing the day of: dark green flannel over faded blue jeans with tears at the knees, along with her favorite scuffed pair of Converse sneakers.

"I haven't seen you in a while," he said.

"Dr. Kaur did say I am a figment of your imagination," Ashini said. "Your guilt for surviving, you called it. And I appeared to you so many times because you wanted me to appear, remember?

You were so sorry and racked with guilt for living when I didn't that you made me up to deal with it. I'm curious, did it feel like a horror movie?"

"It did," he said. Especially in those last few days before he finally left. He remembered once, washing his face in the bathroom, looking up and seeing Ashini standing behind him, a big smile on her face. He had a panic attack and had to be allowed to take leave for the day. Or the many times he'd see her in a crowd. Like the time he'd been the last to board the plane to KK and saw her sitting in one of the rows.

"Let me go, Wes. You didn't kill me. Those stupid bank robbers did. I'm just … well, a figment of your overactive imagination. You got busy with Tommy, and suddenly I'm not there anymore to kacau you. Maybe that's the medicine you need."

"I'm sorry, Ashini," he said.

To his surprise, she approached him. She didn't hover the way horror writers liked to describe it. She walked. One step at a time, like a normal human being. Like she was there, in flesh and blood and part of real life, rather than a terrible effect of his guilt and trauma.

Her hand reached up and out. He saw the friendship bracelet around her wrist that he'd made for her when they covered the anniversary of some international private school – their first assignment as a team. He felt her fingers touch the side of his face.

"No one blames you, Wes. And I'll never blame you."

He closed his eyes and felt a lump in his throat. The corner of his eyes had gone wet.

"Live your life. You're almost at the end here. I'm so proud of you."

"I …"

"Wes?"

He blinked several times. Ashini was no longer standing in front of him. It was just the garden. The last rays of daylight had faded, and darkness was slowly blanketing the town.

Using the heel of his right hand, he wiped away the tears that had formed in the corner of his eyes and turned to face Delilah.

"You okay?"

"Just thinking," he said.

"Lester just got to town."

56

Darkness full and absolute had fallen over Darat Kumut when Lester unlocked the front door and stepped inside. Outside, the wind was picking up. The clouds had grouped together and looked full to bursting. The town was expecting heavy rain, a lightning performance in the inky black sky and the boom and roar of thunder.

"Mabel? You here?" Lester called out. The house was dark, with no lights on, and it was eerily quiet, which was unusual. He carried a box filled with fruit and vegetables that the All-Convenience Store did not sell. Lester went to the foot of the stairs and called out to Mabel again. He was greeted with silence.

"Anyone here?" he tried.

"The kitchen," Wesley called out.

Surprised, Lester moved as quickly as he could. He cut through the living room and dining area and entered the kitchen.

Wesley sat at the kitchen island, his back to the stove and sink. He had a bottle of Tiger next to him as well as his phone. On the stool next to him, away from Lester's line of sight, were the notebook and a sheaf of paper that Rabbil had passed to him earlier.

"What are you doing here?" Lester asked as he set the box down on the countertop. "And where's Mabel?"

"Mabel's out with Delilah. It's just us boys."

"Huh," said Lester. "I didn't know Mabel had plans. Especially with her gout kicking in."

The massive, double-door fridge faced the kitchen counter. Lester opened both doors and began filling up the fridge with the items from the box. Wesley noted that the man was moving slowly.

"Beer?" Wesley asked. "I don't like drinking alone."

"Don't mind if I do," Lester said. He found a bottle, and cracked the top open using the edge of the countertop and the flat of his palm. He touched bottles with Wesley, took a long swig and grinned. "Refreshing."

Wesley just smiled.

"You didn't tell me what you're doing here. Aren't you supposed to be on the island? At the resort?"

"Yeah. But I had some questions."

"Oh. For Mabel?"

"No. For you."

Lester, crouching in front of the chiller at the bottom of the bridge, stood up and grinned once more. Only, it looked less like a smile and more akin to a grimace. "For me? I'm just the assistant, buddy. The mind of murder belongs to Mabel."

"Funny. Murder is exactly what I wanted to talk to you about."

Lester was holding his beer bottle. But once the last word left Wesley's mouth, his hand juddered and the beer bottle slipped loose, hit the top of the kitchen island and fell on its side, spilling beer all over the countertop and floor.

"Fuck," Lester said. His hand righted the bottle.

"That's a good reaction," Wesley said. "Was that the same word you uttered after you killed Tommy Asandu, or before? When Raul Krishnan asked you to do it?"

Lester stared at Wesley for several seconds. He looked shocked, worried and aghast. But the look held for a moment or so before he arranged his face into something like surprise. "I think you've had too much to drink, Wes."

"You can tell me, Lester. I can help you."

"Hey, man," Lester said, "I really don't know what you're on about. Serious, bah."

"Sure?"

"Sure."

Wesley's hand found the notebook. He placed it on the top and pushed it forward.

Lester gasped. He took a step back as if Wesley had just slapped him across the face.

Wesley reached out and flipped the pages, finding the one he'd earmarked. There was a timeline beginning two months ago: Lester's notes as he followed Tommy around Darat Kumut. Lester had recorded where Tommy went, how long he spent in one particular spot as well as the people he spent time with. Lester had also noted down several important things. A location for the murder (*the abandoned jetty past the seaside chalets looks good?*) as well as the method Raul Krishnan wanted – *boss said he wanted T 2 b OD. Promised that the heroin would be arriving soon. By Tue latest. Need to plan by then.*

And finally, on the date of Tommy's murder was another annotation. This one was very simple. It read: *Job done. Debts removed – hopefully.*

Wesley read the five words loud and clear so that the recorder app on his phone could pick it up.

"That doesn't mean a thing," Lester retorted.

"You made copious notes about Tommy's movements in the days leading up to his death. Then on the day of, you write 'job done'. Unless you were delivering drugs to Palace Neptune, of course."

Lester simply stared at Wesley uncomprehendingly.

Wesley waited in the hope the man would spill the beans. Or maybe he needed a small push, something to get him over the edge.

"It must be something, right, owing Raul Krishnan money? I mean, bad enough the man rakes in *billi*ons from his casino. Bad enough he owns the businesses in these towns by paying off their bank loans so that they end up owing *him*. And they can't spoil that because one word and that's the end of their business. I mean, come on Les. In fiction, 278K is nothing. Probably *be* nothing if you have a big paycheck – you could probably scoff at that. But to people like us? The kulis?"

Wesley waited for the man to react. But Lester just had his eyes on the liquid mess on the countertop.

Did he have to add more things? He was running out of script and was hoping Lester would set the nails in the coffin, produce the hammer and start nailing. And if that didn't work, well …

His hand dipped down, found the final item, brought it up and tossed it to Lester.

The T-shirt unfurled.

"Three people saw you following Tommy to the jetty. You tried to stick to the shadows, but you're not a professional killer, so I'm not surprised they saw you. Just had to wear that shirt, didn't you? Borneo Skull Fuckers. Fucked your*self* if you asked me."

That did the trick.

The man's shoulders sagged. His body began trembling. One hand reached up to brush away the stray tear that had formed in the corner of his eye. When he looked up at Wesley, his eyes were red and there was nothing but dread on his face.

"You have no idea what it's like to owe that man money," he sobbed. "I … I thought after the pandemic, when the casino reopened, I'd go at it slower, you know. Like spend a little less money? I swore I wouldn't be wasting money at the casino again. Really, I did. I just … I don't know how everything went wrong. I lost big on the first day, then after that, I just kept losing. I … I made some money back but not enough and …"

And then Lester was bawling. He had his hands over his eyes and was crying miserably.

"How bad was it, Les?" Wesley asked.

"Bad," Lester said softly.

"Tell me what happened."

"I can't."

"Come on, man. You do this and maybe we can work something out. Get you to safety."

"I …"

"Les, listen to me. Tommy was a piece of shit, but he still had family. People who cared for him. Isn't it … I don't know, important that you get this off your chest? Give them the closure they need?"

"I …"

"You're not a monster, man. You were just desperate. I know that. I …" It was Wesley's turn to pause. "I almost killed myself, dude." He stopped for a moment to actually take stock of that line. It was the truth and nothing but. "I was covering this assignment with a photographer. She was my best friend. Two peas in a pod and all that. One day we got this call about a bank robbery in downtown KL. We were the nearest, so we tried to get in close and cover the action. I was driving. She was taking pictures. We got to the roadblock where the cops were gonna cut the robbers off, and … they did, but they decided to gun it instead of surrendering because they'd 'accidentally' killed a hostage. So it was the noose for them. Their car just … ploughed into a cop car and that cop car crashed into us. She … she never made it. The EMT told me it wasn't a peaceful way to go."

Wesley reached into his pocket and pulled out his cigarettes. There were three soldiers left in there. He fired up one and slid the cigarettes over to Lester, who automatically took them and lit the second.

"I felt bad about living after that. Couldn't eat. Barely slept. Wasn't able to concentrate at work. At one point, I thought I was seeing her ghost. It got so bad that I almost took my own life. That's why I'm here. My parents thought a few months in Darat Kumut would help me find the will to live. I suppose I have."

Lester took several puffs and the silence was only briefly interrupted by the sound of the tips of their cigarettes burning.

Lester took a long puff, nodded to himself and started speaking.

"One day this guy … a short and stocky type… pulls me from the blackjack tables. Takes me to the bar. We get drinks, and he says he's been seeing me around and asks me why I'm wasting so much money at the casino that even the cashiers are surprised I could fork out cash for chips.

"I told him that I manage, but things are a little... tight. Mabel doesn't see it because I'm here and food is covered. And I live with her rent-free. Plus, I don't spend much in town except for a couple bucks over at the pub. This guy, he nods and we chat, share stories about each other. And then at the end, before I leave, he gives me his number. I was like 'Buddy, you wanna suck my cock, is that it?' but that wasn't the case. He just wanted to make friends. I should've known that it would be more than that."

Lester took several strong pulls from the cigarette and dropped the butt into the beer bottle, hissing in death as the last dregs of the liquid snuffed out its short life.

"Mind if I take the last one?" Lester asked, nodding at the box.

Wesley nodded.

After taking a seat and firing up the cigarette, Lester continued his story. He'd returned to the casino and played his games. He'd seen Mr. Short & Stocky, but the guy just smiled and waved in his direction.

The man finally made his approach the following month, after Lester blew a full RM1,000 at a poker table.

"My poker face, man … it's … well, it needs improvement. And those YouTube channels are shit. They don't work at all," Lester said.

Short & Stocky brought him to the bar once more, but this time he asked if Lester was interested in recuperating his losses. Making some money on the side.

"I said yes, of course. I mean, I'd just blown a thousand ringgit. What other choice did I have?"

Plus, Short & Stocky promised that the casino would give Lester, a nobody who worked as a writer's assistant, store credit as well as a little fee for helping them out from time to time. Limited, of course, but with the extra job he was being offered, he might be able to support himself at the tables.

"I agreed. Back then … this was last year, when the government just started opening up business sectors following the vaccination drives. And I'd been doing nothing during the pandemic except play online poker, so I didn't mind. Anything to be at the tables, right? And then, about two weeks after the proposal, Short & Stocky calls me up and tells me that his boss would be on the mainland that night. I said I'd meet him and we did it … at the abandoned jetty."

And that had been the start of the business. Lester had agreed to the very simple job. Bring the drugs – that Raul Krishnan had collected and personally inspected – from the casino to Palace Neptune, the club on the mainland. The contact person in Palace Neptune – the head bartender – would take the package, and voila, job done. Lester's payment would be given when he got back to the casino.

"How often did you do this?" Wesley asked.

"It depends. Sometimes I wouldn't get a job. Sometimes I go there every week. Sometimes once. Twice. It depends on the boss."

And so, Lester began racking up his debt at the casino. Before he knew it, he was in too deep.

"Short & Stocky pulled me aside one day. This was … three and a half months ago, I think? He said he had something important to talk to me about. He took me to the bar, but this time we weren't alone. There were a couple security guys there and this skinny dude with glasses who had some papers and a calculator.

"Short & Stocky told me that I was the biggest debtor in the casino."

"You didn't realize this?"

Lester shook his head. "I just played, lah. Plus, I took it as payment for bringing the drugs over to the mainland. Only I was spending a lot more time in the casino. Especially since Mabel had Delilah over and didn't know what kinda book she wanted to write this time. I was spending so much time there that I didn't realize I was almost 300K in debt to the casino. When the skinny guy with the calculator told me the amount, I almost shit myself."

"Weren't you keeping track of your money?"

Lester smiled, took one more pull from the cigarette – which had burned down to the filter – and shoved the butt into the beer bottle. "Whatever money Mabel paid me was going into the casino. Whatever money I made from moving the drugs from the casino to the club was also going into the casino," Lester managed a bitter chuckle.

Not too long after that, Short & Stocky called Lester back to the casino. There was hope, it seemed.

"The boss wanted me to do something about the town's local jerk. Tommy Asandu."

"'Do something'?" Wesley said.

"He wanted the problem to go away. I asked him to elaborate, and he just snapped at me. Asked me if I thought he sounded retarded. 'I want him dead', he said."

"Raul Krishnan?" He needed Lester to say the name out loud. Acknowledge the person who'd ordered Tommy to be killed. That was the clincher. So far, he was the only person saying Raul's name. Lester was doing a very good job of not saying things out loud. Maybe he was more terrified of Raul than the law.

Lester simply nodded when Wesley proffered the name. Wesley thought of another attempt at getting Lester to say it. There was no time for long thoughts or brainstorming or deduction. He was going entirely on faith.

"You stalked Tommy. How long?"

"A whole month. I followed him around town at night. Just watching him. Seeing where he went. What his routine was." Lester had the T-shirt in both hands and was speaking down to it, not looking at Wesley. "*He* said it had to be thorough. The cops wouldn't suspect anything. Half the job was done because Tommy's a drug addict. And *he* was specific about how it had to look."

"An overdose?"

Lester nodded. "Like an accident. That way, the cops wouldn't think too much about it."

What Lester hadn't been expecting, Wesley reasoned, were the cops from KK. Or the fact that the medical examiner in Tawau was very good. Real-life murder mirrored television shows and movies – Wesley had experienced it firsthand when he covered the crime desk back with the paper. Nine times out of ten, the culprits were caught almost immediately.

"Who supplied the drugs?"

"*He* did."

Come on man, Wesley thought, *give me the fucker's name.*

"*He* had a special batch cooked by his supplier. Made sure it was cut with fentanyl or PCP or something like that. Something to make it potent. To make sure Tommy would die instantly. I think his cook got the numbers wrong or something because ... well, it didn't really work."

Wesley thought about the summarized version of the medical examiner's report that Inspector Rabbil had given him earlier and said, "You weren't alone, right?"

"What?"

"When you killed Tommy. You weren't alone."

"I was." Lester sounded agitated.

"No you weren't," Wesley said, trying to sound calm. "The needle mark was found on his neck. The jugular. To do that, you'd need someone to hold him down while you administered the lethal dose."

Lester turned pale. "*I* was the only one there."

"Who are you protecting, Lester?"

"No one," Lester snapped. "I told you I was alone when I killed Tommy Asandu."

"You're telling me you managed to hold Tommy down and inject the lethal dose into his neck without any resistance?"

Whatever it was that Lester planned on saying was swept away into the realm of the unknown, because in the silence that followed Wesley's question, a creak came from the staircase.

Lester glared at Wesley and said, "We're not alone in here, are we?"

Fuck, Wesley thought.

57

"Who was that?" Lester shouted.

"No one," Wesley said, "it was probably the wind. One of the windows was left open and–"

Lester grabbed the beer bottle by the neck and smashed its lower end against the countertop, turning it into a very sharp weapon.

Wesley raised his hands. "Lester, let's not do anything–"

"Shut up. Just *SHUT YOUR MOUTH, YOU LYING LOGIUT!*" Lester roared. Waving the broken end of the bottle in Wesley's face, he said, "Tell me the truth, Wesley. Who else is here?"

"Lester," a voice called out from the staircase, "my name is Rabbil. I'm an inspector with the Royal Malaysia Police, and …"

Hearing the word *police*, Lester moved. In seconds, he skirted around the kitchen island. He wrapped one arm around Wesley's neck. Wesley's heart raced as he felt the sharp end of the broken bottle press against his neck.

"Lester …"

"Shut up," Lester snapped as he continued gripping the bottle.

Wesley felt something trickle down his neck. He was very sure Lester had cut him.

Rabbil entered the kitchen. He had his gun out in one hand and the other was raised in a calming gesture.

"Lester," Rabbil said calmly, "Wesley wasn't lying when he said you'll be safe. Come clean to me and I'll make sure you get a lenient sentence."

Lester laughed harshly. "Yeah, right. Toss your gun, inspector, or I'm gonna slice this lying logiut's neck open. Lower it. *NOW!*" The sharp end dug deeper in. Wesley didn't bother playing macho. He cried out in pain.

"Do what he says, inspector. Please."

"Damn it," Rabbil said. "Okay, okay, just get that bottle away from his neck."

When the gun clattered to the floor, Lester moved the bottle away. Lester's breathing was ragged. His free hand was wrapped around Wesley's neck. "Stand up."

"What?"

"You heard me. Stand up. I'm getting out of here."

"Lester …"

"Shut the fuck up," he snarled. "Get up."

Wesley stood up.

"I'm getting out of here, inspector. You make one wrong move and I will cut off his toli and bulak and leave him to die. I swear.."

Suddenly, Wesley's bladder was ready to burst.

"Okay, but please don't hurt Wesley."

Lester didn't reply. He looked around the kitchen and his eyes fell on the woodblock with knives, by the sink to his right. He tossed the broken bottle. His free hand reached for a chef's knife.

"Inspector," Lester said. "There's one more thing I'd like you to do. Your handcuffs. Slide them over the kitchen island."

"What?"

"Slide your handcuffs over to Wesley."

"Do it," Wesley said.

Slowly Rabbil lowered his right hand to his gun belt, and his fingers inched around to the back, just above his pocket where his cuffs were. His fingers wrapped around the cold steel bracelets and he pulled them out, placed them on the kitchen island and slid them towards Wesley.

"Pick them up," Lester ordered. When Wesley had the cuffs, Lester said, "Cuff yourself."

With shaking hands, Wesley wrapped the left cuff around his left wrist, clicking it shut. He then went to work on his right wrist. The cuff slid into place with several sharp clicks.

"Make sure it's secure, Wes."

Wesley lifted his wrists. *This is a dream*, he thought. It had to be, because cuffs, a cut on his neck, and now a fucking chef's knife pressed against his kidney? He wriggled his wrists. The metal felt real enough against his skin.

"Alright," Lester said, "inspector, I'm leaving. You follow me, you get too close, I will kill him. When I'm far enough, I'll drop him and he's all yours."

Rabbil burned with anger. This was the first time he'd been in a hostage situation. His speciality was homicide, not whatever this had devolved into. *Next time*, he thought, as he watched the killer and the jack-off who'd decided he was smarter than a killer slowly make their way out of the house via the backdoor, *I'm not going to let a civilian, much less a kid, tell me how to do my job.*

Once they were out of sight, he reached for his walkie-talkie and then fished out his pack for cigarettes from the breast pocket of his shirt.

"Ticks," he said, doing his best to not scream and throw something at the wall, "we got a big fucking problem. Make sure Delilah doesn't know, okay?"

58

"You've got to be shitting me," Rabbil said.

"Get in, boss," Atiqah said.

"Not a word," he said to Delilah, who was sitting in the front seat. "Not one fucking word from you."

"I thought he would be safe," Delilah said in protest.

"He decided to hold an exclusive interview with a killer," Rabbil said through clenched teeth. "Managed to get the story, from what I heard."

"What happened?" Delilah asked as Atiqah shifted Mabel's ancient Volvo's gear into drive.

"I was going to make a grand entrance," Rabbil said. "I was creeping down the stairs and–"

"The fifth step, right?"

Rabbil nodded.

"Cibai," Delilah said.

"That idiot Lester snapped and he took Wesley hostage," Rabbil sighed and ran his hand over his face. He was tired, high-strung and craving a pint of Guinness – no, keep the Guinness, he wanted a real drink, a hard shot of Red Label if the pub had any.

He reached for his walkie-talkie and asked for a status report from Rudolph, who'd been stationed at the town entrance on a lookout for Lester. He was still there when Rabbil had radioed him with an order to trail Lester's car, a white Myvi with a spoiler at the back and a fluffy Hello Kitty visible from the rear screen.

"How far?"

"He's still on the kampung road, boss. Uh … he'll be hitting the trunk road in about … uhm …"

"There's a reason they invented the word *guesstimate*, Rudolph."

"Five minutes," Rudolph squeaked back.

"Ticks. You aced the driving thing, kan?"

"Full marks."

"Can you make magic here?" The unsaid words being: *because I don't want to end up with a dead hostage, a shit ton of paperwork, Integrity and Standards crawling up my ass, and my wife giving me a lecture about the importance of human life while she's pushing our baby daughter out of her womb.*

"I can," Atiqah said. "Strap in, and make sure you don't vomit."

Rabbil rolled down the window and reached for his cigarettes.

X

"You're making a mistake, Lester."

"Shut up," Lester barked. "Just *shut up*."

Wesley was undeterred. "You could have surrendered. Played the good guy. I would have testified. Told them you were willing to help prosecute–"

"Prosecute? Testify against *Raul Krishnan*?" Lester shouted. "Kau sot ka? Testifying against Raul Krishnan will *kill* me. We're talking about the son of a billionaire. Who has the best lawyers in his pocket. Who can call a politician who will then force the police to cut him loose. Who will then be a threat to me. My family. You're crazy if you think I'll say anything, Wes. And don't you try anything. I still have the knife."

Wesley, who was lying on the backseat, hands cuffed, thought about wrapping the cuffs around Lester's neck. That could work, but then what if Lester lost control of the car? And Wesley was determined not to get Lester hurt at all. He wanted the man to testify against the bigger villain in the picture: Raul Krishnan.

He could see the pitch-black sky and droplets of rainwater on the windows from the steady rain.

"Are you gonna drop me off?" Wesley asked.

"I'm not going to kill you," Lester said.

"You sure?"

"I'm not some psycho, man. I just … I did it because of the money."

Wesley said, "Then stop the car and let me call the inspector."

"After what I did to you, yeah, right."

"I won't press charges, Les."

Lester let out a strangled laugh. "Even if you didn't, what happens after? I get sent to jail and then what, you think everything magically resolves itself? Raul Krishnan is gonna come after me, Wes. We both know that. He'll remind me that I have an obligation to not talk about anything that's going on in town. And I know that I won't because if I do, if I say …"

Lester went silent.

Struggling from his position, Wesley tried his best to see what had captured Lester's attention. He couldn't see much, but when Lester spoke, his voice was tight with tension.

"We're being followed."

"What?"

"We rounded a turn and I noticed a very familiar car. An old model Volvo."

Wesley's heart sank. He should have felt hope, he *wanted* to feel hope, but none of that came because the one thing he had tried to avoid – getting Delilah involved in this last-ditch effort to get Lester to confess – was happening. They had argued about it earlier as he laid out his plan to Inspector Rabbil. He'd be alone in the kitchen, Rabbil upstairs, and Delilah and Mabel tucked safely away in Zara's cottage. He'd get Lester to confess and that'd be that. Delilah hadn't been too happy with that decision, but he'd persuaded her that nothing would happen. He was just gonna do what he'd once (upon a time) been a pro at.

Seeing how things were going, Wesley didn't feel much like a pro.

"It's Delilah," Lester said, eyes constantly shifting from the rearview mirror to the windshield. "But she's not alone."

"What?"

"She's not even driving."

X

The roads were devoid of any other vehicle. The last few they had seen were heading in the opposite direction, towards Tawau. Lester, it seemed, was heading north. The next town, according to a milestone, was Kunak, followed by Lahad Datu.

"He's picking up speed," Atiqah said. She pressed her right foot hard on the accelerator and the Volvo's engine roared in protest, though it did a good job of shooting forward, wheels spinning fast on the wet black asphalt. The wipers did their best to clean up the windscreen and through the constant falling rain, three pairs of eyes were focused on the tail lights of Lester's Myvi.

"Faster, Ticks!" Rabbil said. One rear passenger window was halfway down. Cool air blew in but rainwater spattered onto the backseat of the Volvo. He'd smoked his last cigarette. His right hand clutched his service Glock, ready for anything in this trunk road car chase. "I want this bastard."

"You and me both," Atiqah said.

Delilah had been quiet throughout the drive; occasionally, she'd chew on her left thumb, her right hand tightly clutching the seatbelt.

"When was the last time this car was serviced?" Atiqah asked.

"Ten years ago? Maybe?" Delilah said.

"Ya Allah," Atiqah muttered.

"Don't mengucap just yet, Ticks," Rabbil said. "Just keep your foot on the – *what the fuck is he doing?*"

Ahead of them, Lester was swerving the Myvi from the left lane to the right – into oncoming traffic, should there be any.

"Is Wesley fighting him?" Atiqah guessed.

"Or is Lester messing with us?" Delilah asked.

"Tail him hard," Rabbil ordered. "I wanna try and get this guy to stop whatever he's doing and pull to a stop."

"And your best bet is to keep poking him in the butt with a car?"

"At this point," Rabbil said, annoyed because he didn't have any more cigarettes and was craving one right now, "I'm willing to try anything. *Anything*. Now, Ticks, better start doing whatever it takes."

Atiqah didn't need to be asked again. With a quick word of warning to the other occupants, her foot pressed against the accelerator. In her mind, she sent a quick prayer to God, hoping that He would guide her towards apprehending this jackass of a suspect. The front end of the ancient Volvo continued to creep closer and closer into the orbit of Lester's Myvi.

Lester gave up his constant lane-switching and now focused on the left lane.

Seeing the sash on the window of opportunity rising up, Atiqah gunned the car forward, and as fender kissed bumper in a very loud *thunk*, everyone in the car winced.

"He's trying to put some space between us," Atiqah said, "ah sial lah, he's switched lane again."

Without a word, Rabbil scooted over to behind the driver's seat. He checked the Glock's safety and turned the switch from on to off.

"Ticks," he said, "keep on this lane. Don't speed until I give you the signal."

"Umm, what's the signal?"

Rabbil didn't bother replying. He lowered the window with the hand crank and then leaned out of the car.

The cold, wet wind hit him and knocked away the growing headache and need for nicotine. His red power tie (which Syafiqah had bought him when they visited Metrojaya at Suria Sabah Mall) slapped his face.

Rabbil took a moment to appreciate how alive he suddenly felt. With a sigh, he tucked his tie into his shirt, brought the Glock up, squinted and, seeing the target he wanted, fired a warning shot, which hit the Myvi's side mirror.

If that didn't mess with Lester's morale, Rabbil didn't know what would. As a precaution, he decided to squeeze off three more shots.

When the driver's sideview mirror was blown off, Lester screamed.

A few seconds later came a second shot, whistling somewhere over the air.

"What is he doing?" Lester cried in panic. His eyes kept drifting up towards the rearview mirror. "Why is he shooting?"

Wesley, who'd buried his face into the Myvi's seat when he heard the first shot followed by the crack and crunch of the sideview mirror breaking apart from the car, pulled his head up and–

A third shot.

Lester shrieked in fear and threw himself to the right, the steering wheel going with him.

"Watch out!" Wesley shouted.

"Fuck!"

The front wheel on the right veered off the asphalt and hit the grassy ground, bumping over sharp rocks and bouncing into and out of holes.

"Lester, control the fucking car!" Wesley shouted.

Lester shouted something in reply.

But to Wesley, it was drowned out by a sudden thought that was the only thing he could hear now: *Lester has lost control of the car and something bad is going to happen.*

Lester gained control of the car and the wheels went back on the road.

With some effort, Wesley pushed himself up so that he had a clear view of the road ahead. He heard it first, the long blast of a horn as it cut through the rain and occasional roar of thunder. His eyes then picked up the bright, golden glow of headlights coming directly at them.

"Fuck!" Lester screamed.

It was the last thing Wesley heard, followed by the shriek of rubber tires burning against the asphalt, and finally, the massive bang. But by then, everything had gone dark.

59

Atiqah pulled the Volvo to a stop.

"Oh God!" Delilah cried, clapping her hands over her mouth.

"*FUCK!*" Rabbil cried.

The Myvi had gotten back on the road, but in the confusion, Lester had not seen the 5-ton truck barreling down the road towards them. Thankfully he'd skidded, sending the car barreling back onto the right lane and then off the car went, flying over grass and mud before slamming into a tree.

"Delilah," Rabbil said slowly, "I need you to sit here and wait. Don't do anything. Just wait for our all-clear, okay?"

Delilah, trembling in fear, just nodded.

"Ticks," Rabbil said, "check the back passenger seat on the left. Priority is Wesley. He has to be alive. I'll do the driver's seat. And Ticks?"

"Yeah?"

"Weapons free if Lester so much raises a hand to you."

Atiqah, who'd only pulled her gun twice in her entire career, nodded. He could see that her left hand, which was still on the steering wheel, was trembling.

"Deep breaths," Rabbil said. "Just like we practiced at the course."

"Okay, boss."

"Don't lose your shit, okay? The bosses aren't here. You'll be fine."

"Okay."

His version of a TED Talk done, Rabbil took a deep breath and tried to ignore his dry throat and the pounding drum that was his heart. He'd been in one (very brief) gunfight. He'd pulled out his weapon just five or six times in the course of his career. Not too long ago, just when Atiqah had been partnered with him, he'd been called to clean up a cop's death. The cause of death: accidental dumbfuckery. The jackass had been drinking with a couple of pals and had decided to show off his service weapon because it was 'cool'. The safety had been off. The drinks had been plenty. Something was bound to go to shit. And to shit it did go.

His legs trembled as he stepped out of the car. His gun was pointed down towards the asphalt. He rounded the front of the car and switched positions with Atiqah.

Rabbil nodded once, then made for the driver's seat.

The lorry driver had stopped by the side of the road and clambered out, shouting at them over the rain, asking what happened. Rabbil told him they were cops and the car that had crashed contained a suspect and a hostage. The driver, a burly man with a Chicago Bulls cap, asked for ID. Rabbil, twitchy and worried as he was, almost told the man to go fuck himself.

His steps were slow and cautious. But the nearer he got to the crashed Myvi, the faster his heart pounded because to draw your gun was one thing, to fire the damn thing at a person... Rabbil knew he could never do it. Even the last gunfight had been three shots from him, all meant as warnings.

The suspect is carrying a knife, he told himself. *The suspect needs to be up close and personal, and within striking range from you to actually warrant making a move. Other than that, you are FINE.*

He was now three feet away from the driver's door. Inside, past the smoky, tinted glass, he could see Lester's prone form, slumped over the steering wheel.

Rabbil took a deep breath, brought his gun up to chest height and tucked it in, his free hand reaching for the door handle. He heard nothing. Not the boom of the thunder, not the crack of the lightning, not the patter of rain as it drenched him. He wrapped his fingers around the door handle and pulled.

The door flopped open. And there was Lester, knocked out cold. In the corner of his eye, he saw Wesley but ignored him. Wesley was Atiqah's problem for now.

Using his index finger, he prodded Lester's form. Rabbil grabbed the man's right shoulder and pulled him back.

"Sial," he said.

Blood flowed from the left of Lester's forehead. He placed a couple of fingers on the man's carotid artery and sighed in relief when he found a pulse.

He turned to Atiqah. She was leaning over Wesley, who was also knocked out. But unlike Lester, there was no blood on his face. His eyes were closed though, and–

"Breathing," Atiqah said.

"Call back-up," Rabbil said. "And tell Rudolph to find someone with cigarettes."

Atiqah nodded and made for the ancient Volvo. He didn't have to tell her to update Delilah. He was sure it was the first thing Atiqah would do.

60

Two weeks later

The bright morning sun woke Wesley up. Blinking several times, he stared up at the ceiling. At the fan that slowly twirled around and around and around. He didn't move, but took in everything around him: the sound of the waves lapping against the beach, the smell of salt in the air, the gentle breeze that blew air into his room. And slowly, he smiled.

The silence was disrupted by the sound of bare feet on the faded maple wood floor in Zara's home. Wesley turned his head toward the door, which was slightly ajar, and watched as Delilah entered. She was smiling and carrying a tray laden with breakfast.

"Sleep well?" she asked as she put the tray on the bare nightstand. Wesley was sure that either his notebook or laptop had been there just last night, but then again, Delilah could've moved it.

"The miracle of painkillers," he said, pushing himself up and leaning on the headboard. His forefinger traced the lump above the scar caused by Priscilla's loafer. That had been the worst of it. The doctor at the Tawau hospital had told him that if Lester had been going any faster, it would've been worse. They had checked him for concussion or any other brain damage, but so far, the only result he'd received was that his blood pressure and uric acid levels were a little higher than average.

"Don't get hooked," Delilah said as she sat on the bed. Her hand snaked out and found his.

"I won't. I'm not really into pills."

"You better not be. I see the swelling has gone down." She pulled her hand away from his to check on the bump that now decorated his forehead. Delilah had been scared shitless that night when Atiqah came running towards the car. She'd expected the worst. And he'd survived. She suddenly leaned forward and kissed him on the forehead.

"What was that about?" Wesley asked.

"For luck," she said.

"Alrighty then," he said. "So, what's for breakfast?"

X

As they ate, Wesley pored over the notes he'd made since he got discharged from the hospital the week prior. So far, everything was coming together perfectly. The only aspect of the story that left a bitter taste in his mouth was the ending. It was not going to be a happy ending, but a realistic finish to this blood-soaked drama.

A day after the hospital had let him out to a very relieved Aunt Zara, Margie and Lucky, Inspector Rabbil came calling, knowing that Wesley would want answers.

"It's not a good picture," he said as he sat down. It was the first time Wesley had seen Rabbil since the inspector showed up in his hospital room two days after the accident to see if he was alright.

"Is Lester still …"

"In a coma, yeah. The doctors aren't sure whether he'll wake up or not. And if he doesn't, we can't drag him before a judge to charge him with murder, right? Like everything else in life, it's a wait-and-see game."

"What about the second guy? The one who held Tommy down while Lester administered the dose?"

Inspector Rabbil snorted. "I'm sure there was one. But unless Lester gives us a name, we have no proof. And I don't feel like pointing fingers, so just pray that when he wakes up, Sleeping Stupid does the right thing and points the law to the other idiot that *might* give Raul Krishnan up."

"What about Priscilla?" Wesley asked after a beat.

"Well, the good news is that she's confessed to selling drugs at the casino. She's also agreed to spill the beans about the whole operation. But ..." Rabbil paused and fished out a pack of cigarettes, contemplated lighting one, then shoved them into his pocket, saying, "While I was out of the station, Jude Ambrose visited Priscilla. He used the lawyer card and got a private meeting with her. No one knows what was said, but now she's decided to change her story.

"This time, there's no mention of Raul Krishnan in her story at all, just that Tommy and company sold drugs on his own. Nothing to implicate that rich fuck. And guess what, she has a top-notch defense lawyer in her corner now. The lawyer was shipped in from KL and said she's doing it pro bono as a favor to Jude, which we all know is a steaming pile of shit."

"What about the recording Delilah made?"

"It's worthless. It wasn't done by cops, but by civilians. That defense lawyer will chew it up."

"And Su Yen?"

"Passed over to CID. But knowing how things are going, I won't be surprised if it ends up as another cold case. Tawau CID will work it, file it as active, but when something bigger comes along..."

The inspector sighed and Wesley could see the bags under the man's eyes and the sag in his shoulders. They had a suspect for Tommy's death, but that suspect was knocked out cold and no one knew if he'd wake up. They had another body with barely anything to form a proper case. The only thing Rabbil had at the moment was Abigail's body. And that wasn't even murder.

"I'm sorry about your case, inspector," Wesley said.

Rabbil shrugged. "Sometimes you win and sometimes you don't. I'm spending another two days here and then we're leaving. With Tawau CID taking over, all that's left is to brief them so they don't get lost."

They exchanged small talk, and after a while, Rabbil stood up, shook Wesley's hand and said: "No more playing detective, okay?"

Wesley smiled. "I'll try not to."

"You better."

X

"What happens after you finish it?" Delilah asked.

Wesley looked up from his laptop. The Word document was now just over 200 pages long. His notes and Delilah's recordings had been boosted by the soft copy of the files on Tommy Asandu, Su Yen and Abigail Martin Supian that Inspector Rabbil had collected and left for them before leaving town.

"I don't know," Wesley said. "I think I'll call up some old contacts, see if there's a publisher in KL interested in airing the sordid details of our little town."

Su Yen's murder had been featured in the local papers, but tucked away in the back pages. The stories had been short and with minimal details, which had surprised Wesley. Tommy's death had been an even smaller 150-word piece. Just another dead junkie, the story said, nothing to see here, move on, the business pages are just up ahead. The lack of attention the press gave this massive story shocked Wesley at first but provided him the fuel to write this story. He had to tell it, and even if no one wanted to read it, he would find a place for it, say a blog or public postings on Facebook. People had to know. The story must be told. That was the job of the journalist.

"You might ruffle feathers," Delilah said.

"Part of the job."

Delilah placed her laptop on his desk. She had been transcribing what Priscilla told them and had been at it for over two hours. Wesley had his notes on the bed along with his laptop and printed copies of the files on Tommy, Su Yen and Abigail spread around him.

"Okay. Enough of this," Delilah said, standing up.

"What are you doing?"

"I need fresh air," she said. "And so do you. You've been holed up in here since the hospital discharged you. Now come on. Let's get some exercise."

"Seriously?"

"Yes." Delilah offered her hand. Outside he could hear Lucky barking cheerfully as he chased a giggling and squealing Margie around the house.

Wesley threw a quick look out the window at the beach. At the golden sand, at the palm fronds that danced in the breeze. At the clear blue sky, the puffy white clouds. It looked beautiful out there.

He took Delilah's hand and got off the bed. The book would be completed, of course, but for now, it could wait.